Old Music for New People

Old Music for New People

David Biddle

THE
ST●RY
PLANT

The Story Plant
Studio Digital CT, LLC
P.O. Box 4331
Stamford, CT 06907

Story Plant paperback ISBN-13: 978-1-61188-318-3
Fiction Studio Books E-book ISBN: 978-1-945839-54-2

Visit our website at www.TheStoryPlant.com

First Story Plant Printing: December 2021

Printed in the United States of America
0 9 8 7 6 5 4 3 2 1

For Ellen Horgan who taught us that everybody's an individual, and that's probably all you should ever assume about them.

1. Things Get Weird

Zaxy stuffed the last of a hot dog into his mouth, then came skipping across the concourse, chewing with what I guess you'd call gusto, mixing in strange little hops and jumps along the way. As he approached us, he managed to swallow that last bite, then said, "He's coming. He's here!"

I clicked out of my e-book, pounded through the half cup of Dr. Pepper I had left, then stood up and slid my Kindle back into the cargo pocket of my shorts. We all followed Zaxy as he bounced back to the window.

"All right everyone," said Daddy, "remember to be inclusive and supportive and whatever else makes sense."

Our parents had not told us we were going to have a summer-long visitor until the night before that visitor arrived. We'd already been at our vacation house, *Casa Cielo*, a full two weeks. Once again, I'd gotten over my frustration about being taken away from summer softball competition. My older brother, Delmore, had found new ways to kind of be a jerk, and Zaxy had his sailing lessons. Already, Zaxy seemed happy enough as part of the mob of summer vacation kids that forms up there in Maine every year—a mob I'd once been a part of, and Del before me. Of course, for Zax it would be a much different experience. There is no one else in the world like my little brother Zachary Dean Scattergood.

And if you're wondering, I think it's okay being a girl trapped between two brothers. You learn a lot about boys that way. Some of it's good. Some of it's bad. In fact, that summer I learned a lot about boys *and* girls—maybe more than your average fifteen-year-old learns, but not exactly in the way you might think.

Passengers began coming through the red security doors.

"Will we recognize him?" I asked.

"Just look for the only male wearing pink shoes," Del murmured, "and a purple bow tie."

We watched as travelers entered the terminal waiting area in little groups, wheeling and lugging carry-on bags. It occurred to me that it was odd we'd all come for this pick up. Usually, Daddy chose just one of us to keep him company collecting visitors.

They kept popping out of the red doors—a mom and two little kids; a businessman; some touristy-looking couples with camera bags and cylindrical fishing rod carriers (these people were very loud, like they'd been drinking); a pretty young woman with surprisingly beautiful, somewhat frizzy hair, wearing a bit too much makeup; another woman, in her sixties, looking lost and confused. Maybe someone she'd expected wasn't there for her.

A few more people straggled out in batches. Then nothing.

"Where is he?" said Zax.

Daddy checked his phone to see if he'd gotten a message from Uncle Edward. He looked up again at the doors and leaned on a railing. A few minutes later another family came out, and right behind them a woman pushing a little kid in a stroller. Maybe a minute after that, a man came hurrying through the red doors, then another man, more waddling than walking. Then nothing again. We just stood there.

"What's happened to Robert?" Zaxy asked.

"I don't know," Daddy said. "Should I call Uncle Edward?" He stared at his phone like it might be magical.

Just then, the flight attendants came through the door. Mom stopped them and asked if there were any more passengers still coming off. They said nope, the only people left were the pilots and cleanup crew.

We were all a bit confused. We turned to head back to the main part of the building. The pretty young woman with frizzy hair and too much makeup leaned against the wall across from the waiting area. She was rather tall and thin, and really quite beautiful in an interesting way, but I did not like that makeup. Her hair fell to her shoulders. Sunlight flashed in its brownish color, making it glint with a milky gold shine that even seemed to flick red a little. Something was up with her. For someone so attractive, she didn't seem to be very comfortable with her body. Maybe her blouse and jacket didn't quite fit. It was hard to tell.

She raised a hand and smiled. "Hey, Scattergood family." Her voice was strained, like it didn't know what to do with itself. "If you're looking for Robert you're not going to find him."

"I'm sorry," said Daddy, "do you know my nephew?"

She giggled and chuckled at the same time, then shook her head knowingly. I turned to look at Delmore. His mouth had dropped wide open. He seemed frozen in place. Mom had her eyes closed, pointing her face toward the ceiling, shaking her head back and forth.

"Did you travel with Robert?" Daddy asked.

She chuckled again, then pushed off from her lean against the wall and took the several steps across the waiting area to us. Sticking out her hand, she said, "My name is now Rita Gomez. I had the name Robert when my father put me on the red-eye last night in San Diego. But I turned into Rita after we left Pittsburgh just before they served coffee and tea. I hope you don't mind."

She still had her hand out for Daddy to shake. I noticed how long those fingers were. My father had now assumed the exact same expression as his oldest son, Delmore. Neither of them seemed able to move.

10

They just stared at this person with slightly open mouths and buggy, unblinking eyes.

We could have dealt with this situation in many ways. I like to think we're pretty good as a group when things get weird. *Was this person really Robert?* I got the implication if it was a practical joke. But it could also be a serious problem that we were going to have to deal with for a long, long summer. Still, Robert could have been kidnapped and this was an elaborate ruse to hide the fact that he was being held against his will. He was, after all, the child of a somewhat famous scientist.

I looked at this person as carefully as I could, trying not to be obvious. I couldn't see any facial hair, but her hands really were oversized. And even though she was wearing women's high-heeled shoes, those feet stuffed in were much larger than the shoes seemed to want.

Everything added up. I tried peering into her eyes. The makeup seemed as well applied as that on any girl's face at Cliveden Friends School, where we all went. Could a boy really have accomplished that, even if it was overdone? I knew I couldn't, and I was an actual girl—well, not in the way a lot of people think, but still.

My older brother and my father were now breathing through their noses in a funny way. They looked ridiculous—like they'd been punched or something. Mom continued gazing all over the place except at this person standing right in front of us. I was really worried the wrong thing was going to come out of someone's mouth.

Finally, I just stepped in front of Daddy, looked up at this person who was definitely a lot taller than me, and took her hand to shake. "Hi," I said. "I'm Ivy. You're freaking us out."

The hand I held had long bones and weird young muscles. I wanted to let go and jump away. But that would have been mean, and quite stupid. I go to a Quaker Friends school, I kept thinking. I'm trained for this kind of thing.

"Hi Ivy," she said, with a big happy smile. "I remember you. I'm Rita."

"But you were Robert when we were little, right?"

"Well," she said as she let go of my hand and hitched her backpack higher on her shoulder. "I was *kind of* Robert back that one time you visited. I didn't want to be. I know you all thought I was weird. I thought I was weird, too. And couldn't ever stop feeling sad. But, well . . ."

She gave a great shrug—kind of happy, a bit embarrassed maybe, relieved, goofy, and a whole lot more. ". . . I also knew I was a girl all the way back then."

"But you're a guy." This was Del coming to life.

"Not right now."

"Really? So you've . . . you've . . ."

She laughed. It was so relaxed and calm, that laugh. I wanted to hug her. There was something about this kid. I felt like I'd known her all my life. It was an odd sensation.

"No. I haven't been *altered,* if that's what you mean. It's called gender reassignment surgery. But what's under these clothes is not who I am. It never was."

Daddy, too, was coming to life, but not in a good way. "Excuse me . . . *Robert.*"

"It's not Robert, Scat," said Mom. "It's Rita, right?"

Our cousin nodded patiently.

Mom stepped right into it all and just enveloped this completely beautiful girl in her arms. "We are so happy to see you, again . . . Rita."

She pulled her head back and held our cousin by the shoulders, then just stared at her. It was one of Mom's hard smiles, the kind where she was saying to life: *"Nope. Not gonna freak me out. It's weird, but that doesn't matter. Because everything's weird."*

Mom was pretty good at that kind of smile. You learn it as a weapon if you live in Cliveden. Also, of course, she was married to our father. It wasn't a fake smile like she might give to one of the moms in town who annoyed her. It was more the hard smile she might give a nice babysitter who spilled milk on the couch, or our housekeeper Kayeesha when she showed up late. Mom probably uses that smile a lot at the hospital where she's an eye surgeon and teaches laser techniques to medical students. Everything's a thousand times more intense at Jefferson University Hospital than the suburban Cliveden social scene.

"So you've gone and done something a bit big here," Mom said, still smiling and holding this girl by the shoulders. She was shaking her head back and forth a little more vigorously than she probably intended.

"Excuse me," Daddy said from behind her. He had his phone out. "Do your parents know about this?"

Mom dropped her hands and turned around. "Scat . . ."

"No, Rikely," Daddy said. "Seriously. Eddie would have told me . . ."

Rita laughed carefully, then looked at me and said, "Well, actually Eddie knows my intentions are to change, but he didn't know I was going to just jump in with both feet today. My mom, too. I didn't know it would happen myself until I was somewhere over Kansas at five o'clock in the morning."

"You *just* did this?" Mom asked.

"Yeah, I guess I did. I got to Pittsburgh and had a three-hour layover. Time to think, you know? I bought this dress and top, some skinny jeans and a few other blouses, these shoes. Aren't they nice?"

I looked down and didn't find them nice. They were dark blue high-heeled things to match her dress.

She was still talking. "And then, well, the makeup I had with me. I've been practicing that for the last two years. It's all—"

"I'm calling your father," said Daddy.

"Oh, please, Uncle Scat, no," Rita said. "Not yet. I need—"

Zaxy interrupted, "Are *you* Robert?"

"Um . . ."

"It's Robert all right," Del said quietly.

"But Robert's supposed to be a boy."

"Well . . ." Rita looked down at our little brother.

"Do you like SpongeBob?"

"Of course . . ."

"Are you sure?"

Zaxy's confusion got Daddy silently more upset, which kind of set Mom off in her strong "*defender of children*" mode.

"Scat, stop! Now, Zachary, we will discuss all of this in the car. Rita . . ." she stared again into that face. "Rita, you're coming with us. We had planned for a Robert-type person, but that's all changed now, obviously. You're coming with us regardless, and of course you're staying the summer like we planned. You are part of this family now."

Mom squinted at Daddy. "And we will not call Edward Scattergood, because Rita is now our responsibility, not his or Samantha's. We're going down to luggage. Delmore, please take Rita's carry-on. Scat, put your phone away." She placed her hand on his wrist. "Please, Scat!" Then she looked me right in the eyes. "And Ivy . . . well, Ivy . . ." I thought she was going to burst into tears.

Daddy trailed behind as we headed for the escalator. He'd put his phone away and was shaking his head and mumbling to himself. That's when the summer of 2013 really began. Right there, with Daddy following us and my cousin and brothers leading the way to get her luggage.

2. Rhino Butts

Casa Cielo is the name of our family's summer camp. It sits on the side of Captain's Mountain above the Resonance Hills boat club. People from Boston named Waverly bought the property back in the 1920s and turned it into their special family summer vacation place. The land had been a big farm back when the village of Resonance Hills was just a couple fishing docks and a hunting lodge at the bottom of a bunch of mountains and hills next to Resonance Lake.

I don't think the Waverlys had a name for their camp. But Daddy's a writer. He once lived at a villa in Mexico that villagers called *Casa de Cielo,* which basically means "house in the sky." They called it that because of the way the villa glowed when the sun rose out of the ocean every morning. The same sun rises out of Resonance Lake and sometimes lights up our camp on the surface of the water below, reflecting the sky as well so that it looks like we're floating both in the air and the water all at once. Daddy says his Spanish has never been very good, but *Casa*

Cielo seemed the best poetic name possible for our summer camp—"Sky Home."

I know it's weird to call our property a "camp." There are two separate houses on it, along with a little barn thing where Daddy works, an old shed where we keep our small boats in the winter, and a special picnic area and barbecue pit up the hill behind the house where we can see the whole bay off in the distance. Our place is separated from the rest of the mountain by a ramshackle, broken-down fencing system—part wood, part stone, part just places where something used to be. Every year when we arrive, Daddy tells Delmore to get out of the car and open the main gate. Then we drive through and Delmore gets back in. The gate stays open all summer. We're so lucky to live inside those old fences every summer. The village is about a ten-minute drive from us—twenty minutes by boat.

It was midafternoon when we arrived in our van back at the driveway leading up to the property. Rita got a kick out of seeing the huge, weathered sign that said *Casa Cielo* with our family name underneath, and the fact that we had this long gravel drive winding up the hill to the parking lot in front of the big house.

Daddy pointed out the barn where he wrote his most famous book, *Between the Rise and Fall*. I was impressed that Rita understood the importance of that novel—both to him and, actually, to the whole extended Scattergood family. It's interesting how one book can turn a kind of opinionated man into a weirdo celebrity author. The whole thing is a story about a rich white guy in college who falls in love with a mixed-race girl. She loves him too, but breaks off their relationship for some reason, but the reader never learns why. The guy thinks it's possibly because he's white and has too much money. Over time, the guy basically goes insane because his love has been thwarted simply because he's an American of European descent—something he can't do anything about. Daddy wrote it a long time ago. I guess people would say he's very white.

Mom's ethnicity is strange. Her father was African American and her mother is Norwegian. Mom's first name, Rikely, was her Norwegian grandfather's last name. That means us Scattergood kids are serious mutts, plain and simple. None of us have what you'd call light skin except Daddy, and even his is freckly and kind of smeary. I have brown eyes that sometimes seem hazily orangish. Delmore has darker eyes. Very brown. And Zaxy has bright blue eyes that can almost seem white sometimes. He's got very gold-blond hair, too, and kind of looks like he's from somewhere like Norway, except his skin is a dusty dark tan. All three of us have hair that's hard to control. Mine's the worst—it gets quite frizzy sometimes. That's why I would almost always wear it tied back somehow or under a baseball cap.

Between the Rise and Fall brings up all sorts of weird discussions about race. It's supposed to be funny, even though the story is also very sad. We don't really talk that much about race in our family, though. I don't know if this makes sense, but when you're a mixture of a bunch of things like all of us are, you kind of feel like you need to be a racial atheist. None of what other people say about race makes a lot of sense. Everyone's always pointing fingers at each other. It just makes us Scattergoods feel bad. I think that's partly why Daddy wrote the book. Maybe that's why it was so successful, too. No one can do much about the color of their skin and their hair and the shape of their faces. That stuff should have very little to do with who you are as a person, but everyday people still make decisions about each other based on appearance. In a way, then, no one can do anything about their skin, hair, and face, so sometimes people feel the need to do something about the way other people look. I know the whole thing should make me mad, but sad is the best I can do—at least, the best I can do where I am in my life so far.

I've tried to read *Between the Rise and Fall* several times but couldn't get past the third chapter. Delmore says he read it start to finish two years ago, but I think he's lying. He can talk about the beginning really well and the ending, but the middle stuff never comes up. And now, two years later, he claims his memory isn't so good.

Rita told us she'd read it, too. You're going to think this is weird, but she's mixed as well. Her dad, Uncle Edward, is like our dad—they're British and Scottish and Irish, supposedly. The Scattergood family was

19

very Quaker way back in history. But Rita's mom, Aunt Samantha, is Honduran on her mother's side. I don't know about the other side.

Talking about that novel to Daddy sometimes makes him unhappy. He wrote four other novels after that, but none were as well received. He'll tell you that having a "prominent anything" can be the kiss of death. Everyone just expects another version of that same major accomplishment. But you, as a writer, want nothing more than to top that first success. It's kind of like the Red Sox second baseman, Dustin Pedroia. He was named the most valuable player of the American League in his second year with the team. He's still pretty good every year for the most part, but unless he gets another MVP trophy, is he really going to feel that good? Poor Daddy. Poor Dustin.

Sometimes, though, it makes my dad happy when people tell him they like the parts about music and romance in *Between the Rise and Fall*. The guy in the story realizes that there are certain things in life that are impossible to explain or even understand—like music and love. And they're the things that matter most.

When Rita piped up about it, I couldn't tell what he was feeling. I think she still weirded him out. I know she still had my older brother in a tizzy. As soon as we got out of the car Del was almost sprinting across the driveway to the trail that leads up to the little house. Mom and Zaxy headed inside. We were standing with Daddy at the bottom of the front porch stairs. He seemed distracted all of a sudden. Probably because he'd been reminded of his book. Rita's gigantic suitcase sat at the edge of the drive.

"We're going to go get Rita set up in the little house, Daddy."

I said that to him, but I was smiling as an apology, looking at my weird cousin because I could tell Daddy was lost in his thoughts.

"Oh. Okay. I'll see you later then . . ." With that, he patted my shoulder, then turned to Rita, looking like he was going to give her a hug, but he stopped himself. He just patted her shoulder, too, then headed off toward his barn.

I offered to take her suitcase. When I tried to lift it, though, it was awfully heavy. "What have you got in here? Boulders?"

"Besides my clothes, it's pretty much full of books. I need to read at night. Mostly stuff about gender and being a woman, you know? I'm trying to catch up." She hoisted her backpack, then picked up her a carry-on book bag.

"You could have spared yourself the weight here," I said. "This is Scat and Rikely Scattergood country. Wait until you see the books we have in the great room." I pointed back toward the main house. That room is the most wonderful place I know of in the world, with bookshelves everywhere, a billiards table, couches and chairs for reading, a super-high ceiling, and windows that look out front to the lake and out back up Captain's Mountain.

"I'm sure you've got a lot of good books here, but there's stuff I *need* to read in that bag. I'm putting this summer to good use."

"We only read around here when the weather's bad."

"Just when it's bad?"

"Well, at night, too, of course. There's no TV. No Internet. No cell service. But we've got tons of books."

She stopped walking. "Wait. What?"

"Yeah, no media. No Internet."

"None? Not even cell?"

"Cell is spotty at best. You gotta use the mountain. Maybe twenty minutes up—if you want to talk to someone or even text."

"No one told me this."

"We've got a landline if you need to call your dad or mom."

"We can just hook up an old modem."

I laughed at that and started up the hill, lugging her case with two hands. "Nope. Del and I tried that last summer. We bought one of those old things at a yard sale way down in Blue Hill near the ocean. But there's something really crappy about our phone line. You'll hear it if you use it. A lot of static. Sometimes we get other people's conversations floating in. It's weird. Modems can't handle that much noise on the line."

"How can you deal with no media, then?"

I sighed. "I kind of like it."

She was silent. I could feel her frustration sprackling in the air behind me.

"You get reception okay in town," I finally offered. "Sometimes I use the library computers. Delmore and Zaxy play plenty of computer and video games that they bring up, so . . ."

We were at the top of the trail. It turned left at that point on flat ground winding through trees, and then broke into the clearing where the little house was.

"You know," I said, realizing what she was about to see, "it's really okay not having any electronic stuff connected to the outside. It really is. Just give it some time."

She didn't say anything to that. I was in the lead, popping through the trees first. Behind me I heard, "Oh, my God!" Then a laugh.

The "little house" is not so little. It was designed to be the house we stay in during the winter. The walls and roof are super-insulated, and there's triple-glazed, solarized silhouette windows that absorb heat in the winter and repel it in the summer. Half its power comes from solar panels arrayed on the south-facing roof. They've never worked that well, but we love them anyway.

The structure is built partially of stones and boulders that had been piled up on the property since before we bought it. The rest is wood salvaged from a warehouse that was being torn down in Portland. Daddy bought the whole thing and had it shipped up here for the architect and builders to puzzle over. The front of the place is where they used most of the stone, except the porch, which is made of the biggest timber pieces from the old warehouse. That front is startling to everyone, which is why Rita said, "Oh, my God." It looks like some modern sculpture that's supposed to also seem primitive.

Delmore was lying in a hammock on the porch with earbuds attached to the sides of his head. Smoking a cigarette.

We stood kind of staring up at the house, but also watching my older brother make an ass out of himself, blubbing smoke rings into the air and flicking his fingers like he was the coolest guy in the state of Maine.

Rita swung the backpack off her shoulder and dangled it around in front of her while she opened up a small pocket. "Wow. Your parents let you smoke?"

"Absolutely not," I said. "Del's just a rhino butt."

My cousin screwed up her face a bit as she reached into the pocket of her bag. "He's a rhino butt because he smokes? Or he's just a rhino butt in general?"

"Well, kind of both," I said. "But mostly the smoking."

At that point, she pulled out what she was looking for—a yellow lighter. Then she reached in the pocket of her jacket and took out a pack of cigarettes.

"I guess that makes me a rhino butt, too."

She seemed very amused as she removed a cigarette from the pack. I glanced up at my brother on the porch. He was oblivious to the fact that we were there. It also occurred to me that he had run off as soon as we got home. Was that because he wanted to smoke? Or was he just trying to get out of lugging Rita's suitcase up the path to the house?

"I get the picture," Rita said. "You don't approve of smoking. Sorry about that."

She lit her cigarette and seemed very pleased with herself. Blowing smoke out of her nose and mouth simultaneously, she said, "You can leave my bag here. I'll deal with it. Go inside or back down to the big house or whatever it's called. I'm just gonna chill a little."

She waited for me to say something. It felt like she was my big sister for a second.

"Are you really going to smoke?" I asked, trying not to sound disappointed.

She took another drag and exhaled. "You want one?" She held the pack out to me.

"No way," I said. Then I stalked up the porch steps.

I hate being mad in any way at all—ever, actually. If I get mad, it makes me even madder to think that the person I'm mad at is so mean or stupid that they've made me mad. Mom says it's one of the biggest challenges of being a middle child. She also says that girls sometimes have it worse than guys expressing their anger. I've been good at not always telling people what I'm thinking most of my life. Or, maybe I should say, that's been one of the bigger problems I've created for myself, as you'll see.

Delmore was wagging his head back and forth, listening to his iPod with a cigarette smoldering in the fingers of his left hand. His legs were crossed at the ankle near the end of the hammock. I walked past him, heading for the door. At the last second, I gave his feet a backward ninja kick, which knocked him out of the hammock onto the floor. I stood over him for just a moment, noting how confused and lost he looked, then went inside and slammed the door. I thought about locking it, but decided that would make me look like a rhino butt myself.

I could hear Delmore yelling and cursing at me. But I could also hear our cousin chattering away and laughing at him, so I figured it was pretty unlikely he'd come after me. Besides, what could he do? Neither one of us really knew how to fight. We went to a Quaker school. And he couldn't exactly tell on me.

3. How to Be a Girl

I made some lemonade, then poured a glass over ice for myself. In the back utility room, I flicked the switch that turned on all the overhead fans in the house. The air felt so much better once it was circulating. I went back out into the living room, slid the Kindle out of my cargo shorts pocket and sat down to read, positioned in just the right way so as to be able to keep an eye on my brother and cousin. Rita was sitting on a boulder in the drive, smoking, and, it looked like, trying to get her phone to work. Del had climbed back into the hammock and was smoking as well.

Both of them were stupid, of course. Either one of the parents could come up the trail at any moment. Worse, Zaxy might come running up. I tried to busy myself back into my story, but it was hard. We had a kid staying with us who was very challenging to think about. I usually don't think so much about how girls look, but even I noticed that she was attractive. I mean, she was attractive to *me*. What did that mean? Once you start thinking about this sex and gender stuff, you find yourself in a hole that's hard to climb out of.

I tried harder to read my book and was just drifting into a nap when I heard the door open. It was Delmore. Shaking his head, he glared down at me and then out the window, then back down at me again.

"I'm not going to last the summer," he said.

"Yup. You're going to die of cancer in about two weeks."

"It's not funny, Ivy. That kid out there . . . I can't deal with it."

He started pacing from the living room past the bar into the kitchen and then back out again. He actually looked pretty freaked out.

"Dude," I said, trying not to laugh, "didn't you take Life Studies in seventh grade?"

"Of course I did."

He looked out the window and kept pacing.

"What is the big deal then?"

"You don't understand."

"I do so." I set my Kindle aside, sat up on the couch, and watched him trundling back and forth. *"Our cousin is a transperson,"* I said in a fake, spooky whisper.

He stopped and stared at me for a moment, then closed his eyes and kind of shook like he was being electrocuted in slow motion.

"Pull yourself together, Del. She's our cousin, and she's not going away."

He resumed his pacing, now a bit more franticly. It looked like he had to pee. He kept blinking his eyes and breathing funny.

I stood up and positioned myself at the counter that separated the living room from the kitchen. As he came near, I braced myself. Head down and mumbling, he rammed right into me like he'd marched blindly into a boulder.

"What is your problem, Ivy?" he demanded.

"You need to calm down." I expected him to get mad. But he didn't. Instead, he slumped forward and dropped his head.

"You don't understand."

"What?" I said.

He lowered his head even further, then shook it back and forth. "You know when we were waiting at the airport and everyone was coming off?"

I nodded.

"And then," he tilted his head toward the window, "*she* came off?"

I waited.

"Well . . . I looked at her and . . ."

I inhaled and waited some more.

"I thought she was really . . . you know . . . hot. I mean . . ."

I tried to stifle myself.

"No. Really! I thought she was super hot, Ivy. I thought . . ."

He looked up now, first at me and then out the window.

"I mean, I was really attracted to her." He dropped his head again.

I burst out laughing. It wasn't a teasing laugh or a *you're so stupid* laugh. It was more like, *"I love you Del, and you are a funny guy to have as a brother."* I'm sure you know that kind of laugh.

"Dude, she *is* beautiful," I said. "And smart, and funny . . . and kind of cool."

"I don't want anyone to ever find out about this," he said.

Rita was clunking up the steps with her suitcase. It didn't look so heavy the way she was carrying it—and she was in heels.

"Your secret's safe with me, big brother. No worries."

My back was turned, but I heard the door opening.

"Wow," Rita said, "what a great place." She just sort of stood there at the threshold looking around, then dropped the suitcase and kicked off her stupid shoes.

"Heels kind of get to you after a while," she said as she turned and went back out and down the steps to retrieve her backpack and carry-on. When she came back, she leaned her bags up against the suitcase and went into the living room to look around.

"Let's get you set up in your room," I said.

I gave her a tour as we went toward the back of the house. She was getting the best room in all of *Casa Cielo*, except maybe the great room in the main house.

When we got to her room, she took off her jacket and carefully hung it in the closet. I hadn't noticed what I should have seen from the very moment she introduced herself as a girl named Rita. It wasn't really that big a deal, and you'd kind of figure this would be obvious, but I realized for the first time that even though she had shaved her legs, her arms were kind of hairy, and, she had no breasts whatsoever. Just a chest like any other guy who was fifteen. That made me feel sad for her. But not sad like, "Isn't it terrible you don't have breasts like I do." More sad like, *"What you're trying to accomplish is harder than anything I can imagine a standard person ever trying to do."*

><

I left her to unpack and take a nap. Back out in the main area of the house, Delmore was playing a video game on the TV and having a snack of Sun Chips and lemonade. I felt bad for kicking him out of the hammock. Taking my glass from beside the couch, I poured myself another lemonade and went back into the living room to say something that might work as an apology. He was sitting cross-legged on the floor. I positioned myself just to his right on the end of the couch so that I could see the side of his face and the passageway into the back of the house at the same time, just in case Rita came out. He was playing this funky submarine battle game that he'd ordered through a Japanese website. The game was called "Toku-Tai."

"So, yeah, it *is* weird," I said quietly. "*She's* weird, I mean."

31

He didn't glance at me or anything. "You mean *he's* weird."

"Whatever," I shrugged.

He kept playing the game. He'd turned the volume down to a tinny insect-sound level, much lower than usual.

"Del, you're wrong about her. She makes us feel weird, but at the same time," I glanced up past the kitchen down the hall, "whoever that is back there sure did show up happy today."

That got to him. Mom says: *"When you show up happy, the world responds the way it's meant to."*

"He did *not* show up happy."

"Yes, *she* did." I laughed carefully. "That's what you were attracted to."

"We can ask Mom if he showed up happy."

I sighed. "She?"

"Whatever . . ."

"No. Not whatever, Delmore."

He kind of drop-threw the controller on the carpet and turned to face me.

"You didn't see him out there just now in front of the house. Ivy, you need to watch people carefully. I watch them. Carefully, you know? The way Dad says to. His hands? I noticed it right away when he was smoking. His hands were shaking. He might seem like some big-shit sophisticated girl with his dress and his makeup and those stupid little heels he scrunched his feet into, but you could see it all in those hands. Just like Daddy says. The cigarette was

wobbly and the phone was as well. He's on the edge,
Ivy. It's always in the hands."

"You'd be shaking too, coming all that way, deciding to go through with a change like that, hoping people you hardly know will accept you."

"Yeah, well, I'm not trying to be something I'm
not. That shaking is confusion and fear. That's what
Dad says it is and I saw it."

"She's going to be here for the rest of the summer,
Del. She's our cousin. She's Daddy's . . . niece. She's
family."

"You had to think whether you were going to say
niece or nephew."

I shrugged, trying to calm down. "Doesn't matter.
She's family and she's here."

"Don't get used to her."

"What do you mean?"

"I heard Daddy leave in the car just now. That
means he needed to make a private phone call.
They'll be sending that kid home very soon. Probably
tomorrow."

><

About forty-five minutes later, Rita came out of her
room. She was dressed in baggy shorts, a long-sleeve
black T-shirt, and flip-flops. Her toenails were painted
a glowing cornflower blue.

Somehow her hair didn't seem like it had been
slept on or anything. It was still quite luxurious, so

blond and brown and red all at once, and so much more feminine than my scruffy, dinge-brown hair.

Something new I noticed, though, was just a little bit of boobs somehow on her chest. She caught me staring. Del had his back turned, gooning out on his submarine game.

She looked down, then back up at me, and kind of closed her eyes like a cat squinching up its face.

"Just practicing," she said, rolling her eyes and shaking her head.

I nodded, but didn't know whether or not I was supposed to say something intelligent in reply. Finally, I said, "We go over for dinner at six every night. Are you a vegetarian?"

She shook her head.

"Good. Daddy usually grills. Mom does salads and pasta, or rice or potatoes. It's my job . . ." I turned to look at Delmore. "It's *our* job to do a vegetable or fruit something."

"Okay . . ."

"I was thinking fruit salad tonight." My brother made a blubbering sound in disgust.

"Okay . . ."

"I'd rather have *your* help than Mister Video Game's, for sure," I said.

Rita made a crazy, sort of sickly face. "I don't . . . I mean, I never . . ."

"What? You don't like fruit salad?"

"No. I've never had to help make food. We always go out to dinner. Or order in."

"Yes, well, Delmore doesn't make food either as far as I know."

I wanted to yell, "*If you want to be a girl, you better learn how to prepare food!*" But that would have been really stupid, because I know lots of guys who are great cooks, and there are probably more girls who stink in the kitchen than anyone's stereotype would admit.

All of that flashed through my mind, but something bigger showed up as well. I realized that what I really should ask her is if she might like to learn how to cook—and learn other things that maybe she didn't know would be helpful for her in the future. That would be a foolish question, of course, since I myself didn't know that much about being the standard kind of person people mean when they say the word "girl."

Then bigger *Somethings* came to me. Do you plan to date guys? Are you going to get an operation and change things around? Does this mean you want to be a mom someday? Are you going to compete in girls' sports? Is there a license or something you need in order to make being a girl official? And why do you need to be so drastic with your change? Why does it matter how your body is made? Can't you simply be a guy who likes girl stuff? Shouldn't we all just be who we are? I mean, let's get real. It's just a stupid penis . . . well, and no breasts, I guess. Not much different than your skin color, hair type, or the shape of your face. Would you change those, too?

Before I could get going with any of that, though, she said, "This is going to piss you off, Ivy, but before we head over I need a smoke."

I'm sure I looked at her like I wanted to kill her. But before I could say anything, Delmore the idiot scrambled off the floor. "Good idea. Me too."

He quickly jogged through the kitchen to his room, then back out past me and held the door for Rita. The two of them went out onto to the porch. Delmore picked up his special Coke can ashtray. They sat about halfway down the steps with the can between them and lit up their cancer sticks.

><   ,

A while later, my brother and cousin came inside laughing at something. At first, I thought I'd ask what was so funny. Then I realized Delmore would probably get grumpy with me. What was the point?

We left the house after they'd both washed up at the sink. I followed the two of them down the path. Del was telling Rita about this group he'd started listening to called Ott. He said there was one song he didn't know the name of that was really good, and that a lot of their music was kind of wild, but really catchy in an atmospheric way. Rita said most of her childhood she had only liked to listen to classical music and jazz and sometimes the Beatles. She was somewhat apologetic about that. But then she told us that in the past two years she'd made friends who finally clued her in. Now she listened to everything—from rap to rock to reggae, even country. She told us that music should be like candy. Only a fool would eat just one kind.

I kept my mouth shut. I can tolerate practically any song, but for some reason, I decided a few years back to only like one group or singer at a time. That's weird, I know. It's a seasonal thing sort of. Maybe it's also kind of snobby. I usually fall in love with music that no one my own age pays much attention to.

During that spring and summer, I was only happy listening to this amazing husband and wife duo who call themselves Johnnyswim. They had just one album out, and it was one of those short EP things, but I loved it so much. Pretty much it's all I had been listening to since April. Their music was mostly about love. Real love—hoping, longing, heartache, and joy. I know that sounds corny and sentimental in this day and age, but Johnnyswim (their real names are Amanda and Abner) had burrowed deep inside my heart by that time. I should mention as well, it seemed like they were mixed race, kind of like us Scattergoods. That may have helped cement my devotion to them.

Before them, I'd gone through a season of Bonnie Raitt. And before her, all I listened to last fall and winter was Bruce Springsteen. The summer before it was Hall & Oates, one of the ultimate Philadelphia groups of the '70s and '80s. I had a big Elton John phase too—his early stuff like "Your Song," "Tiny Dancer," and "Rocket Man." There was Michael Jackson, of course. That was the summer I was twelve. Also, Stevie Wonder one winter and Joni Mitchell one spring. Some of my friends call that stuff old music. But there was always something in each of those musicians that touched me and helped me understand something new about myself.

When I was little the only music I really liked was Fleetwood Mac. What can I say? Sometimes it's not so much that other music is bad or inferior, just that what you love never fails to make you feel good. That's the way it was for me. I hear whatever's being played, but I mostly only let myself get transported by one group a season.

So, I guess maybe a warning is important here in this story. A lot of different kinds of music had weird effects on our family all summer long. A lot of it was older music. Johnnyswim was a part of things, but so was music by The Modern Jazz Quartet and Miles Davis. There was a secret musician that I wanted to know about, too, but wouldn't until a kind of perfect moment near the end of the summer. And then there was Fleetwood Mac. Everyone should listen to them. I didn't really understand that until things had progressed pretty far for all of us. In a way, you could say Fleetwood Mac saved the day for people in our family. Mick Fleetwood, John McVie, Stevie Nicks, Christine McVie, and Lindsey Buckingham are the heroes of everything.

I've been hearing Fleetwood Mac songs since before I was born. Daddy had been a fan from the group's early days as a blues band, and Mom supposedly used to sing their song, "Landslide," all the time to Delmore when she was pregnant with me. Mom said that she and Daddy and a bunch of their friends used to listen to Fleetwood Mac and have wild dance parties when they were older teenagers and even in college. That was hard to believe. Dancing to anything was still beyond me right then.

Music has such an interesting way of touching everything. Sometimes I think of it as a form of light you can't see.

Anyway, we were on the path to the main house. Rita was telling Delmore that she had all this new music with her no one anywhere had heard yet, and that it was all going to be big. Then she said she'd also started listening to these two bands at the beginning of the summer and they were awesome. Of Monsters and Men was one of them. The other was a group she called Eddie Sharp.

Delmore said, "Edward Sharpe and the Magnetic Zeros."

Rita laughed, "I know, right? Where do these people come up with these names?"

All three of us kind of grunt-laughed, and then we came into the clearing above the big house.

"Where did that hotel come from?" Rita cried.

The main house actually is ginormous. We have no need for the little house at all. It has eight bedrooms and six trundle bed couch things that fold out all over the place.

In the kitchen, I turned to Rita and said, "We really are going to make fruit salad, okay?"

She took a deep breath. "You're going to need to show me what to do."

I could feel Del inching out of the room behind me. Zaxy was in the great room playing a game, on an iPad. Our big brother was happier watching and advising Zaxy about little-kid computer games than helping make dinner.

"We're going to start with the strawberries," I said. I took a quart basket out of the refrigerator, rinsed them in the sink, then handed Rita a serrated paring knife. I had another one for myself and started slicing the strawberry tops off, then piling the berry parts on the cutting board in front of Rita. "We need them smaller," I said. "Bite size. Cut them in half, maybe in quarters for the really big ones." I figured that was a simple enough thing to do.

But I watched out of the corner of my eye, just in case. Rita was handling the trimmed strawberries like she was trying to make mushy red scrambled eggs. Rather than holding the knife with her fingertips, she had it mangled into her fist. She didn't so much cut as mash down. Even with the sharpened blade, little pieces of strawberry shot through the air around us. I watched her destroy three of them. We were definitely going to have a mess on our hands. All of a sudden, Mom was standing to Rita's right.

"Stop," she said with her hand hovering over the cutting board. I could hear the smile in my mother's voice and see it as well by the way her hand was bobbing in the air. Rita squeezed her eyes shut tight. I couldn't tell if she was about to freak out somehow or was just counting her blessings for Mom's help.

"First of all, you need to relax," Mom said. She put her hand on Rita's wrist. "Calm down. Never hold a paring knife like you want to kill someone. It's not a weapon. It's an instrument. You need to learn that. Maybe someday you'll want to become a surgeon."

"I don't think I want to be a surgeon," Rita said.

"Yes, well, no matter what you become in life, you want to hold a knife with your fingertips when you're cutting soft fruits and vegetables. And you must relax. But also, no hesitating," Mom said. "Slice. Just slice. Let the blade do the work. You are in charge of both the blade and the strawberry."

We both kind of spluttered at that. Rita let her hand relax, held the knife handle with her fingers, then sliced, and the berry became two. Not perfect, but so much better than she'd been doing.

Mom moved down the counter and picked up her wine glass. "Another."

Rita cut. This time she did it perfectly.

"All right. That's good," said Mom. She took a sip of wine. I could hear Zax asking Delmore a question out in the other room.

"You're going to be a great surgeon someday," Mom said to Rita. "Just keep slicing strawberries and it will all work out."

Rita smiled. I went back to work rinsing and cutting off all the bad bits, piling berries up on the side of the cutting board for Rita.

Mom watched us for a while. Finally, she said, "We need music. I'll be back in a sec." She bustled out of the room.

"Wow," Rita said.

I nodded a couple times, then said, "She's kind of scientific about things in the kitchen."

"No. She's so cool. I mean . . ." She shrugged. "I don't know anything about kitchens or food. But now I want to learn. I mean, I *need* to learn."

"Stick with us, then. Mom's full of that kind of thing."

4. Questions and Answers

We were eating dinner but not saying a word. The jazz Mom had put on floated around us, drawing sadness and beauty into the air the way it sometimes seems to do. Finally, Zaxy started to laugh in this silent way he has sometimes. He was holding a green bean in one hand, his other hand over his mouth, blinking at the lamp flame in the center of the table. When he looked up, he stared at me. Then he looked at Mom to his left, then Del, who was sitting next to him. He let his eyes drift across the table to me again and, I think, to Rita, and then finally to Daddy, laughing without a sound the whole time.

Finally, Mom said, "We like it when you enjoy yourself, Zachary. Be careful, though, no beans until you've stopped laughing."

That made the kid start shaking he was laughing so hard. Daddy took a sip of wine and cleared his throat. A pack of Marlboros rested at the edge of the table near his elbow.

Del said, "Such a strange little kid." Then he put a fork load of fruit salad in his mouth. Zaxy rocked

43

back and forth, still holding this long, green stick of a bean in his one hand. Tears were pouring out of his eyes. Rita and Del tried to eat as if nothing was happening. Zaxy seemed like he might start hyperventilating pretty soon. He'd done that in the past.

Rita asked, "Are we listening to Miles Davis?"

Mom nodded. "Yes, as a matter of fact."

"*Kinda Blue*?" Rita asked.

Before Mom could answer, though, Daddy cleared his throat again, took another sip of wine, and said somewhat louder than you might expect, "So, Robert. Tell me, why did you change your name to Rita Gomez?"

Zaxy's whole body jerked to a stop. He got very small and stared at our cousin, waiting for an answer, a bean poking out of his fist.

Rita said, "It's a *trans* thing, Scat. The name kind of just comes to you."

"I see," said Daddy. He took another sip of wine, seemed to consider what he'd heard, then asked, "Kind of a mystical experience?"

Rita raised her napkin from her lap and dabbed around her lips. I felt her thinking and gauging the situation. "It's weird, Scat," she said. "It's not really *mystical*, exactly. I've had to deal with it all my life. Some people—trans people—can remember the first time they realized they weren't the gender people told them they were. Sometimes parents remember for them. In my case, I always felt like I was going uphill but never getting anywhere. Maybe it's because I'm an only child. I don't know. So, no, it wasn't mystical. It's just this nagging sense that things aren't right, like you're stuck driving around in a weird car and you absolutely cannot just stop and get out. The funny thing, of course, is you actually *can* get out." She looked down at her plate.

"But the name?"

"Right. I don't know. Robert's a very male name. I've always known it was wrong for me."

"Bobbie can be a girl's name," Daddy offered.

"I never really felt like that was an option."

"So . . . Rita? What's that?"

She took a bite of fruit, maybe for time to think. After she swallowed, she said, "We had a housekeeper once with that name. Rita Jones. She was black and kind of young. I was maybe four or five. I really liked her. She was more or less a nanny to me for a while."

"What happened to her?" Mom asked.

"Not sure. You know how my mom is. She's a hard person to work for."

Daddy chuckled. Mom nodded. They glanced at each other for a second.

"So, yeah, *Rita.* I always liked that name. I went through a long period there where I listened to the Beatles' song, 'Lovely Rita, Meter Maid,' over and over. I was maybe ten or so. I felt sad when I listened to it. I missed *my* Rita. She'd stuck hard in my memory for, like, five or six years."

Daddy leaned a bit over his plate. "And Gomez?"

Rita nodded, then tittered. It really was a titter. I was impressed. "I came up with it on the plane." She shrugged. "What can I say? I'm from San Diego. There's so many Mexican families. I don't know. My mom's from Latin America. I'm mixed race. A lot of times people in San Diego blather Spanish at me out of nowhere. Just assuming, you know? That's always been fine with me. Makes me proud. I can usually follow what they're saying. I've always felt more accepted . . ." She shrugged and made a sour face. "It's kind of stupid, I know, but the name Gomez just came to me at sunrise, thirty-thousand feet in the air. It sounded right. Rita Gomez doesn't feel like I made it up at all. It sounds like that's who I've always been."

"Don't you think you should have talked to your parents about it first?" Daddy said. "I mean, you're thinking about giving up your—*our* family name."

Rita had managed to keep eating through much of this—quick small bites when Daddy spoke. Now she dabbed at her mouth again with her napkin and sat up very straight in her chair. "Excuse me, Scat." She turned to our mom. "Aunt Rikely? What is your full name?"

Mom nodded. You could see approval in this very sly smile she flashed. "My full name is Rikely Thomas Scattergood. But I was once Rikely Virginia Thomas."

"A woman changing her name after marriage isn't exactly the same," Daddy said. "It's a custom. Common in most civilized cultures."

Mom shot that hard smile of her's at Daddy. "It's not really a custom, so much as a choice *I* made, Scat."

"It's a custom."

"Well, it may seem like that to you, but I assure you, I did not make my choice of taking your name based on a *civilized* custom. You know that, Scat. I chose to take your name because I didn't want to complicate things. I wanted to have the same name as my children—and you. But it wasn't custom, husband dear. Don't act stupid to prove a point."

"It's just a name, though. Right?" Rita offered. She put down her fork. "I mean, you changed your name maybe because you got married, but you were still the same person. Going from Thomas to Scattergood didn't really alter who you were."

"No. No it didn't." Mom looked across the table at Daddy.

"So, no big deal, maybe. But what about someone like me? They gave me this super common boys' name. Only inside, all my life, I feel like I'm a girl. And now I think I may want to change and become that girl *outside* as well as inside. Certainly, you can't expect me to want to be a girl called Robert. Who wants to be known as that weird girl, Robert?"

"So perhaps you need a girl's first name," Daddy said. "But you've also done away with your surname."

Rita just stared at him.

"Does being a Scattergood embarrass you?" Daddy asked.

Rita kept staring at him. She didn't seem angry or defensive.

47

He went on. "You need to think all of this through pretty carefully . . . Rita."

Mom spoke up. "When I took the Scattergood name, I didn't know all that I know now. But even so, I'm proud to be a member of this family. The Scattergood Clan did a lot in early American history and they continue to do a lot. Obviously. It's a big statement, Rita, to swear off your family name. It really is . . ."

Our cousin continued to stare in Daddy's direction. Her eyes were a bit glazed. They'd penetrated Daddy's head. Her vision was floating somewhere out the window behind him.

"I guess that's really why they sent me out here," she finally said.

"What?" said Daddy.

"To think this through."

Daddy looked puzzled. "Really?"

"Makes sense."

"How?" Mom said.

"I *need* to figure this out. All of it. Seriously. My parents know that probably better than I do. You all are distant enough from us—and smart enough—to challenge what I'm trying to do here, but you're still family and you have my parents' best interest to guide you. Sending me out here for the summer is a good way to figure out what I'm going to do."

"Figure out?" Mom said.

"That's the thing," Rita said slowly. "Before I made that change on the plane, I had never been in public as Rita. I didn't know how it would feel. I'd talked to my parents about how weird and confused everything seemed, but I had no idea. They kept saying they'd support me in whatever I wanted. They said they were there to talk. They said I needed time. Distance . . ."

"Did you tell them you might do something drastic when you came out here?" Mom asked that in a funny voice.

Rita tipped her head to the side, then looked across the table at Zax. "Not really . . ."

My parents locked eyes. If they'd been angry with each other a few minutes earlier, now the expression they shared was concern.

"All of this is a bit funny," Daddy said. "Strange funny."

Rita waited. I looked down at the hand holding her fork. I hadn't noticed until right then. It was shaking a little.

Daddy went on. "I called your father this afternoon." He looked at Mom. "Your aunt here was against it, so don't be mad at her. I had to call. He's my brother. We weren't expecting this."

Rita put up her hand and said, "I understand, Uncle Scat. It's just—"

"Yes, well, your father was very surprised. He didn't seem to have any idea."

"What?" Rita's hand started to shake more.

"To learn that his son Robert showed up at Bangor International Airport as someone named Rita Gomez."

She closed her eyes for a moment. "I guess he might choose that angle."

"It was a difficult conversation," Daddy said. "He claimed he'd talked to you about waiting. You need time to think things through more thoroughly. And your hair? When I mentioned your long hair there was dead silence. Is that a wig?"

"What did he tell you?"

"Your father was upset," Daddy went on. "He kept apologizing to me."

I was all of a sudden quite curious about my cousin's hair. So was Del. I'm sure Rita could feel us eyeing her head.

"Did you speak at all with Samantha?" Mom asked.

Daddy shook his head and began to knead the sides of his cigarette box with his fingertips.

Rita's hand had stopped trembling. She said, "All of this feels unnecessarily uncomfortable."

The Miles Davis had stopped sometime earlier. You could hear the wind outside. Night birds called to each other, preparing for the sun to go down. But inside, none of us made a peep. Daddy's hand on his cigarettes had even stopped fidgeting. I guess we were waiting for Rita to say something else.

My eyes came to rest on my little brother. He stared back at me sadly, then let his eyes float again to the flame in the lantern. I kept watching him. He looked back up at me after a few seconds, then allowed his face to go sad again. Finally, he asked, "Is that really a wig?"

Coming out of that silence it was like Zaxy was yelling on a playground. I think we all blinked five or six times to help us float out of the trance we were in. I swiveled my face around carefully, squinting at Rita from the side of my eyes with a hopeful wince on my face.

She seemed to hesitate a beat or two, then smiled and let out a soft chuckle. "It's a nice one isn't it? I've had it for a while."

"You look very beautiful," Zaxy said flatly, like he was trying to explain something he knew he was too young to really understand.

"Thanks."

Delmore snickered. "I don't think I want to see you without it."

"You won't," Rita replied. She turned to Daddy after saying that. "My father apologized to you?"

Mom said, "For now, Rita, you need to just be who you think you need to be." She looked across the table to Daddy for agreement.

He let out a long breath and scratched his forehead. "I think there are a lot of difficult issues you bring up, young . . . lady. With all of this, I mean."

Daddy does this thing where he breathes only through his nose and sits up very straight, very noble, like he's some kind of emperor. He didn't give Rita a mean stare or even a disapproving one—just a hard one. I'd seen him do that with some of the young writers who came to visit him. He used that look on me sometimes, too. Not so much on Delmore. And certainly not Zaxy. It was very intense, and it seemed to make it hard for him to breathe properly, smoker that he is. But I also felt right there that maybe it was a look of resignation or even respect. Rita stared right back at him the same way, her back just as straight, only she wasn't having trouble breathing. Her shoulders arced behind her. I looked down at her hand again. It wasn't trembling at all.

"I can't tell you what to do," Daddy said finally. "I—"

Rita held up her hand. "Actually, Scat, you *can* tell me what to do. I just might not do it."

"Yes, well," he reached for the second bottle of wine and picked up the corkscrew to begin peeling off the seal. "I suppose you're right about that. What I mean is, I will *not* tell you what to do."

"Did you tell Edward that?" Mom asked.

Daddy was now working the opener into the cork. "No. I didn't say much. He did the talking. As usual. My older brother."

He began to tug the cork out of the bottle. Looking down the table at Zax, he said, "Big brothers can be such . . . such . . . help me out here, Ivy. What is it you say?"

"Asses?"

"Ah, asses, yes, that's it. Big brothers can be such asses."

Zaxy liked that and elbowed Del. Poor Del.

Mom was Mom, though. "Don't worry about what your father says, Delly Belly. I was the oldest in my family, too. For those of us without older siblings, dads are the asses. In fact, they're not just asses, they're rhino's asses."

"Hmm," said Rita. "I think you mean rhino *butts*." She turned and tapped the top of my head twice.

5. The Problem with Super Boys

After supper, the kids did the dishes as quickly as we could—which wasn't too quick since Rita had pretty much never done dishes before, either. When we finally finished up, Rita and Del had to have smokes as soon as we got to the top of the hill beyond sight of the main house. I left them to their stupid behavior and went inside, put Johnnyswim on the CD player, and sat in one of the two reading chairs near the fireplace. We had no need for a fire that night, but it was still nice sitting there reading with the smoky scent of burned ashes and a couple half-charred logs to keep me company.

Rita and Del came in about ten minutes later. Rita plopped on the floor while Del turned on the TV and game console, then fumbled around on the shelf until he'd found the second controller. He finally sat a few feet to Rita's left, handed her the controller, and started pressing buttons on his until he'd called up his submarine game.

"Wait a minute," Rita said to him.

"What?"

"Is this Johnnyswim?"

Before I could respond, they both burst out laughing. I felt really lonely right then. Why do people make fun of music other people like?

Rita turned to me like nothing had just happened. "He's going to teach me how to play Toku-Tai. Are we going to bother you?"

"Don't ask her that. Of course it'll bother her."

Rita waited for my answer.

"He's right," I said. "But don't worry, I can just go to my room when the music's over."

"I don't—"

"There are certain things Ivy doesn't like in this world," Del said. "Twitter, Facebook, texting, maybe cell phones as a principle—although she has one that she uses a fair amount when no one's looking. Oh, and boys *not* named Bailey Cooper. Also, there are certain things she totally despises, namely video games and reality TV."

I had a choice there. It was truly embarrassing just to hear the name Bailey Cooper, let alone feel like I had to respond to that. But Del was right about stuff I don't like. I also don't like makeup and high heels (as you know), perfume, dresses, snobby vegetarians, and cat lovers who think they hate dogs. In all fairness, I don't much care for dog lovers who think they hate cats, either. I'll admit it here: I've always been a bit too caught up in my own opinions. Some might even say I'm a bit immature and uncool. What can I say? I know what I think and feel.

"I don't know if I *despise* reality TV," I said. "But it's true, I despise video games. That's just for myself, though. I don't despise people who play them. Go ahead. Really. If you get too loud or crazy, I'll just leave."

Rita hadn't stopped staring at me. She asked, "Who's Bailey Cooper?"

My cheeks began heating up and my hands seemed a bit numb. And then there was my heart, pounding up and up and up through my throat into my jaw.

"Well, he's just the most dashing and best-est of baseball players in the whole of lake country," Delmore, the camel's ass, said. He fanned his face with his controller.

My first impulse was to slam my book on the floor and stomp out of there. My next was to search for something to say that would get back at him. Finally, it just seemed like I needed a sharp retort. Only nothing came to me on any front. The best I could do was this: "Blanche here thinks I'm in love with a guy named Bailey Cooper."

"I get that," Rita said. She waited. My whole face was now quite possibly as hot as a baked potato in August, and I had honestly lost the feeling in both my hands and my feet.

"Well?" Rita tried. "Are you?"

"Am I what?"

"In love with a guy named Bailey?"

Delmore went, "Oh, it's love, all right. Love *sick*! She's in love. Luh-uh-uh-uh-ve!"

"Delmore!" It took a lot to keep my voice from quivering.

"And this guy's up here?" asked our cousin.

"All year," said Del.

"Well?" She directed that at me.

"What?"

"What's he like?"

I could've just said I don't want to talk about it, then calmly walked out of the room. But something opened up inside of me right there. I wanted to answer her question. It seemed like it would feel okay to do that. Also, it seemed like answering would show that I wasn't over the moon and smitten like a little idiot.

"Del here is being dumb about all of this," I started. "Bailey Cooper is a nice person and a really good baseball player. He's only seventeen, but he plays on the Resonance American Legion team with older guys from all over central Maine."

"So he's a *baseball* player?"

"Yup. People say he's getting recruited by Dartmouth and Harvard."

"Smart, too?"

"And cute," said my brother. "Apparently . . ."

I closed my eyes and inhaled.

Rita smiled softly in my direction. "Are you going out with him?"

I laughed. "Hardly. He's seventeen and barely knows my name."

"So you . . . you don't even really know him?" She sounded disappointed.

"Oh, she knows him," Del said as he went back to setting up their submarine game.

"He used to teach sailing," I said. "In fact, he still does. He'll be teaching Zaxy tomorrow."

"He's a sailor, too?"

"The dude is a stud," said Del. "He won a whole bunch of junior offshore races at the Down East Regatta a few years ago. I mean, he went from lake sailing to ocean racing and smoked every one of those snobby rich kids out of Penobscot Bay. He's supposed to be good at tennis, too, and cross-country."

"So he's one of *those* guys," Rita said. "I'm going to guess he's *seriously* cute, too." She was looking at me again. Waiting for an answer.

My face was now pulsing, and my cheeks were probably glowing bright orange. I sure felt weird. Was my voice shaky?

"*Those* guys?" I asked.

"We have a lot of them out in California." She glanced over at Del. "I call them super boys. The problem with super boys is they only like super girls . . . which, of course, can mean a lot of things depending on the super boy."

And there it was. I most definitely have never qualified for the super girl club. Such a stupid conversation. Yes, I liked Bailey Cooper. Every girl in Resonance Hills liked Bailey Cooper. A lot of the moms "liked" Bailey Cooper, too—and not necessarily in a mom kind of way. He was tall and lean, with dark wavy hair always just a little bit shaggy and bouncing too close to his eyes. His hands were big and looked very strong when you watched him do things with them, like swing a bat or cleat down a mainsail, but there was something gentle about them at the same time. T-shirts hung off his broad shoulders like flags of perfection. He had a wide mouth and full lips, and he spoke quietly and confidently.

Yes, he was a super boy. And I was not a super girl. Plus, he was my older brother's age. A bit beyond reach for someone like me.

But I wasn't really interested in how handsome he was, or even that he was a star baseball player. I knew guys like that down in Cliveden. It was a stupid little thing, but there was something that connected us. At least, that's what I felt.

I'd more or less known Bailey all my life. He used to run in Delmore's group of friends before they all became teenagers. Every summer he'd be down at the water with all the other boys, throwing rocks, chasing frogs, fishing, swimming, getting into mild forms of trouble with grownups on the docks and in town.

Then, all of a sudden, at thirteen Bailey gets a job usually only the kids who are already driving get. He was running sailing camp for the under-tens. The next year he had the under thirteen group, which included me.

That was the year I started to like sailing a whole lot more. I didn't really know why. Daddy said Bailey was a good instructor. But Bailey was only around about half the time because he was off down east near Bar Harbor, competing in regattas. I used to hear the older boys talk about him with reverence. The older girls giggled a lot around him and said really stupid things.

Somehow I learned that he was playing on the Junior American Legion baseball team in the area. He was well over six feet tall by then and pretty skinny, but, you know, it was Maine, and I guess they just needed guys who could make contact with a baseball and look like they knew what they were doing catching and throwing.

We went to watch the team play a couple evenings that year. He played outfield and batted sixth, which was pretty amazing to me since he was at least two years younger than everyone else. I didn't know I was feeling crushy, though. I just wanted to be best friends with him. Of course, I didn't tell anyone about that. It seemed stupid. He probably knew my name, but I was just a dumb little girl to him.

It became a very powerful and dreamy need one night watching him play. He'd gone out to his position in center field during the middle of the inning, maybe in the fourth or fifth. The right fielder was warming up, playing catch the way outfielders do in between innings with a teammate on the sideline. Usually, the center fielder and left fielder throw with each other. Only, that night the left fielder wasn't out there. So Bailey played catch with the second baseman.

I'd just finished my twelve-year-old season of Little League. I'd been the starting second baseman all year. As I watched Bailey throwing back and forth with this kid who played the same position I did, it just dawned on me that what I really wanted, more than anything in the world, was to play catch with Bailey Cooper. It really seemed like that—*more than anything in the world.*

Playing catch with him would be an equalizer, a way to show him that, yeah, I was a dumb twelve-year-old girl, but I was good enough with my glove and had a decent arm. We would have a good time doing that. He'd like me. It wasn't even about respect. There wasn't a single one of those giggly girls with breasts and flowing hair, and makeup even, who could play catch and have it actually be fun for a guy like Bailey Cooper.

This vision of playing catch with him got the better of me the rest of that summer. I obsessed over it. Sailing lessons were over at the end of July, but I went out of my way to show up at the club, carrying my mitt. Sometimes I'd come down with a hardball and toss it in the air, playing catch with myself. A few times, when he was within earshot, I asked groups of kids if anyone wanted to play catch. Of course, no one had a glove, including Bailey, so my suggestion went out the back door of everyone's conversation.

It was sad, really. I had no idea what I was actually feeling. Things changed the next year. I had a tough baseball season in the spring where the boys were starting to be better players than me. I wasn't feeling too confident about that side of my life. But Bailey

61

had been promoted to teaching senior-level sailing, which I was now part of. Del had graduated and was hanging out at the house doing whatever he wanted. That was quite all right with me.

"Ivy? You there? Hello?" It was Rita.

"She's dreaming about kissing Cooper," Del said. "Super Cooper!"

I made a face at him, then flopped my head back against the chair a few times. Staring up at the ceiling, I said, "Look. Bailey's a good guy. What can I say? I'd like to maybe be friends with him someday."

That seemed enough for my cousin and my brother. They turned their attention to the screen on the wall, setting up their submarines. Delmore was pretty good at quietly instructing Rita about the goals of the game and the strategy. I tried hard to stay focused on my book, but after a few minutes I tiptoed back to my room. I don't think they knew I was gone until they were heading to bed.

6. Secrets

Delmore and I used to get up before seven in the morning so that we could be at sailing class by eight. We each "graduated" early from boat school at thirteen, though, which basically means Mom and Daddy didn't force us to complete the senior level like a lot of the other kids who vacationed in Resonance Hills. Us getting up that early is another reason that Zaxy was still sleeping at the main house. Still, no matter what, one of the worst things about having a writer for a parent is that they've usually been up working for several hours already, every day. Daddy is up by five most mornings, seven days a week. The only time off he gives himself is Christmas Morning.

So, when Rita, Delmore, and I came down to the main house that next morning for breakfast, Daddy was sitting on the porch reading something on his iPad with an iced coffee next to him. He was smoking what I could see was his third cigarette because I counted two butts in the ashtray to his right.

"Good morning teenagers!" he chuckled in the chippery way he's always had before lunch. "My good-

63

ness, Rita, you look smashing in that blouse. Love the toenail work, too!"

It was true, of course. Our cousin looked amazingly beautiful standing there in the morning sun. What a great wig. In that particular light it flickered with hints of marigold and what I guess you might say was dark red honey. Her blouse was mint-green linen with a small, loose collar and three-quarter sleeves. It seemed a bit big for her.

"Mom's got breakfast warming in the oven for you punks," Daddy said. "We have a big day ahead of us. We need to introduce Rita here to the water."

"The water?" she asked.

"Right. The lake. The whole deal about coming here is the lake. Young lady. You'll see. In the meantime, get some eats. We'll drive down when you're ready."

Del opened the front door and we started to follow him.

"Ivy?" Daddy said. "Can you hold up a minute? I wanted to ask you something."

Del and Rita went inside, and I took a few steps toward my father who was just putting his cigarette out in the ashtray. He swiveled a bit in his lounge chair. "They gone?" he asked.

"Yup."

"Good. I just wanted to clue you in to some stuff." He was speaking in his secretive voice, a hoarse, ominous whisper. "Sit."

I took the lounge chair next to him and waited with my hands clasped between my knees.

"I didn't tell the whole story last night."

"The whole story?"

"Right. About my phone call with Uncle Edward."

"Oh."

He swiveled around again to check the door, then took a deep breath and settled back into his chair. "It was a tough conversation. He told me your cousin there is *required* to remain a boy."

"Required?"

"Edward told me that she . . . he . . . shoot . . . I don't know what to call that kid. He was my only nephew for God's sake."

"Just use Rita, Dad. That's what she wants."

He scratched his chin and picked up his pack of cigarettes. "I guess . . ."

I watched him extract another cigarette from the pack, then put it between his lips.

"Your uncle was pretty upset. He made me promise not to tell *her* that he knew what was going on. He made me promise not to let your Aunt Samantha know, either."

"But they're married . . . I mean, they're her parents."

"Right, well, things are rather complicated these days out in San Diego."

"And you did tell Rita that you'd told him what she'd done."

"I did. You're right. And you know I don't play games with people. But here's the thing, Ive, at the beginning of the conversation Eddie seemed confused, almost like he didn't have a clue that his son might be inclined to turn into a girl. A little way into the conversation, though, it seemed like he was more faking that. You know, kind of putting on being baffled."

"But Rita said they sent her out here to figure things—"

"That's why I'm talking to you here, child. A lot of things are going on in that family that we just don't fully understand yet."

"So Rita was lying about why they sent her out here?"

"No, I don't think so."

"Then what?"

"I think she's as confused as we are . . . and maybe as confused as my brother is."

All the time he'd been speaking he had the cigarette dangling from his lips. Now he lit it. I was glad that I was sitting upwind.

"Those two parents are definitely having problems. I got the impression that Samantha is more unapproving of this transition thing than Eddie, but, like I told your mom, I didn't speak with her."

"So you should talk with her."

"Probably. But Eddie's my brother. And by the end of the phone call he had been very clear that we are required to force Rita to change back to Robert."

I didn't know what to say to that. Just how were we all supposed to force Rita to do anything?

"They're getting a separation, those two."

I blinked. "What? That sucks."

"You must have been able to tell your mom and I were holding something back last night at dinner."

I nodded.

"It would seem your cousin is part of their problems."

"What do you mean?"

"I'm not sure exactly. But there's actually a court order that won't let Robert Scattergood go around in public like a girl. Or even dress like that at home in private."

"A court order?"

"A judge—"

"I know what a court order is, Daddy. It's just . . . how could they—"

"Right. Pretty extreme. I guess this judge thinks Robert's wanting to transition is complicating his parents' ability to figure out whether to separate."

"So. What? Aunt Samantha doesn't want her to change and Uncle Edward is confused?" I thought for a moment. "And that's why they're getting a divorce?"

Daddy exhaled smoke, then popped his lips together.

"Honestly, Ivy, I don't know. I would certainly hope none of all this will come to pass. Those two have been married forever. When there's trouble in a marriage that old, the cause is usually a combination of so many things . . ."

"But maybe Rita's *not* one of the causes."

He shook his head. "It's possible she is, though."

67

"That would so suck."

"Yes it would. But it would explain why my brother was kind of weird about the whole thing."

We sat looking out at the lake in the distance. In the morning, with the summer light, it looks like a piece of sky floating out beyond the trees.

"We can't . . ." I started to say. "I mean, it's not fair."

"Right. I feel the same way," he said. "And I honestly can't make Rita—or Robert for that matter—follow a judge's orders. I wanted to ask you if that makes sense."

"Of course it does. Not even a judge should be able to force a kid to do something like that."

"So you think all of this trans stuff is legit? I mean . . ."

"You mean that Robert really feels like he's a girl?"

He nodded. "It's big stuff. The idea is that eventually the change is forever. Don't just answer me with a knee-jerk liberal, Friends-private-school Scattergood response here. Think about it. Are you, at the age of fifteen, ready to make a choice like that? Could you just decide you're going to become a boy, eventually get surgically altered, and never look back?"

"Why do you say it's so permanent?"

"Because that's what we're talking about here, kid. That's what this transition stuff is. I stopped in town yesterday to download a bunch of articles to my iPad. Heavy stuff, when you go through with it. First off, boys need to shut puberty down. Rita would have to take testosterone-blocking drugs. There's also estrogen cocktails to become more female. Some of the articles I found actually talk about designer hormone therapy they're working on to simulate the mental and emotional part of a woman's monthly menstruation."

He looked over at me and chuckled.

"*That* might be a mistake," I said.

He chuckled again, took a long drag on his cigarette, then went on. "There's body sculpting, too. Breast implants, shaving the Adam's apple, sometimes cosmetic surgery to make the face more feminine."

"They can do all that? Shaving the Adam's apple? That's . . ." (I felt squeamish.) "Really?"

"Really."

"I assumed a lot went into the whole process, but we never really talked about it on that level in school."

"No, I suppose you wouldn't."

We were silent for a moment. Daddy took another hard puff on his cigarette, then stared out over the distant lake trickle-sparkling beyond the top of the trees.

"The big one, though, is what they call bottom surgery."

That seemed really weird. Surgery on your butt? Then I understood. "Oh!"

"Right. Supposedly, it's pretty effective now for boys turning into girls. They kind of invert the penis and don't even have to sacrifice much by way of nerve endings."

I held up my hand, feeling more and more uncomfortable. "Daddy, don't."

He took another puff on his cigarette. We sat in silence for a while, staring off at the clouds, the sky, and the lake.

"I just want you to understand what we're talking about here, Ivy."

"I really didn't need to know the details," I said.

"Actually, I think you do. Because you will likely be talking to this *new* cousin of yours. You seem to be getting along. I want you to know what you're up against."

"What do you mean?"

"She's got to deal with the reality of this choice, Ivy. It's not just putting on a wig and wearing a bra stuffed with gym socks. We're talking hardcore life changing issues here. We're talking about the most fundamental and monumental decision a person can ever make—that no person should have to make."

"And Uncle Edward doesn't approve."

"Uncle Edward is confused . . . I mean, right now it's all still pretend. Apparently, Robert's been . . . Rita's been dressing up at home some, wearing makeup. I don't think Eddie's ever seen the wig—"

"All right, but he said—he demanded—that she turn back into Robert."

"He said the court order commands it."

"Yeah, but why did . . . ? I mean, why send her out here and not tell us? It's not fair to her. Or us."

My dad leaned over to stub out his cigarette. I wanted to tell him that he needed to quit. But I tried to focus on the conversation instead.

"I will try to track down your Aunt Samantha. But I doubt I'll have much luck. You know how she is," Daddy said quietly. "But we're not going to force your cousin to do anything. I wanted you to know that, and to understand the details here. But I don't want you to talk to her about her parents and the court order or anything else on that level."

I was surprised all of a sudden by how mad I was beginning to feel. You don't force a fifteen-year-old kid to do anything unless they're hurting themselves. Even then, you can't be a dictator. It dawned on me that Uncle Edward and the judge were being pretty cowardly. Especially Uncle Edward, demanding that his brother deal with something like this and not facing it head-on himself.

"He's being a real ass," I said.

"Who?"

"Uncle Edward. He ticks me off. I mean it. He's an ass-butt and a half." I turned to just catch my father's smile before he let it drop and made his face go serious.

"Yes, well, that's Eddie. The bane of my existence." His face was certainly solemn, but I'd caught that smile. What was that about? Serious or not, I could see little remnant flickers from the lake and the sky reflected in his eyes.

"Are we going to get through this summer okay, Daddy?"

Somehow, right there, with all the complexities that Rita threw at us, I felt very vulnerable and unsure of myself. I wondered about the strength of my own parents' relationship for probably the hundredth time that year. And now I had learned that my uncle and aunt were having problems. So many other friends had parents who were divorced or in the middle of one. Then, too, Delmore seemed so hot and cold all the time, like he couldn't figure out who he was. Sometimes I felt sad about Zaxy as well. He was heading toward becoming a teenager faster than he should. I suppose that was partly because he had two teenaged siblings, but some of it also had to do with our parents. In the way things broke down between those two sometimes, he was forced to change and grow on his own. None of us were able to help. We really didn't understand him.

"Hey," Daddy said. "You okay?"

Nothing would have changed if I'd told my father no, I'm not okay. Sometimes I feel so sad for all of us. I feel sad for the world. The older I get, the more it seems, sometimes, like nobody is equipped to deal with how complicated things really are.

But I didn't say that. Instead, I smiled at my father and said, "Thanks for letting me know all that stuff. Can I go get some breakfast now? And can I drive the boat today?"

"Sure," he said. "It's your turn. Go eat, and don't forget to tell Rita to put on sunblock."

As I stood, he reached out and took my hand. "You can talk to Mom about all of this, just don't share it with either of your brothers. Obviously, not your cousin, either."

I nodded several times. He let go of me as I moved toward the door.

7. Sound of Music Days

Sometimes up here the night air can be sharp, clean, and almost wintery cold. A few hours after the sun has vaulted into the sky, though, everything warms up enough to make it feel like summer. Golden light hums everywhere, very softly. Our early-part-of-the-day uniform is usually shorts and a sweatshirt. After lunch sweatshirts come off.

Daddy calls these *Sound of Music* days because we're in the mountains and the sky looks almost exactly the way it does at the beginning of that movie. You feel like you could spin around just above everything, maybe look down to find a beautiful young Julie Andrews turning and turning under the bright sun and young clouds, singing at the top of her lungs.

Zaxy had camp every weekday until the afternoon, but usually, by late morning Del and I were down at the dock with Mom and Daddy. It was all about the boat. I haven't mentioned the boat yet. I should have. A lot of stuff got going when Rita popped into the picture, so I forgot about the boat.

It seems like summer is always, at least in part, about the boat and riding in it with Daddy, or just drifting on the water. Sometimes we pack a lunch and head out for a long ride to different coves and beaches on the lake. Other times we just troll slowly along the shoreline looking at the scenery.

I drove the boat a fair amount. Sometimes it would get boring. Sometimes Delmore would take over. He was pretty good, to tell the truth, about letting me get my fill of being in charge. That's probably because he was also allowed to go out on his own.

Daddy tried to teach Rita how to fish that day. None of us, including Daddy, really ever knew what we were doing. We just had cheap little six-foot rods and Zebco reels with the thumb button that made casting simple enough.

We had a stringer for anything that was a keeper. Stringers are pretty weird. You slide them through the fish's mouth and then out one of their gills. Then you drop the fish back in the water so they stay fresh until you're done fishing and can take them home to cut up. It must be so frustrating and confusing for a fish hung up on a stringer.

We had a good-sized tackle box in the stern equipment cabinet and a couple of nets. Perch and sunfish were our normal catches—small, boney, useless fish most of the time. The nets were almost a joke. Occasionally someone would land a muskie or a pickerel. I suppose that's why we kept pretending we knew what we were doing.

You need a small boat with a quiet motor to troll like a real fisherman. Since our parents were too lazy or cheap to own two boats, we would travel around to spots Daddy thought were likely places, cut the noisy motor, then drift and cast. We kept a couple places secret where you might get lucky sometimes and catch northern pike. That was fun, but they're so difficult to filet, we would just throw them back in the water.

At first, our new boat attracted a lot of eyes in town when we drove it there to shop at the Albertson's. It was only the second boat we had owned in my lifetime. A 28-foot Cobalt Bowrider, it had a powerful Volvo engine that purred and burbled under water. Daddy was very proud of it, which is why he was so set on spending part of most days out on the water. He'd bought it the year before as a surprise for all of us. It was huge and sleek, with white and red lines near the water, and the most beautiful cobalt blue hull in Resonance Hills. I think boats like ours are really more ocean vessels.

Rita didn't seem to like being out on the water much. From the moment we parked at the boat club parking lot to the end of the afternoon as we were all piling out of the Cobalt, she let this grim look flash across her face when she thought no one was looking. A few days later, I asked Mom if she ever saw it. She laughed a little and grabbed a handful of hair on the side of her head. She whispered, "It's her wig, Ivy. She can't get it wet."

Rita and I read up in the bow seating area. Daddy and Del fished off the stern. Mom read some technical manual she'd brought along. I read the sports section from the Boston Globe to catch up on the Red Sox. I love the Red Sox. If we'd spent our summers in Philly, I probably would have ended up a bigger Phillies fan. But we spent the heart of every year in New England. There's only one baseball team for the whole region. How could I not be a diehard fan of one of the most beloved sports teams in America?

When we saw the after-lunch fleet of training boats heading away from the docks, we took turns with the two sets of binoculars on board, trying to find Zaxy's boat. At least, that's what I pretended to do. I couldn't help myself. The crash boat, a beat-up fiberglass Boston Whaler with a loud and smelly old Evinrude engine, carried the instructors. The person driving it was usually Bailey Cooper. He sat on the top of the driver's seat with his dark hair flying in the wind, zipping from one student boat to another.

I tried to be inconspicuous with my interest, but Del knew what I was doing.

"Cooper's a dud, you know." He faked a brotherly love tone of voice with me.

"What are you talking about?"

"Your boyfriend. You're watching him."

"I am not."

"Yes, you are. You're like some seventh grade boy who's just discovered boobs."

"I'm looking for Zax."

"He's on the one with the light blue fish on the sail. Number 769."

"I lost track."

"Sure you did."

"Why do you have to be such an ass?"

"Ivy," Mom said. "Your brother may be bothering you, but that's no reason to call him names."

"But why does he have to *act* like such an ass sometimes?"

Mom went back to reading her manual. I was actually the ass, of course. What was I doing ogling a boy two years older than me? So what if he had his shirt off on a *Sound of Music* day? It really is sad when girls expend so much energy being interested in unattainable boys.

When I pulled the binoculars away from my eyes, I caught a glimpse of Rita's expression shifting from concern or anger or fear, or something, to a sort of nonchalant half-smile. I felt like I needed to look away and act like I hadn't seen anything, but I extended the binoculars to her instead.

"Ever been sailing?" I asked.

"When I was little. In San Diego. But we were on some rich professor's yacht, not actually sailing something like your brother out there."

"Cruising in a rich dude's yacht sounds kind of cool."

"I remember it as rather unnerving."

"Why?"

She didn't say anything as she put the binoculars up to her eyes and adjusted the lenses.

"I don't know, really," she said, finally. "It just seemed that we were at the mercy of the wind. And so close to the water. They had to keep adjusting the sails, and the direction the boat was going, and everything. This is much better." She patted the side of the boat. "This is like a living room on the water attached to an engine. Much more sturdy, trustworthy, and comforting."

I decided I didn't want to have a discussion about sailboats versus motorboats. I'd had the same discussion with Del and other kids in sailing class too many times over the years. I pressed the button on my Kindle and waited for my book to come up.

I'm sure Daddy liked the silence and calm, just lounging on the boat in the middle of the lake. Technically it wasn't the middle, that was still a couple miles out, but we were certainly in a kind of nowhere. You could hear voices on the wind from the fleet of kids sailing, but they were far away. We also heard birds calling to each other and the constant slap of water against the hull. It was all peaceful and relaxing.

Every once in a while, when Daddy or Del would pull in their lines, you'd hear the click and snap of a reel. A few seconds later the zing of line would come, flying out of the reel, up the length of the rod, and back out over the water. Then the plunk and soft splash of the baited hook and sinker. If you looked over, you'd see a red and white bobber floating ten or twenty yards from the boat and the backs of my father and brother hunched and waiting.

79

I would fish sometimes too, of course. But during that first week Rita was visiting, I just wanted to settle in up in the bow to read and think.

She was still watching the boats when I glanced up. I stared at her chin and cheeks and ears and the way the breeze blew wig hair across her forehead and neck. If you let yourself think it, you saw she wasn't a normal girl. I kept checking for whiskers. So far, her chin and upper lip were smooth enough. I knew I was being unfair and mean. She really was very stunning looking, no matter what gender she had under her clothes. Her hands were long-fingered, but the nails were girlie enough. She had earrings on, too—pearl posts set in gold that day.

Was she heading to a point where she couldn't turn back? It had to be scary, or at least it must have made her feel really uncertain about how things were going to turn out.

Just as those thoughts occurred to me, I realized she wasn't watching the sailing. She was following the crash boat. I tried to decode the expression on her face. Her lips were tucked hard into her mouth like she was sucking on them. Her throat seemed to be pulsing slightly like a bird's. I couldn't see those brown eyes of hers, but her brows lifted just enough to suggest keen interest.

Was she checking out Bailey? Hadn't she told me that she still liked girls? It was hard to remember. I was confused. Maybe there had been a girl in the boat with Bailey. I couldn't remember. It seemed impossible that she would be looking at Bailey Cooper the way I had been looking at Bailey Cooper. I cocked my head and squeezed my face together. It felt like a moment where I could get mad or jealous or confront her or something worse. It would have been easy to be offended, grossed out even (yes, I know that's stupid), if she was interested in a guy. It also felt like a moment where I should just leave things alone.

I turned to see if anyone else noticed what was going on. Del and Daddy had their backs to us, sitting on the transom with their fishing poles in their hands, watching their bobbers and the water behind us. But there was Mom, right behind me, looking up into my face. I could see the question mark in her eyes. I turned away from her, hoping to just let it all go, maybe, figuring she'd possibly just then looked up and hadn't noticed me watching my cousin. I certainly didn't want to acknowledge that look on my mother's face. What I really needed was those binoculars back so I could figure out if there might be a girl on board with Bailey.

"Can I check something out with those?" I asked.

Rita didn't take her eyes off the scopes, but said, "These?"

"Why don't you use the ones back with your father, Ivy?" Mom said.

I didn't want those. I didn't want to be so obvious pointing them at exactly the same thing my cousin was watching. I'd never hear the end of it from Delmore. I glanced back. He and Daddy still had their backs turned to us.

"It's okay. I'll wait."

"You want 'em?" Del called.

"I'm good."

Mom must have caught on. "She's good."

I turned quickly and found Mom squinting at me. Maybe it was the sun. She gave me a brief smile, then went back to reading. I tried to go back to my Kindle, but it had simply become a screen to stare at. I couldn't focus. Finally, Rita stirred, swinging the binoculars in my direction.

"Here you go." She extended them from her seat on the other side of the bow. I tried to be as casual and uninterested as possible as I sat up.

"Thanks."

"Sorry."

"No problem."

I put the eyepieces to my eyes and adjusted the focus wheel. It took a little time to find the crash boat. When I did, my heart began to beat a bit faster. There was Bailey, standing up now, shirtless and driving. And in the bow was Justin Wedge. Behind him in the stern-facing seats were two other guys I couldn't make out. No girls.

As I watched, I felt the Cobalt shift a bit. All of a sudden Rita was sitting very close to me.

"He certainly is quite striking," she said at a volume meant only for me.

If you'd looked at my hands right then, you would have noticed my knuckles had gone bloodless and bone-colored from how hard I was gripping the binoculars.

"A boy like that . . . ," she said.

What was my problem? If she'd been one of my friends from home I would have giggled—and felt stupid, but also kind of giddy. I mean, yeah, a boy like that. He did something to me. He did something to every girl. But for Rita (or Robert, I thought coldly) to say something like that—well, it seemed unforgivable somehow.

"I like his shoulders," she said. "I like his—"

"Don't!" I snapped.

She flinched a little. I was still watching through the binoculars, but I felt that flinch. "I just—"

"Stop!" I said even louder.

I could sense my parents and older brother staring at us. I knew that Rita was startled, and probably quite self-conscious and uncomfortable all of a sudden. Right there, I started to hate her. I understood it was immature and stupidly catty, but I didn't care. It felt good to be mean to her. I watched Bailey a bit longer through the binoculars, then carefully moved the scopes away from my eyes. Rita was still sitting next to me, but she had turned away, staring at the distant shore.

I put the binoculars down on the seat next to her, then moved to the other side of the bow and snatched up my Kindle. As I shifted around to lie back, I caught Mom watching me. Again, the squinty eyes. Del was paying attention as well from behind her. He had one eye closed. Only Daddy seemed oblivious to things. I didn't care. My sharp response surprised me, too, but it also felt like the only appropriate thing to do.

I shook my head hard at my mother, then glared down into my Kindle. With a little effort I began to read again, but it dawned on me that what I'd just done was get seriously mad at someone, and out of nowhere that had spilled into being disgusted with the whole world. I was even mad, somehow, at Bailey Cooper. The only person I wasn't upset with was Zaxy.

And so I began a weird, dumb, stupid, self-centered, idiotic, immature, and foolish point of departure for me in my life. I know how I must have seemed to my family. But I didn't care one whit.

8. Rita-Robert-Whoever

The more I stewed on the idea of Rita wanting to transform into a girl, the more it seemed crazy. It was just so much work. The end result might be disappointing. If she took all those drugs and had all sorts of surgeries, including a boob job and even the bottom operation Daddy mentioned, for the rest of her life she would have to explain to those she cared about that she was transformed from what she had once been.

What if I wanted to become Chinese or Italian? That wouldn't be so bad, I suppose, but it was impossible to actually accomplish. I've been mixed-race all my life. Trying to change that, even at fifteen, would only alter how I looked, not who I actually am.

Daddy used the term "end game" a lot when he talked with his friends about politics and writing fiction. I felt that I saw the end game for Rita, and it wasn't happy.

As angry as I was at her, I swear part of me felt bad for her, too. She would be somebody in the middle of what people expected, kind of a person from another dimension. A facsimile of something beyond easy understanding. Why would anyone do that to themselves?

I was proud of myself for thinking all the way through to her end game. I had completely accepted who she was. But then I'd thought about what that meant. The implications. It seemed like only a matter of time before I would find the right moment to confront her with my conclusions. But the right moment rarely crops up when you're busy hating someone over a boy.

After a few days, though, I needed to talk to someone about my thoughts. One or both of my parents would have been the obvious choice. Or maybe even Delmore. But a funny thing happened. I myself was mad at her and had decided that what she was doing made no sense, but all of a sudden everyone else in the family was getting along great with her. They seemed totally fine with Rita-Robert-Whoever.

She and Delmore got into a schedule of sneaking off to smoke cigarettes both in the morning and after dinner. They also sat on the front porch in the late afternoon when we got back from the lake and listened to music blasting through the living room on Daddy's stereo. Sometimes I had to shut myself in my room and plug into my iPod. They were experimenting with new indie rock stuff and weird electronica—bands like Ott, God is an Astronaut, and this new girl singer with just one name—Lorde. They kept saying Lorde was going to be huge. Rita had managed to obtain a demo tape of this kid. She was from New Zealand and only sixteen. They thought she was the greatest thing in the world, but I thought her songs were all kinds of stupid digital music, an electric beat with these Goth Girl semi-hip-hop lyrics.

I tried to get them interested in Johnnyswim. I loved those two singers so much. But Delmore shut his eyes and wagged his head, saying, "Boring, Ivy. You need to open your ears. They need to figure out how to get more hip or hop, or something."

That made me feel bad. Yes, Johnnyswim was different music in a way. But it was soul music. My dad used to say that in the beginning it had all been about the blues. Then came Elvis and the Beatles and soul music. Everything after that was just people trying to be different for the sake of being different. It's weird how lonely you feel when people make fun of the music you like.

Del told Rita that for two years I'd only listened to Fleetwood Mac, but he could never tell if I really knew what they were singing about. That was true, but so what? Fleetwood Mac was special. They'd always been special in our house. Our parents loved them. Did you have to totally pay attention to what they were singing about to like their music? It made me happy.

They also kept making fun of Johnnyswim's name. "They're just a husband and wife, for goodness sake," said Del. "Who are they trying to fool?"

It was a losing battle, so I spent more time in my room reading and listening to what I knew was great, ignoring them as best I could.

Rita connected with Zaxy, too. She realized pretty quickly that I didn't want her helping with dinner anymore, so she would hang out with my little brother in the great room, playing billiards or watching movies with him on his iPad. Sometimes Delmore hung out with them, too. But Del started disappearing by himself now and then after checking in with Mom at the main house. I wasn't quite sure what was up with that.

And, of course, Rita began to suck up to my parents. She got up early and sometimes helped Mom with breakfast. Or we'd find her sitting on the steps of the main house with Daddy just as the sun was getting warm, talking about God knows what. At dinner, she would ask him questions about books or what life was like as an author back when he first started writing. One time she tried to get him to talk about growing up with her father back in Philadelphia, but he seemed very reserved and disinterested. I noticed that she didn't ask that kind of a question again.

It felt like she was destroying my family. Everyone seemed to be kind of separating from each other somehow. Maybe it was simply my imagination, but I would look around the table at night, and no one was really making eye contact. They only looked at her. Everyone somehow seemed embarrassed to be together—everyone except Rita. What was she doing to us?

Things reached their worst when Mom took me aside and told me she thought it would be a good idea for Rita to help her with dinner one night a week. She looked at me in a funny way when she said that. I understood right then that she was totally aware of the fact that I did not feel comfortable in the same room with Rita.

"But it's *my* job to help you," I said.

"I know, sweetie, but it really would be good for your cousin to learn more about cooking. I mean, if . . ."

I had a dishtowel draped over my shoulder. She'd let her words dangle, waiting for me to say something. I threw the towel on the floor and marched out the back door. My first thought was to head down the road to the lake. Maybe I'd just go for a walk until dark. They would just have to deal with the fact that I'd disappeared.

I'm not sure if I knew I was crying. But there was Daddy, sitting in a lounge chair, smoking a cigarette. He held a spatula like a little flagpole in his other hand. A large glass of red wine rested on the table next to him. I glanced over at the stone barbecue oven. A tray of steaks sat waiting to go on the grill as soon as the flames died down.

"Whoa there, Ivy. What's up?"

All I wanted to do was tromp down the hill and cut over to the road. "Nothing," I said to him.

"Nothing?"

I didn't respond.

"You, um, look like you're upset, kid."

"I'm fine."

"Right, well, that ruddy face of yours—pretty as it is—looks a bit like you want to fight someone."

I shook my head and closed my eyes.

"Ivy, the problem with tough cookies is that when they cry, people who love them know there's something *really* wrong."

I took a few steps down the hill. "I'm not crying."

"Right."

"I'm not."

He took a drag on his cigarette and seemed to consider me for a few moments. Then he patted the chair next to him and said, "Entertain me while I wait for the coals to get right."

I didn't move. He took another drag, then tossed his cigarette butt into the flaming pit.

"Sit and talk to me. That's pretty much an order."

I don't know why, but I started blubber crying when he said that. I covered my face and sobbed. I just stood there shaking with my head bowed and my hands hiding my eyes and nose and cheeks.

After maybe thirty seconds of this, I smelled the wine and the tobacco first, but then I felt pressure on my shoulder, nudging me gently up to the patio area. He put his hands on both of my shoulders and maneuvered me around the tables and chairs, then sat me in his lounge chair.

"Lie back," he said. "There. Now shut up with the crying, kid. It's not you. Very unbecoming. Very . . . very . . ."

I took my hands away from my face and looked up at him. He had his arms crossed, standing over me with the spatula still in one hand, searching my eyes.

I leaned back, closed my eyes, and took several deep, jerky breaths. It was surprising to me as well that I had just lost it there. I shook my head. "Daddy, I know what you were going to say, and I'm glad you didn't."

"What?"

"You said 'very unbecoming,' and then you said 'very' again, and maybe again. You wanted to say *'very girlie'* but you didn't."

He bobbed his chin up and down. "Maybe."

"You were going to say that. But you're too smart."

"Yes, well, this dad-of-a-teenage-girl thing is a bit dicey."

"No it isn't."

"You have no idea."

"Daddy," I said, wiping my face. "You have it easy and you know it."

He moved closer to the fire and glanced at it. "I would agree with you, except you surprise me every once in a while like this, and I don't . . ."

"What?"

"I don't know exactly what to do. Do you remember that time I called you my own special tomboy?"

I shook my head and maybe smiled slightly. "That word is so dumb and stupid," I said. "It made me feel like you're like everyone else. I hate that feeling."

"Yes, well . . ."

He placed the meat on the coals, then returned the tray to the table. Taking a sip of wine, he reached in his chest pocket for his cigarettes.

"She's making a huge mistake," I finally blurted out. He stopped with the pack of cigarettes between two fingers and gave me a questioning look. I went on. "Rita . . . or Robert . . . or whoever that person is."

He closed one eye and tilted his head to the side. "I thought you were on board with that whole adventure."

"Not anymore. I had some time to think about it. What she's trying to do could be pretty reckless."

"Reckless?"

"It's like you said. She's traveling down a scary road and there's no way back. Why does it matter what you look like? I mean, you can be a boy and act any way you want. You don't have to be a guy kind of boy. There's a couple kids at school sort of like that. And I'm a girl, but I don't act like a normal girl. I mean, we're born with our body one way, but our minds can make us anything we want to be. That's the creativity thing you're always talking about. Right?"

I watched as he lowered a twig to the fire, then pulled it out to light his cigarette. "You sound angry, Ivy."

"Maybe I am," I said. "But I've really been thinking about this. You are what you are. You shouldn't change that. You *can't* change that, actually."

"Rita seems to think she can."

"Well, she's wrong."

He checked the steaks by poking at them with his finger, then moved over to me and sat down next to his wine. "Maybe you're right," he said. "But maybe she understands that. Maybe she's a lot smarter than you're giving her credit for."

I shook my head in disgust.

"Here's what I need to know," he said. "Is that why you came out here crying?"

I tugged on my lower lip with my index and middle fingers.

"I was mad," I said.

"Crying mad?"

"Yup. It happens when your mom kicks you out of the kitchen."

"She kicked you out?"

"She said she wanted *her* to help tonight."

He took a swallow of wine. "Ivy, that's not actually kicking you out."

"It sure felt like it."

I was tired all of a sudden. I settled back in the lounge chair and turned my face away from the house and looked up the mountainside. It was steep—basically a lofty hill rising to a track that ran the rest of the way to the top of Captain's Mountain. It was a good three-mile trek. We'd made the hike a few times over the years. Sometimes we'd go up with Mom to watch the sunset and meet Daddy who had driven up in the van. Once we'd all even hiked up to watch the sun rise. It was fun trekking to the top in the dark with flashlights, but exhausting walking home. Still, witnessing the sun poking up over the horizon of water below, was almost magical.

For just a moment I thought I saw movement and then a quick red flash in the distance in the bushes and trees. It was pretty far away, but there definitely seemed to be something or someone moving around. Occasionally people jogged or walked animals up there, but they usually stayed on the trail. This was down a bit and near the upper reaches of our property. Who was it?

"So," he said as he lit up a cigarette. "You got kicked out. What's the deal?"

"I don't want to talk about it."

He remained seated for a few beats, then got up and began to turn the steaks. When he was done, he looked up the hill, too.

"Someone's up there," I said.

"I know."

"Who do you think it is?"

"Delmore."

"Really?"

"He's up there a lot of evenings."

"What's he doing?"

He inhaled hard and long on his cigarette, then held it in front of his face and stared at it. "I don't know. Hanging out with friends, maybe."

"Does he know you know he's up there?"

"Nope. And, to be honest, I don't think it really matters, and I don't care."

"Wait a minute. You don't care?"

"Not like that. I just know it's none of my business, and that's all right."

"I'm going to ask him about it."

"Let him be, Ivy."

"He's sneaking around."

"First of all, you don't know that. Second, everyone deserves privacy."

He turned to look at me very intensely. "Your cousin deserves that respect, too. Let her be. You're acting like your mom did before she had children and knew better. It's not your job to decide what's right for everyone else in the world. Honestly, sometimes I feel like we have let you stay more sheltered than most kids."

And there it was. How do you respond to that? All of a sudden I felt really trapped out there with him. I was still kind of annoyed, but not so much that I needed to hear more pearls of wisdom from my father.

I inhaled deeply. "Time to go back in," I said. "Maybe help Zaxy set the table or something."

"Maybe apologize to your mom?"

I took another deep breath. "Maybe."

"Well, okay then," he said. "Tell her I'll be in with the steaks in about five minutes."

I stood up. "Are you going to call Del?"

"Nope."

"Well, how's he—"

"He seems to know. As soon as I go in, he'll head down. You can pretty much bet on it."

"You sure don't shelter Delmore."

"No, I guess not. But you what? You always figure things out. So does he. Each of you in your own way. That's what's important here.

95

9. Incident at a Coffee Shop

The next morning, us kids were sent grocery shopping in town. We decided to take the boat. It was the weekend before July Fourth. I wanted to let Rita be Rita. But it wasn't easy.

Resonance Hills is a tourist community from April through late September. The town has about a dozen upscale lodges down near the water, plus lots of beautiful, well-kept vacation homes. Main Street and the business sector sit up the hill about thirty yards overlooking a long pier and public boat slip. Downtown on the water has always been a scenic setting to drive a boat into—all rustic New England, wood, stone, and brick buildings everywhere, colorful signs and banners and art.

We pulled into a slip as close to the supermarket as we could get. Shopping carts were lined up at the end of the dock.

"I need to go find a Starbucks and check my email," Rita said as soon as we'd tied up the boat. She was wearing her lime green shirt, cargo shorts, and flip-flops with her wig hair tied back in a scarf. She pulled her iPhone out of the thigh pocket of her shorts.

"We don't have Starbucks here," I said.

She gave me a flat, emotionless expression. "I know. It's a little joke I have with your brother."

Del pointed up the slight hill toward a block past Main Street. "Earth Beans is up there, two blocks down on Water Street. You'll smell it before you see it."

"I need at least an hour," she said.

"An hour?" I asked, then looked to Del.

He closed his eyes and put a hand on my shoulder. "Ivy, chill. Girl's got stuff to do."

"So do we."

Rita was already busy with her phone, which she had now turned on. "Hey, I've got service." She started flicking things around on her screen and tapping and reading.

"There's Wi-Fi all over town," Del said. "It's not great, but you can usually operate pretty well unless you need video or to call someone. You'll drop in and out a bit. Nice and random." He shrugged his shoulders.

"Very last century," she said as she continued to fiddle with her screen.

Delmore had his phone out, too, and had become equally preoccupied. Both of them were walking in that ponderous way people do when they're paying attention to what's coming at them through their screens. I was hoping they'd somehow stumble off the side of the pier into the water.

Turning to my little brother, I blinked slowly a few times. He reached out and took my hand. We stayed a good twenty yards behind Delmore and Rita. When we got up to Main Street, we stopped. "What do you want to do?" I asked.

He peered down Water Street, which both Del and Rita had disappeared into. A good-sized crowd roamed all around us, walking, shopping, eating at little sidewalk tables, enjoying the beautiful summer day.

"Can I get a cappuccino?"

"Coffee?"

"Everyone drinks coffee at school. Except me."

"Really?"

He thought about that for a second. "Well, maybe not everyone. But a lot of kids do."

"Then let's get you a cappuccino."

I turned to head up Water Street, not happy about having to go into the same place that Rita would be, but I wanted to be a good big sister.

"Wait."

"What?"

"Will I like it?"

"Zax! You will drive either yourself or me crazy someday. Let's just do it. Don't think about it. If it works, you're good. If it doesn't, well, then you'll know. Life is too short." I raised my eyebrows and tilted my head at him.

"It could be a waste of money."

"No it won't. It's the price of figuring something like that out. Come on."

I had to tug a little to get him started, but we were finally walking up Water Street. As we got closer to Earth Beans, I felt a hole opening up in the middle of my stomach. Maybe I needed to get a muffin or something. I shouldn't feel hungry, I thought as we opened the door and walked in. What's wrong with me?

As usual, a couple dozen people sat at tables and on sofas working on their computers and tablets and phones, drinking fancy coffees, talking quietly. Half of these people were teenagers. I looked for Rita but couldn't find her. We went up to the counter and waited to order.

"We'll get you a small one, okay?" I said to Zax.

He nodded grimly. I put my arm around his shoulder and tried to draw him in to my hip, but he resisted. Looking down, I found a furious little face staring up at me.

"Yikes, dude." I said quietly.

He shut his eyes for a moment, then shook his head. I took my arm away and stepped to the counter to order one small drink for Zaxy and a blueberry muffin for myself. That's when I detected a bit of a commotion behind us and to the side, the creepy kind of laughter you hear from boys in the school cafeteria—mean, whispery, and what they call smug. Deluxe ass-butt, boy sounds. That's what I thought, anyway. The hole in my belly got bigger.

99

I stepped back from the counter to wait for our order and turned in the direction of the ass-butts. There were four of them. I knew two of the kids from sailing lessons years ago. The other two seemed familiar, but I couldn't place them at first.

One of the kids that I knew puffed up his cheeks. His eyes were bugging out of his head. Then he went "Bah ha ha!" really loud, and the other three laughed even louder. They had enough sense to realize they were calling attention to themselves, so they moved their chairs closer together at their table, and leaned their heads toward each other. But that didn't make them any less obnoxious.

". . . not a girl" . . . "Faggot" . . . "Really? Breasts?" . . . "Homo" . . . "Unreal" . . . "Wanna bet?" . . .

They actually said other stuff that I don't want to repeat. I'm sure Zaxy heard it one way or another, but he didn't react. It was disgusting. They were worse than deluxe ass-butts.

I scanned the room until I found her. She'd been pretty smart and had chosen a table near a back corner of the room. She was bent over her phone—it looked like texting someone—and she seemed oblivious.

The ass-butts made more noise again. "I dare you."

"Put money on it."

"A bet?"

"Oh! Homo bet!"

They snickered and whinnied and guffawed. One of them burped. People in the shop were now eyeing them. I didn't feel so bad about what I was about to do.

100

Behind the counter, a girl called out our name. I paid, then took the hot drink in the big porcelain cup along with the plate with the muffin and quietly told Zaxy to follow me. We wound our way past a couple people over to the table next to the jerks. I felt the hole in my stomach getting even bigger.

Sitting down right next to those four guys shut them up pretty quickly. But it only worked for about ninety seconds.

"I want to say . . ."

"What?"

"I actually thought he was pretty hot. First glance I mean. Just saying."

Snickering. "You think half the girls in the universe are hot."

More snickering. "I do. They are."

"You just need to get some, man."

"Seriously . . ."

"What?"

"We wouldn't have noticed a thing. Not a thing, if . . ." They were whispering now. "Really! You have to stare for a while until, you know . . ."

"Yeah. Hands and the neck."

"The neck?"

"Shoulders. I don't know."

"It's weird. Look."

They went silent. I glanced up quickly to find them all staring into the corner at my cousin.

"Oh, shit! She's looking at us."

For a moment I thought they were talking about me, but then Zaxy said, in a normal, matter-of-fact way, "Hey, it's Rita."

I didn't want to acknowledge our connection, but he was pointing and looked so happy to see her that the only thing I could do was turn my head in the direction of his finger. Rita was half-smiling at us. Then she gave a short wave before looking back down at her phone.

The ass-butt table remained silent for a few beats. I figured maybe they had shut it all down now that they understood there was a connection to the people sitting next to them. But I was wrong.

"Hey. Do you know that . . . that . . . *thing* over there?"

I turned. All four of them stared at us. I'd taken a few bites of my muffin, but my stomach still hurt. Ignoring them, I turned back to Zaxy. "How's your cappuccino?"

"Haven't tried it yet." He stared down at his drink.

"Well, it's not too hot. They're never too hot. Eat some of the whipped cream, then take a sip with your straw."

It sounded like the guys next to us were climbing on the table. "Hey. Really! Are you related to that *thing* over there?"

I tipped my head down and rubbed my left eyebrow. Right then it dawned on me that I'd never wanted to punch somebody before—not even Delmore. It kind of felt good having that feeling. It was anger, but it was more than anger, too. It was something bigger than that.

Zaxy's blue-white eyes were now popping out of his head. He was sitting up stiff and straight like a robot, letting his head swing back and forth slowly. He mouthed, "No" to me, blinking his eyes rapidly. I ignored him and rubbed my eyebrow again, then turned to the four jerks.

It occurred to me that if I punched one of them, and it didn't really matter which one, they wouldn't be able to do anything back because I was a girl. That seemed very funny all of a sudden. I looked from one to the next to the next and figured I'd just hit the ass-butt that made the most disgusting face in our direction. It seemed like a very logical and easy situation to be in. All of a sudden, the hole in my gut had disappeared.

"He asked you a question."

I nodded. "I know."

"Are you related to . . . whatever *that* is?"

"Yeah," said another one of them. "You look a lot alike."

I didn't know how to take this. I'd never thought about the fact that Rita actually looked like us, but she would, of course. Except for the weird coloring of her wig, we all had skin darker than most people's, our faces were all kind of long, and our mouths were somewhat wider than usual—and we had full lips and big eyes and pronounced cheekbones.

"You look like *its* little sister, or something," said another one.

103

"Sure," said the first one who I was beginning to remember had always tended toward being a bully when we were in camp together. "You look like *it*, only not quite as strange. Probably because you're a *real* girl." He stopped with that, waiting to catch my eye. I turned to face him. "You've always been one, of course," he continued. "Pretty attractive, too."

They all snickered and whinnied again, like they were watching a dumb comedy show.

"He wants to ask you out," said one of the older boys.

But they were tongue-tied now. That last comment had backed them into a corner. Unfortunately, I was in that corner, too. No boy had ever talked like that to me. Ever. That's when I noticed in the periphery of my vision a lime green shirt appear between me and their table.

"Hey guys," Rita said. She'd put on a fake, sexy voice. I let my eyes shift to Zaxy for just a moment. He was busy using the tip of his straw to eat whipped cream. There was a dab of it on the tip of his nose and a big splob on his shirt.

The four ass-butts didn't seem to know how to respond to my cousin. They just sat there staring up at her. I was still ready to hit one of them. I figured maybe Rita would follow my lead.

"So," she said, looking down at the four of them, "I couldn't help hearing everything you said over here."

One of the older ones shrugged. "So?"

"So, you seem confused."

They let their eyes move from her to their drinks to me and Zax, then back to Rita again. Finally, one of them said, "We're not confused, asshole. You're the one who's confused."

I shifted around in my seat so I could see who said that, but all of a sudden I felt Rita's hand on my shoulder, gently, but somehow very firm at the same time.

"I know it seems like I'm confused," she said, "but, really, I'm not."

"You're a . . . ," he whispered here, "*fucking freak.*"

She put her other hand to her chest and hunched her shoulders up. "That is *so* mean."

She'd let her voice shift ever so slightly. I felt her squeeze my shoulder again just a bit. Then she used her regular voice.

"Actually, guys," she let go of my shoulder, made sure to stand to her full height, put both her fists on her hips, and thrust out her chest with the fake boobs just enough. "I think I'm transgender. Really! Can you believe that? That's what I've become. Boy to girl. You write that B-2-G. Get it? Bee, then the number two, and, finally, Gee. Like Gee Whiz. See? It's simple. B2G."

They stared at her. "That's sick," one of them said.

She closed her eyes for just a second. When she opened them she said, "Right. Why would you say anything else? You have every right to feel that way and to make fun of me. But . . ." She rested her hand on my shoulder again then swiveled around and extended her other hand to Zaxy's shoulder. "I don't like it when people give my cousins a hard time about me. They didn't ask for this weird human being to come into their lives."

The four of them continued to stare at her. She shook her head back and forth sadly. The obvious thing for her to do right there was to clock the jerk closest to me. Instead, she walked back to her table, picked up her coffee cup, returned, and sat down next to me.

The four ass-butts watched her do this like a pack of confused dogs. Rita took a sip of her drink then turned to Zaxy and smiled.

"Is that a cappuccino?" she asked.

He nodded with his mouth open.

"Have you tried drinking it?" She pulled her head back a little to survey him. "You've clearly tried the whipped cream."

I had myself positioned so that I could see the four boys out of the corner of my eye. They each seemed to be staring a hole into the center of their table. It dawned on me that I should be really ticked at Rita right now, since it was her fault we were in this mess, but I wasn't. I was happy to have her sitting at our table, and proud that she was our cousin.

I turned to the boy table and said to all of them, "Her name's Rita. She's from San Diego."

They looked at me like I was insane. In a way, it felt like I'd actually punched them—or Rita had.

I leaned closer to their table and whispered, "It's time to leave, guys." The youngest-looking one lifted his eyes. "It's okay," I said to him. "We don't mind."

He was about to say something, but one of the other kids backed his chair out and stood up. The other two flinched. I think they thought *he* was going to clock *me*. But he just stood there, looking kind of stupid until he finally said, "Let's go."

The other three made a lot of noise standing up. They each gave us one last look, then moved together toward the door. An older woman and man were just trying to enter Earth Beans as the ass-butts got to the door. Rather than letting the couple come in first, three of them brushed through the door quickly. The last of them turned and looked at Rita one last time.

"Faggot!" he yelled across the room.

Then he moved quickly through the door, bumping into the man trying to come through. You could see annoyance on the face of the woman as she held the door.

Once they'd left, the air in Earth Beans calmed down immensely. My hands were still a bit shaky, but my stomach now felt quite normal. Rita had gone back to fiddling with the screen on her phone. A few people seemed to be staring at us, but when I caught their eyes each of them dropped their gaze.

Zaxy finally said, "I'm gonna drink this. Really. But I need a spoon for the whipped cream."

Rita got up and went to the counter, then came back with a spoon and handed it to him. I put a piece of muffin in my mouth.

"I was ready to punch one of those jerks," I said quietly to no one in particular.

"Yes, I know," said Rita without looking up from her phone.

"You were, too."

She took a deep breath then looked up at me. "Why would I do that?"

"They were insulting. They were . . . they . . ."

"What?"

"They were ass-butts."

She laughed, then shook her head. "I truly appreciate the support, Ivy."

She turned to my little brother who had positioned the straw in his cup but still seemed unsure of whether he should drink. "You too, Zaxamillion. You guys did a good job. But . . ." Her phone buzzed and she went back to reading the screen and fiddling around with it, writing a text.

"But, what?" I asked.

"What? Oh, that kind of thing is supposed to happen. Folks just aren't used to people like me."

"Still, that's no reason to be jerks."

She laughed again. "Yeah, but punching them? Ivy? Are you kidding me? That is not very ladylike."

"I'm not a lady. And I don't want to be one. Ever."

She looked at me, then at Zax. "Are you actually going to drink that?"

"I'm trying to."

"Okay, but your big brother is going to be here any second, and he's probably going to want to get going. We need to find some ice cream and then do our shopping. And we said we'd get gas for the boat."

"Del's coming here?" I asked.

She held up her phone like it was a badge. "Who do you think I was talking to just now?"

I was about to say something when Del came through the door smiling and laughing. He sat down on the other side of the table from Rita and said, "I just saw them. I'm pretty sure it was them, anyway. Four guys, right? Yeah. I know those creeps. The Mahoney brothers, some kid named Cyrus, and Billy Chissers who lives here year-round. Cyrus and Jake Mahoney did sailing with me. Matthew Mahoney was with you, Ivy. That kid is a total asshole."

"Wait, was she texting you the whole time this was going on?" I asked.

"Nope. Just at the start of things and once they were out the door."

"Ivy was going to fight them," Zaxy said. He leaned over his straw and sucked on it carefully. His whole face jerked for a second when the drink hit him. "Whoa!"

"Dude, are you drinking coffee?" Del was surprised, but obviously very impressed.

Zax let the straw drop out of his mouth. "This is my first cappuccino. Ever in my life's history."

"I see. How is it?"

Zaxy leaned down, took another pull on his straw, then sat back in his chair, smacking his lips. "Ahhh!"

All three of us laughed.

"Careful," said Rita.

"Yeah," Del said as he tapped Zax on the arm. "You already have the look of an addict."

"Caffeine can be pretty potent," I said.

"So can all that sugar," Rita offered.

Zaxy leaned over his straw again and took a couple extra hard pulls until we heard the squawking gurgle sound that comes with straw sucking when a drink is almost done.

"I want another."

"No way," I said. "You are kind of scary. We're going to get ice cream next."

"One for the road? Like Daddy says?"

"Nope."

Zax turned to his brother and then to Rita. They each shook their heads.

As we all stood up, we saw an older woman staring at Rita. I bussed my paper plate and our cups to the dirty dish stand, then followed my siblings and cousin. As I went out the door, I looked back into the coffee place. The older woman put both of her thumbs up and gave me a shy smile.

10. Rita Gets Flirty

We returned to the boat club just before one o'clock. It took three trips each to haul our grocery cache from the Bowrider to the van. I was sweating as we finished up, which felt nice. Going back for the last two bags, I considered for the twentieth time in four weeks that I really needed to start a workout routine. As I returned with a bag in each arm, I saw Delmore packing the back of the van—and Bailey, leaning up against his car, talking to Zaxy and Rita. It looked like he was saying funny things to Delmore as well, but I was too far away to hear anything other than the hum of his voice. All of a sudden, he and Rita began laughing at something. I stopped behind a mini-van and a Volvo station wagon to watch.

She was doing all the little things I'd seen older girls do around cute guys: the flash giggle; touching the back of her neck when she said something; tilting her head, creating this totally fake admiring glow; both hands in back pockets, rocking from the balls of her feet to her heels, her extra-long legs stiff like a cheap doll's.

The whole game had always made me sick. It was so fake. Couldn't guys see that? I was getting mad at her all over again, probably Bailey as well. Or was I mad at myself? Honestly, I didn't know. I'm not sure I know even now.

At least she was talking to him. I, on the other hand, was hiding behind cars. My arms were getting tired, but I figured I just needed to wait there a bit longer. Which way was he going to come through the parking lot when he left them? All I had to do was make the right guess, position myself accordingly, and then come strolling out from behind the proper vehicle. We'd pass each other and . . . and what? I had nothing to say to him. He might mutter a hello at me, but he also might not even go in the direction I'd guessed.

What was I even thinking? Ugh!

Eventually, I bumbled out from behind the cars and did my best not to pay attention to him until I got all the way to the last row of cars in front of ours. He was talking to Zaxy as I came around to the back of the van where Delmore was packing stuff in before we drove up the hill to the house.

"You just keep with it," Bailey was saying. "Sometimes things don't seem like they're going to come to you and then . . . bam, you got it."

Zaxy's face drooped a little. "What if you're the type of kid that never gets it? Ever!"

"Ha, little man, you need to have some patience. Just give it a . . ." He looked up as my shadow touched the ground near Zaxy's feet. "Hey."

I still had no idea what I was going to say.

"Hey." Pretty sharp and profound and exciting, right?

"Your little brother here thinks he's a terrible sailor." He looked back down at Zaxy. "Give it time, Zax. Time." He tapped him on top of the head, then turned his eyes to me.

"I just met your cousin here," Bailey said. He stepped over to take one of my bags, then lifted it for Del to take. I moved to Bailey's side and handed Del the other one.

"Thanks," I said.

He flashed me a quick smile, then said, "You guys stole the super boat from your parents and went shopping." I couldn't tell if he was talking to me or to Rita or to Delmore or Zaxy. I was so flustered. But no one said anything. When I looked up, it seemed like everyone was waiting for me to respond.

"What? Oh. Yup." I stepped back and waited for a response. No one said a thing. It all made me feel kind of strange. Finally, I came up with, "Just slowly breaking in the parents."

"You all have such a nice boat." Bailey said. "Nothing finer than a Cobalt."

"Better than that old Crestliner." I picked up another bag for Del just as Bailey did the same thing. Our shoulders bumped.

"Whoops, sorry," I said. We both straightened up at the exact same time. He looked over at Rita and laughed.

113

"Hey, Cooper," Delmore said as he took the bag from me. "You guys playing night games like last year?"

Bailey wrapped an arm across his chest and grabbed his opposite shoulder. "Every Tuesday, Thursday, and Saturday night. Come out and see us. We're playing on the Fourth too, of course."

"People say you're going to be playing in a big college program after next summer."

Bailey extended his other arm across his chest, maybe realized he looked silly, then quickly dropped his hands to his hips.

"I hear all sorts of things about myself," he said to Delmore. Then he turned to Rita. "Life in a small town can actually be pretty frustrating."

She nodded. Then Bailey turned to me. "Rita was just telling me how much she liked this quaint little New England village we have here. But when she told me she was from San Diego, well, I don't know about you, Ivy, but I think there's a lot of places in California that make life in a small backwoods town seem rather boring."

I put my hands in my pockets. "And then there's Philly."

"Yeah, Philly," Bailey said. "Never been there. I hear they have some great schools."

"College baseball there is pretty dismal," Delmore said. "You're way better off in San Diego, I'd think. Ivy keeps saying she wants to go west to play softball. Arizona or Southern California. If my sister wants to go west, there must be something to it."

"Where are *you* going to go?" Bailey asked Del.

"I'm going to NYU," Rita said.

"New York City? Really?" Bailey said, sounding excited. I noticed Del had put this kind of fake smile on his face, like he was relieved somehow.

"So, what do you think, Delmore Scat Man Fondue?" Bailey asked again.

I loved the way Bailey was able to let some weird name flow out of his mouth and be so relaxed with himself. People were always playing with our name. The way Bailey did it had always been quite special.

Still, how did Rita already have an answer to the question of college? I understood that NYU was a cool school to have as an answer. No older kid had ever asked me that question before— just adults. And while I'd fantasized for years that maybe I'd get into Arizona State or UCLA or even just the University of Miami and play softball for one of them—any of them—I had never had the name of a specific school ready and waiting in the front of my mouth.

I checked myself there, though. What an ass-butt I was being. Ivy Scattergood was jealous of her boy cousin Robert because he was practicing life as a girl, flirting with a cute older guy, trying to be cool. The whole thing was starting to weird me out. It also seemed to be weirding out Delmore. He had crawled out the back of the van and was now leaning up against it with his arms crossed, staring daggers down at the ground.

Bailey understood there was something awkward going on. He looked at Del, still waiting for an answer maybe, but I could also tell he was probably ready to head back to work on the docks.

Finally, Bailey said, "Well, we don't need to come up with real school options for another four months or so at least. You got plenty of time, Delmore. Besides, as they say, it's all just a crap shoot."

My brother kept his eyes on the ground for a few beats after that, then looked up and shook his head. "I'll be lucky if I get into Temple or Rutgers." He pushed off from his lean against the car. "But, really, I don't know. I wish I did, but I've never been that great a student and, you know . . ."

I glanced at Zax. Ten-year-olds have a hard enough time thinking about sixth grade, let alone college. I saw that he sensed an odd resonance in Delmore's voice. It was a kind of sadness, like he'd made a joke that no one had laughed at and he knew he wasn't being funny.

"Hmm," said Bailey. "Those are pretty good schools."

"They've got decent athletics," Del said. "I've heard that, anyway."

"Yeah," said Bailey, and it was obvious he was going to head out. "Great athletics. Great schools. Well, I gotta go."

He put his hand on the top of Zaxy's head. "See you on Monday morning, right, little guy?" He held up a hand to Rita and Del, then started to walk away. Just as I was beginning to really hate my cousin even more, since Bailey hadn't said bye to me, he turned and said, "Good to see you, Ivy. Come to the game on the Fourth. It's not softball, but it's still . . . I don't know . . . fun to watch?" Then he swiveled around and disappeared into the rows of parked cars.

"Wow," said Del as he closed the tailgate, "I've never heard a baseball player apologize because he's not playing softball."

Rita said, "That's not exactly what he was saying."

I had no idea what she was talking about, but I never wanted to hear her talk about Bailey Cooper again.

11. Fireworks and Duds

On Thursday evening, July Fourth, the whole family took the boat into town. Del and Rita, of course, were on their phones as soon as we tied up at the dock. It was one of those summer nights with light blue air and a wavering sunlight ready to shift toward gold or orange, or something else promising and unreal. We had come to town for the annual Independence Day picnic and baseball game. After the game, fireworks.

Daddy and I walked along the edge of the sidewalk, just behind the two idiots staring at their phone screens. We guided them forward and kept them from wandering off the sidewalk or into telephone poles. Daddy said we were herding phone maniacs. Leading, along with more than a few hundred others, Mom and Zaxy carried our blankets down toward the picnic field. Mom had her backpack slung over her shoulder as well.

We paid a flat fee of twenty dollars a head to get into the dinner area, got the backs of our hands stamped with a blue eagle, and lined up for food. The line for lobster was the longest, but it was worth it. They piled all these claw and tail pieces on top of our fried potato wedges and corns-on-the-cob. I even decided to try coleslaw and the five-bean salad they were serving. We ate our blueberry pie desserts on the move, wandering with everyone else over a little bridge into the baseball section of the park.

The players were finishing up their infield practice when we got to the bleachers. Zaxy wanted to go toward the top, so that's more or less where we ended up. I made sure I sat close to the aisle stairs in order to get out of there once Rita got too annoying.

The lake was to our left. You could see the fireworks crew—mostly volunteer firemen—setting up on some barges just off the beach. Even though a lot of people had just finished a lobster dinner, folks were still heading down to the snack bar for ice cream bars, hot dogs, and soda. I looked to my right and saw that both Delmore and Rita were engrossed again in their phones. Zaxy, sitting between Mom and Daddy, was still eating the last of his pie with his fingers. His lips were purple. Mom opened her backpack between her feet. I figured she either had some beers in there or a bottle of wine. Instead, she pulled out a newspaper and handed it to Daddy. Then she took out a paperback for herself. I'd seen enough. Without a word, I left my family in the stands. My plan was to wander around the outside of the field and be as close to the action as I could.

The game started a few minutes later, after a husband and wife sang the national anthem. Bailey was out in center field. His pitcher had short, thick legs, but threw pretty hard. The Resonance team was called the Seals. We were playing the Greenville Lake Monsters from over near Moosehead Lake. You could hear that they had a good number of fans on their side of the stands.

The first Lake Monsters batter smacked a hard grounder to third base but got thrown out. The next guy tried to bunt his way on, but our short-legged pitcher was surprisingly light on his feet, fielding the ball with his bare hand and throwing underarm to first for a close out. The next guy, their best hitter, I figured, because you always have your best hitter bat third, hit a long fly ball into the outfield. Bailey had to run back at an angle, but he caught the ball easily.

I turned and stared up at my family as the Seals came jogging off the field. Both of my parents were still reading. Del and Rita, apparently, were magnetized to their phones. Only Zax seemed to be paying attention, resting his chin on his hands. The sky had shifted to a blend of green slowly turning into purple.

The game remained close all the way to the end. We were down 2-1 in the bottom of the ninth inning. Bailey played okay in the field but had been impatient at the plate, swinging at bad pitches. Our first batter was smart and drew a walk. When the next batter came up to the plate, Bailey, because he was on-deck, sauntered out of the dugout. The guy at the plate was maybe insane. He kept swinging at every pitch, just barely tipping the ball foul each time. Finally, he shot one right back up the middle through the pitcher's legs. The player who had walked was on his toes, rounding second and scurrying to third base. We had the tying run on third and no outs, plus the winning run at first.

The crowd was cheering pretty loudly when Bailey stepped in for his turn. He took a few practice swings then settled into his hitting stance. Most people were clapping or cheering the whole time he got ready. Just before the pitcher finished his wind up everyone went silent. It was like we were all holding our breath together. My palms were sweating. I wondered right there in that very short moment whether a good hitter who hasn't gotten a hit all game stands a better chance of getting a hit the longer they go without one. At the same time, I realized that I didn't even know if the Lake Monsters had brought in a relief pitcher to close the game out. It's funny how you don't notice the faces of players from the other team. You notice their size. You notice, sometimes, their skin tone. You might notice the length of their hair and whether they have a beard or a mustache. But you just don't really register them as individuals.

Whoever was pitching, he'd released the ball. It was in flight. Close to pure silence hushed the stands.

I thought: *First pitch. Don't swing. Make the pitcher work. Do not under any circumstances swing.* I thought all of that just before Bailey's bat began to

121

move, flashing down, following his hands as they streaked toward the ball.

We heard the dull clink from Bailey's metal bat. The ball instantly disappeared into the darkness above the lights. A few people got to their feet. The left fielder moved back, squinting into the darkness. A tick later the ball came out of the night sky into the gleam of the outfield lights. The fielder stopped near the wall and pounded his glove once, then began to lift it for the catch. I held my breath to stave off disappointment—maybe also to hold onto the last remnants of hope.

They say it's a game of inches. Sometimes it's a game of feet. The fielder was poised to catch the ball right in front of the wall, but at the last moment his head swung to the right, and he watched as the ball cleared the fence beyond his reach. Home run, Bailey Cooper. The crowd went wild. I moved as quickly as I could to get back to the stands. I needed to be a part of everyone's joy.

The excitement didn't last too long, though. It was, after all, the Fourth of July. The fireworks team stood out on their launching barge ready for the show. Behind them would be dozens of boats with families aboard watching from the water.

We decided to stay in the stands to watch. It meant swiveling around sideways, but there was room to spread out and stretch. I leaned against Mom, wondering when they were going to turn off the last of the field lights.

Zaxy sat in front of me. He turned with a big, exasperated sigh. "When is it going to start?"

"Pretty soon," I said. "The players need to clear out of their dugouts and find their families."

"I want fireworks."

"Good things come to those who wait."

I felt Mom's hand squeeze my shoulder.

Delmore shook his head. "Good things come to those who don't wait, too."

"The idea," Rita said, "is the waiting."

We all let that sit in the air. It occurred to me that she maybe understood that little statement better than most people.

Out of nowhere Bailey and his parents came clomping up the bleacher steps. He was in front. He kept climbing until he was standing a few rows below us, his parents trailing behind. I think everyone in my family felt at least a piece of what I was feeling. He was such a star. It felt good just to know him. Mom squeezed my shoulder again.

"Hi there, Scattergood family," Bailey said. "I want you all to meet my parents." He swept his hand in their direction. "Mom and Dad, this is the whole Scattergood crew, including their cousin, Rita." He gestured toward her first, then each one of us individually and said our names. Daddy was last. Bailey said that Daddy's name was Scat, then he turned to his mom and said, "But you all know that anyway." Then he looked back at Daddy. "They've read your books."

Bailey's mom stepped forward first. Her name was Jean. Bailey's dad seemed a bit of a sourpuss, which was kind of sad, if I can say that. I mean, his son had just hit a game-winning home run. That's something every dad should be proud of in a major way. But Mr. Cooper had this way of pinching his lips shut and swiggling them back and forth, like he was totally unimpressed with anything his son had just done. He wore gold, wire-rimmed glasses, and a po-nytail trailed down the back of his neck. Daddy had been a hippie early in life, and Mom, too, in her own way, but both of Bailey's parents still had that '60s look. Mr. Cooper was introduced as Coop.

"Hey!" said Zaxy. "My dad is named Scat. Coop and Scat! That's pretty funny. Last-name dads."

Everyone laughed. I recalled something I'd heard once about Bailey's dad being a pilot for companies that sent executives up to Resonance Hills and Moosehead Lake for fishing and hunting expeditions. He certainly didn't look the type, standing there all poopy faced with his long hair. Bailey's mom ran a nursery school.

Just then the lights went down in the field area. The Coopers were left standing in the dark. Before the first *phump* from the fireworks, Mom stood to move over a little and said, "Come sit?"

"Sure," said Jean Cooper. Mom settled on the bench a few feet down from me, then Jean moved up to sit next to her. Bailey let his dad scoot in over clos-er to my dad and Delmore. And Bailey sat right next to Zaxy, just in front of me.

That first shot of light into the night sky feels like they're offering you a promise of magic that you'd forgotten about all year. There's a single volley with a tail of faint light opening up a crack in the black, then a big bang followed by a shower of sparkles and glitter swirling and falling. You wait maybe ten seconds, then you hear two quick phumps, one by one, and then a big spray of sparks and a bunch of small spider flowers burst against the black sky. Masked by the explosions those two made are a bunch more phumps and then more sparks and glitter light.

Bailey was laughing. He turned to me. Then he spun the other way to peer down at Zaxy next to him. More phumps. I noticed music playing very faintly over the ballpark public address system. As the sky lit up again, brighter than ever, Bailey glanced over his right shoulder and laughed again.

"What?" I called over the fireworks.

I cursed life right there because turned away from the light show as he was, flickering shadows made his face hard to admire.

"The music." He pointed at a speaker mounted below us on a telephone pole.

It was hard to hear. I bent forward so that my head was closer to him. "What is it?" I asked.

"Not sure. It's funny, though, because we can barely hear it. It's almost like insects trying to catch up to us."

Just then a huge series of cracks and explosions went off in the sky. He glanced past me and his whole face lit up in rainbows and splashes of light.

They were playing a new song out over the field, a bit easier to hear. It started out kind of cutesy and sweet, but then the singer kept going, "Hear me roar." Was that Katy Perry? Bailey moved up a level, and for a long time, we sat side-by-side watching the sky light up and catch fire. I had no idea what to say to him. Once the song was over it looked like he wanted to say something, but what came out of my mouth was, "I hate Katy Perry." Poor Bailey.

><

When the show was over, Bailey walked us back to the docks. Somehow, my whole family managed to leave me at the top of the hill alone with him.

"I like your family a lot," he said.

I still didn't know what to say to him. I was squeezing my hands together behind my back.

"I've always liked your brothers. They're both kind of oddballs, but still pretty cool."

I still had nothing. I tried smiling at the sidewalk.

"You, on the other hand, have always been quite a daunting person to be around. I don't know why. I guess it's because I didn't understand girls when I was younger."

"I don't understand girls now," I said.

He laughed. "You're not like most girls."

"I guess," I said. And what did that mean? Was that why he liked Rita instead of me? What was I, compared to any girl—even a fake one?

"That's what I like about you. Most girls are . . . aren't . . ."

"Most girls are what?"

"Okay, this is going to sound really crappy, but I don't mean it that way."

"Just say it."

"Most girls aren't that interesting to me. But you are."

I could see my mom looking up from the dock toward us. I scratched my head. I thought, *"Oh, you're so interesting, Ivy Scattergood! Maybe we can put you on a TV show. 'America's Most Interesting Girl.'"*

"So I guess that's, what?" I finally offered. "A compliment?"

It was his turn to scratch his head. "Well, yeah. I suppose it was."

"I guess it's not crappy. I mean, a crappy thing to say."

"A lot of people—"

"I think I have to go," I said.

He turned away to look down at the dock and my family. He waved at them. I saw him take a deep breath. "Would you want to go for a walk sometime?"

All this stuff started zipping around in my belly and my legs. Was he asking me? Alone? Or was he maybe wondering if Rita and Del and Zax and I wanted to go for a walk? And, a walk? What was a walk?

I took a step backward down the hill and turned to see that both my parents were standing with their fists on their hips.

"Um . . ."

"I mean, if you don't want to—"

"No, it isn't that."

"Maybe we could do something else?"

"Are you talking about a walk with *just* me?"

"Well, yeah. I mean, if that's okay. I mean, *is* that okay? With you? With your parents?"

"I don't care what my parents think."

He glanced down the hill again. "They're looking kind of impatient," he said.

"Yeah, well, they're impatient."

"So?"

"So, sure. I'd like that. A walk."

He seemed to relax all of a sudden. "Just me and you," he said. "Tomorrow? There's no camp. We could go walk the Resonance Rail Trail."

I glanced quickly over my shoulder. Daddy was heading toward us, back up the dock.

"Okay then."

"How about I pick you up at noon?"

I glanced back again. Daddy had almost reached the steps. No way did I want him back up here saying one word to me. I headed down the hill walking backward. "See you, then. At noon."

He put up his hand. I couldn't tell if he was waving at me or Daddy or even the rest of them waiting on the dock, but it didn't matter. I turned to hurry down the hill. Rather than impatience on my dad's face, he looked a little worried, but also amused.

12. A Very Serious Bump in the Night

When I woke up later that night, it seemed like I'd been dreaming for years. There had been a noise. I was sweaty, which was odd, since the room was chilly. It felt like I'd been going from ride to ride to ride at a carnival and now I was awake. I needed to use the bathroom. What had I heard? It really felt like I'd been dreaming for a surprisingly long time.

The last thing I wanted in the middle of the night was to go blind with all the special energy-efficient lights in the main bathroom that Del and I used. I decided to use the bathroom down the hall where you could simply switch on a single dim bulb that lit the shower stall. No big deal. I was wearing a Red Sox T-shirt and my special Cliveden Friends athletic shorts. It was pretty likely that Rita slept with her door closed, but I wasn't sure. I knew Del slept with his open a little, though. Being quiet seemed important.

The bathroom door was mostly closed, but the crack was lit like a line of lightning frozen by the dark. Rita, probably, had left every single light on in there. It was just the kind of thoughtless thing she would do. I slid my hand in through the opening and groped gently along the wall until I found the light switch panel. I needed to shut down the one over the sink, and the big overhead one in the ceiling, and the fixture behind the toilet. So, I did that. The room went dark for a moment, meaning the shower light had not been on.

Nudging the door further open, I sideslipped into the room. Groping again along the wall, I found the single switch for the shower light and flipped it on. I was facing the wall as I did that. When I turned around, my breath caught. A stranger with short brown hair wearing blue shorts and an over-sized T-shirt sat hunched over on the shower floor. His hands were covering his face and he was shaking. Was I still dreaming?

I needed to yell. Nothing came out of my mouth. So I looked for something to throw at this person. Then, out of the corner of my eye, I saw the wig on the floor and the pile of clothes that had been worn earlier that night. And an open jar of Noxzema on the counter near the sink.

He was bunched up in a ball on the shower floor. He slowly dropped his hands and turned to look at me. It was the same face in some ways, although it was smeared crimson and seemed tired and quite defeated.

But it was also not the same face.

He sighed. His chest heaved a little. He said, "Hi, Ivy. I'm Robert."

Now *I* was shaking. Hopefully, it wasn't noticeable, but that voice was not the voice I'd come to expect over the past few weeks. It was deeper than Del's, craggy somehow—a smoker's voice.

"Rita?"

He shook his head sadly. "Robert. Rita's dead."

Okay, freak me out. I got the situation, sort of, but dead was a bit much.

"What's going on here?" I finally asked.

Robert, or Rita, or whoever this was, began to bump the back of their head softly against the wall tile.

Eyes closed, breathing deep, I felt a very peculiar creepiness floating around the room.

"Can you put those lights back on for me?"

Again, the scraggily, deep voice. *Go back to your real voice*, I thought. *Let me help you with the wig. This is way too spooky.*

I wanted to say all of that, but instead, I flicked all the switches on with the flat of my hand. The room instantly swarmed with a glaze, making me squint. The boy—whoever—held both hands out in front of him and cocked his head.

I waited. He dropped his hands and turned to face me.

I'm going to guess I looked pretty weird there with my mouth still half open and my eyes probably honking out of my head, bright light everywhere making my face pale and pasty. I was focusing really hard on breathing through my nose.

I closed my eyes for a count of five, thinking that might change things. Then I opened them, and just like that, there wasn't a shred of Rita in that face. It was all boy. A handsome boy, except for the obvious pain he was experiencing. Cute, maybe, is what you'd say in normal circumstances. A boy. Without doubt. No question.

"This isn't a dream, is it?" I asked.

He laughed. It was not a happy laugh. "Did I wake you?"

I shook my head. "I don't know."

"I've probably been making a lot of noise." He snort-inhaled the way people do when they've been crying. Then he rubbed his nose with the back of his wrist.

You really don't want to have conversations like this with someone in the middle of the night. Especially if you've simply gotten up to pee. But there I was, and it looked like I was actually going to have to talk with this bummed-out person for a bit.

"So . . . What's up? Robert."

He sighed. "I don't know. I went to my room and started feeling sad. I couldn't sleep, so I came in here. I've been here ever since. What time is it?"

"Very late."

"Or early."

I waited.

"Obviously, this was going to happen."

"What was going to happen?"

He shook his head. "They call it lots of things. I've read about it and seen people talk about it on YouTube. It's called dysphoria sometimes."

132

"Dis what?"

"Dysphoria. The opposite of euphoria. You go through it when you try to transition. It also affects people who can't or won't try to transfer. I just never thought . . . I mean, I was just playing. Well, not really . . . but still. I'm supposed to be deciding. It's not supposed to be real yet."

He pulled his knees up close to his face and hugged his legs tightly, then rocked a little back and forth. "You get confused, I guess is the best way to put it. You get sad and frustrated and lonely. It sucks. I feel like I want to . . . you know . . ."

He was going to say something there that I didn't want to hear.

"I started feeling weird watching you up there at the top of the hill with Bailey. And then later, when you got down to the boat I studied your face. You looked a little embarrassed, and your cheeks were flushy, but your eyes seemed so clear and happy. I started thinking, I'll never . . ." He swallowed, and his Adam's apple bobbed.

I *so* needed to pee.

"It was very simple watching you two up there on the hill," he finally said. "A nice guy trying to get up the courage to ask a nice girl out. Totally simple. The best thing about the whole world. All our lives. But what about someone like me? What about those of us who decide to change? That is not simple."

"Stuff with boys and girls is never simple," I said.

133

"Easy for you to say."

"Look. I didn't know what was going on at all when he and I were standing there. I'm sure it was difficult for Bailey. It was difficult for me, too."

"Okay, maybe simple is the wrong word. How about straightforward? Bailey likes you. You like him. Trust me, if I liked someone it would not be straightforward."

I felt like I needed to say something reassuring or positive, but I couldn't figure out what would make sense or be honest.

"You know, I used to love *The Little Mermaid*," he said. "The Disney cartoon movie. I didn't understand why I loved it, but I did. I watched it all the time when I was little. I had posters of Ariel up in my room and a bunch of her figurines. When I was eight, my parents took me to Denmark on summer vacation just to see the sculpture they have of her on a rock. The expression on that mermaid's face seemed so sad. It made me love her even more. I'd probably watched that movie five hundred times. When we got home I watched it for three days straight. Over and over. Remember how I had all that mermaid stuff everywhere that one time you all visited?"

"I remember," I said. "Del thought that was strange."

"Yeah, well, it didn't seem strange to me. But now I think it's pathetic."

"What? Ariel is awesome." There, that was something positive. I so *seriously* had to pee.

"I loved *Beauty and the Beast*, too. And *Cindy-rella* with those stupid little mice. And all those other

134

Disney movies. I related to the girls. They were my heroes. So dumb."

"Dumb? Why?"

"Because each story was about them somehow being saved from a horrible fate by a prince charming, then riding off into the sunset to marry the guy. What a crock."

Oh, how I needed to pee.

"I *want* to be Rita," he said. "I *need* to be Rita. But it's all too complicated. I mean, there's so many things that are weird about this stuff. My parents sent me to the other end of the universe because they want me to understand how scary life is." He sighed. "My life is scary, all right. Becoming someone else of a different gender means destroying so many things.

"I wasn't happy, you know? I didn't feel right, inside or out. Ever. It was like I was wearing these clothes that didn't feel right on me somehow, but I couldn't figure out what I was supposed to do about it. And I knew that if I took them off, I'd have to find other clothes to wear, only I didn't know what those clothes could possibly be. I felt so lost and helpless." He let out a small, barking laugh.

"I totally related to all those princesses and fairies and whatevers," he said. "But you know what? I mean, seriously. Do you know what?"

"What?"

"I also really liked the idea that they got married at the end to prince charming. I mean, I loved those girls so much. I was so happy . . ."

"What's wrong with that?"

He closed his eyes all of a sudden and began to bump his head softly against the wall again. I *so* needed to escape just for a second, head down the hall to the other bathroom.

"I was happy," he said, "because *I* wanted to marry them. I wanted to be the prince or whoever, too. Do you understand how messed up that is? I wanted to be those girls, but I also wanted to marry them. Only I didn't want to marry them as Robert. I wanted to marry them as them. That is some twisted crap for a little kid to go through."

I really, really had to pee. All I needed to say was that I would be right back. But it also seemed like I shouldn't leave him alone, not even for a few minutes, no matter what.

"And that's the dysphoria of it all," he said. "I'm a girl in my heart, but I want more than anything in the world to find a girl to love and marry—a Belle or an Ariel or a Cindy-rella."

I held up my hand to stop him. "Can we just wait on this a sec?" I'm sure I was kind of doing the full bladder dance there. "I really need to pee." I began edging toward the door.

"Just go in here."

"Yeah, I don't think so."

"I don't know what planet you're on, Ivy, but it's just peeing. I won't watch. Just go!"

I often wonder what would have happened had I left the room that night. Probably nothing, but you never know. Ever since my cousin showed up I couldn't shake this feeling that she (he) was able to completely disappear and never come back.

So, what was I supposed to do? Put my foot down and be a prissy with this part-girl, part-boy cousin and refuse to pee in the same room?

I shrugged, giving in, and moved to the other side of the room. It's true he couldn't see anything from where he was sitting. And it was weird how he'd so easily forced me into doing it. He'd just let himself slightly sound like Rita again, just for a moment. It wasn't until I was sitting down with my shorts around my ankles and getting serious relief that I realized, no matter what, someone in the room was hearing me pee into the toilet water. That felt so personal. And then I had to wipe. That was personal, too.

Maybe he understood how the tinkling sound was making me feel, though, because after just a few seconds he said, "The first thing I ever realized about all this stuff was that I didn't want to stand up when I peed. You know? I was probably two. My mom kept taking me in the bathroom and I kept trying to sit down and she kept making me stand up. And I kept wanting to sit down. I remember getting really mad once. Or maybe she got mad at me. It was horrible."

I'd finished and had managed to quietly snake some paper off the roll so that he couldn't hear.

He laughed, a short, sarcastic burst of sound. He went back to bumping his head against the shower wall again. "That fight probably pushed me further along learning to use the potty than anything. I refused to let her in the bathroom with me anymore. I needed to sit down. So I made her stay out with the door closed. I made my dad stay out, too. What a great feeling. It seemed so normal and natural. Finally! Just sitting down to pee with no one telling me it was wrong. Where did that come from?"

I'd finished and decided I wasn't going to flush the toilet. That, too, seemed far too personal a thing to do, even if Robert couldn't see me at all.

Standing quickly, I pulled my shorts back up, rinsed my hands in the sink, then moved over closer to him and sat on the floor. He didn't turn and look at me.

"Funny thing is I didn't learn to wipe myself for at least another year. No one told me. They just thought I was standing and peeing, you know? Like a red-blooded American boy. I probably learned in fourth or fifth grade about wiggling and jiggling to get those last drops out, but for little me, when I was done I just stood up and pulled my underwear back up."

I said, "This is a weird conversation."

He banged his head and closed his eyes.

"I saw a friend's babysitter wipe herself once, though. We were hiding in the bathroom closet to spy on her—me and Mary Wellington. She was kind of a pervert. She liked to show me her . . . you know. It was very confusing. I understood the difference between boys and girls. She wanted to see mine. I was not about to show her. They'd made a mistake.

I knew that very well. She got very emotional when she made me look. I wasn't exactly emotional back. Just jealous."

"All sorts of girls wish they could pee standing up," I said. "On my softball team. Two of them. They giggle a lot when they talk about it, but it's very obvious they're jealous."

"Real penis envy."

"Yeah, I don't know. They're just weird. I think they'd like to just have the convenience. You know, not having to pull down your pants or your underwear, not even having to find a bathroom to go."

He almost laughed at that. Then he said, "Once I started wiping, I felt really proper. I know, it sounds strange, but when I wipe, I feel like maybe I don't have a penis after all. I mean, I try not to look down. I've gotten pretty good at barely touching it. I just dab."

He looked up at me finally. It was hard to tell if he was waiting for me to laugh or just hoping that I didn't think the whole conversation was pathetic and insane. To be honest, I was surprised that I was able to have it at all. If he'd been a regular guy I would have been mortified. But there was something about how direct my cousin was being, how matter-of-fact about it all. It was so quiet I could hear the lights humming.

It hadn't occurred to me until right then, listening to the humming light, that this was a perfect time to explain to this person, this cousin of mine, that they were making a huge mistake trying to change genders. I just needed to find the right moment to take over the conversation. My statements needed to be firm and defined, but also concerned and gentle. It was important not to sound judgmental or dismissive. Maybe it would be easier than I'd expected.

"There's also the problem of being here," he said.

"What? In the shower?"

"No. Here. In Maine. Like I said, the other end of the universe. They sent me away. They're ashamed. They said they wanted me to figure things out. I'm trying, but it's not easy."

All of a sudden, I knew that the talk we needed to have was going to be difficult no matter what. "Maybe things aren't the way you think they are," I said after a pause. "With your parents, I mean."

"Oh, you don't know. You don't know. You don't know what it's like."

"Maybe not totally, but—"

"I don't want to insult you, Ivy, or anyone in the family, but I hate it here. It's a joke. I hate it."

That ticked me off. But before I could respond, he said, "I get the whole nature thing and the water and boats and the whole Yankee rah-rah New England vibe. But that's just so not me. I come from a place where trees are just decorations—even the palm kinds. And it's always sunny. It's never cold. And there's a frickin' Starbucks on every other block. Plus, you can use your cell phone whenever you want."

He looked me right in the eye and said, "It's called civilization. It's called the Golden State. It's called

Southern California, Ivy. It's the place where dreams are made."

I sighed. What do you say to someone like that?

He went on. "Being here is making things worse. It's depressing. Really. I mean, I love you all. You're family, but I don't want to read, I don't want to spend all day fishing, or talking, or swimming. Nothing. I'm depressed. And it's as much because I'm here as it's because I'm supposed to make a decision about who I'm going to be. When I grow up."

I hesitated for just a moment, but I knew what I had to do. It was time. If this person was going to hate on our summer home, they needed a taste of their own medicine. But I needed to start in easy. It would all need to end up with an explanation of why, if you were born a boy, you need to stay a boy. Maybe I could find a gentle way to say he was acting like a spoiled only child. I'm sure that's why they sent him out to visit us. They'd had no choice. This kid needed to be bounced back and forth by brothers and sisters. We were the next best thing. This was about starting up the conversation then advancing to the right topic. I could do that.

But I didn't get a chance. Out of nowhere, I thought of something completely different. It all of a sudden became very obvious that if Robert instead of Rita was going to show up at breakfast the next day, it was going to be pretty depressing for all of us. And they were all going to miss Rita. I wasn't, personally— at least I didn't think I was—but I knew Delmore and

Zaxy would. There was definitely something wrong with this person plopped down next to me in the shower. More importantly, he'd just told me he hated being with us in Maine. That was depressing too— depressing to me because I loved it here so much. Because of his lousy attitude, he was going to miss out on all the things I loved. Yeah, there was stuff that sucked about leaving the city and coming up here for the whole summer, but still, it was Maine and it was pretty darned amazing and beautiful.

I took a deep breath. "You know what you need?" I finally asked.

"A lot of stuff, probably."

Ugh, I could hear that depressed and self-centered tone of voice settling in.

"A sunrise hike! I have no idea what time it is, but if we leave just as it's getting light . . . I mean *just . . . right* as the birds are starting to stir and the air is still nippy and there's barely enough light to see what you're stepping on. Just that first glow, you know?"

"What are you talking about?"

"It's just the timing. You need the right timing."

"Timing for what?"

I thought for a moment. "Climbing Captain's Mountain. It usually works out. We do it every few years. If you start right, you get to the top just as the sun is coming up. It can be truly amazing." I turned to look at him. "I'm not going to say any more, you just have to trust me. Come on. Let's go to the kitchen to see what time it is and check the sky."

"What if I don't want to?"

I looked right into his eyes. "You know, you're very smart, and you're pretty headstrong, which is a major Scattergood thing, but if you're too scared or lazy or whatever, to climb Captain's Mountain and maybe see something really fantastic, you're not going anywhere in your life."

He held my gaze with a cold stare. I did my best to match that stare right back.

Finally, he said, "Okay, then, I guess. Should I bring a sweatshirt?"

"Uh, yeah. It's cold out there." I watched him squiggle around to stand up. "You're going to need boots, too. You do have hiking boots, don't you?"

"That was something they got me especially for this trip," he said as he eased out of the shower stall.

"Well, that was smart."

He picked up his clothes and the wig piled on the floor. "I need to take these to my room and get my sweatshirt and boots."

I nodded. "By the way," I said. "It's not Cindy-rella. It's Cinderelly."

"What?"

"In the movie. The mice call her Cinderelly, not Cindy-rella."

13. Climbing the Captain

While Robert was in the back of the house getting his stuff, I dressed quickly, put on my hiking boots, and went out to the kitchen. I grabbed a daypack off a hook in the kitchen, took a couple water bottles out of the pantry and filled them at the sink. The clock over the stove said it was nearing four. Through the living room windows, I could see that it was still pretty dark, but the color of the air above the trees was just starting to soften. When I opened the door and stuck my head out, I could hear birds mumble-chirping.

Ten minutes later Robert and I were heading around the back of the house, and my eyes were adjusting quickly to the semi-darkness. Just enough pre-dawn light filtered through the trees so that we didn't need flashlights. Still, we had to watch our step.

"You should stay just behind where you can see me," I said. "It's an easy walk uphill most of the first mile or so."

He didn't respond.

"Oh, and whatever you do, as we go up, don't turn around. Okay? That's very important. Do *not* turn around until I tell you to. Even when we get to the top. Wait 'til I give you the word. Okay?"

I heard grunting behind me and figured the message had been accepted.

We walked carefully in the dim light. There wasn't really a trail to speak of until we got up pretty high, but I knew the best way to weave through trees and find stretches of open space.

Within about ten minutes we were both breathing hard. I slowed down some and aimed for the least steep terrain that I could remember. The sound of night insects still filled the air, but birds were grumbling awake, practicing morning tribbles and trills.

When we'd started off, it truly did feel almost cold. Both of us were wearing hoodies with the hoods up. We had on shorts, of course, but after that first ten minutes heading up, I flopped my hood behind me and could feel the prickle of heat on my neck and cheeks.

I heard Robert cough a couple times and could tell he was giving some distance to me, so I slowed a bit more. It occurred to me that I couldn't just turn around and point out smoking wasn't good for him. No turning around! I, too, did not want to see anything until we reached the top. It had to be just right.

After a few more minutes of climbing and the occasional hacking cough, I waited for him to catch up. Taking off the backpack, I pulled out the water bottles.

"Don't drink too much," I said, offering him one. "You wouldn't think it, but you're going to want water coming down more than you're going to want it going up."

We each took a few gulps. "Remember, no turning to look," I said. He was close enough that I could see him through the thick gray murk, shaking his head as he twisted the top back onto his bottle.

We stood for a while, still catching our breath.

"Pretty hard work, huh?"

He nodded. I could still hear a bit of labor in his inhales.

"I'm surprised, really," he managed. "I don't . . . I shouldn't . . ."

I waited. "What?"

"Doesn't matter."

The air had this kind of glowing silver pulse to it now. I took his water bottle and put it back in my pack, then said, "Okay, we gotta get going or we'll miss it."

After a couple dozen yards, he said, "Walking in these boots is weird. It doesn't feel right. My feet are like wooden clubs poking at the ground."

"They give you stability."

"Whatever."

We were getting up high enough now to where the trees started to thin out. After another ten or fifteen minutes we came across the road that runs around most of the mountain and stopped again for a little water.

"Don't turn around," I said.

"Jeez. You are too psycho."

"Trust me."

He sighed. "Better be worth it."

It was my turn to sigh.

We started to climb again. The going was steeper. It took a while, but I finally found the trail that runs up the last piece of the mountain. It switched back and forth, so we made easier progress.

"This trail will take us to the top now," I said. Within a few minutes I started to sweat and breathe heavily again. Then Robert said something that almost made me feel like diving off the mountain.

"I'm not happy. That's what I'm saying."

Those words sent a chill down my back. It wasn't Robert's voice. It was Rita's. There wasn't one person behind me, there were two.

We hit the first switchback on the trail. It got steep again.

"I'm not trying to say that I hate it here." Still Rita's voice.

"Would you quit that?"

"What?"

"Talking in your Rita voice."

"What?"

"You're talking like Rita. You sound like her. You're not Rita. You're Robert. Remember?"

She was silent for about ten steps and then started laughing—in Robert's voice.

"It's not funny," I said.

"Sorry."

I kept walking. We would reach the top soon enough. The sky was beginning to spread and glow. Our timing was very possibly going to be perfect.

"Do not look."

"Right," he said.

It really felt like I was talking to two people. "Either one of you," I added.

He laughed again. "It's getting light."

"Need to hurry."

We hit the next switchback and kept going. Then another and another. I glanced up to my right and could make out the top of the mountain above us.

"Just a little farther."

"I hope so. You're moving pretty fast."

"Gotta make it."

"What . . . ever."

We kept climbing until we got to the three steps. "Okay," I said. "Here's the deal. This path goes straight up to the parking lot. It's very steep. The trail does a few more switches. We're going up these steps to the path. It's like a shortcut. We should be right on time." I started up the steps.

"Parking lot?" I heard behind me.

"Right. You can drive up here or even ride bikes."

We moved quickly now. I kept sensing that special feeling on the back of my neck, but it had to be an illusion because the light still wasn't quite right for it. Overhead it was still kind of murky and dull. But that would change soon enough.

We hit the bottom of the parking lot, went about halfway up into open space, then I stopped. The wind had picked up, which was a good sign. I'd learned that from Daddy years ago. Tugging my pack off, I said, "Okay. Now. Wait until I give the signal." I looked him in the eyes. He had sweat dripping down his forehead, and he was breathing pretty hard. "We're not turning around until I say so."

"What is the big deal?" he asked, finally.

I wanted to answer that by saying, do you remember you were crying and feeling sorry for yourself? Do you remember that you were hinting at something that I didn't even want to think about? You were smacking the back of your head against the shower wall and crying? Do you remember that you said you don't want to be here?

But something far more important was about to happen. We waited. The wind picked up a bit more. I knew we had just a few more moments.

And then it was time.

"Okay," I said. "Now."

I watched and waited for him to obey that command. Just as his head began to move, I let myself worry the whole thing was going to be a dud. That happened sometimes. Maine's summer sky can be fickle.

But it was perfect. He had half turned. A little flame of light started to kindle on his cheeks. A spark caught on the edge of his eye.

I turned, too. And there it was.

It's always a different shape. Sometimes it's the long edge of a wafer. Sometimes it's a stretch-mark smear of orange or red, pulsing where the lake meets the sky. Today, though, it was a sharp diamond rising out of deep blue emptiness. I let my eyes swing right—enough to see Robert's smiling face and the full force of the diamond of light coloring his cheeks and eyes.

"Amazing!" he said.

"Just wait."

We stood watching. And then it happened. The diamond floated high enough above the water to become kind of a rooftop peak of light, and then the lake lit up right down the center, shimmering and sparkling, the light of the new sun running like a magic wand, extending, streaking from the distant horizon directly at us, spreading onto the shore below.

"Oh. Wow," murmured my cousin.

I gave my head a shake. "Just a bit more . . ."

Before he could respond, we could feel it. It wasn't exactly heat. It was more a sense of being embraced by this shimmering beacon, or touched by everything in the world all at once—not so much warmed as started up.

I bent down and pulled out a water bottle. Handing it to him, I said, "See?"

He took the bottle, nodding and blinking. "Does this happen here every day?"

I chuckled. "Zaxy asked Daddy that exact same question a few years ago. Do you know what Daddy said?"

"What?"

"It happens every day all over the world."

That wasn't funny to Robert, but he did nod a bit as he said, "We should do this every morning."

"Some people do, I guess, somewhere."

"Seriously."

"No. Right? I agree . . . although, it has to be a morning free of clouds or haze or fog."

"It was like a fire starting out there and then running right at us."

"Yeah. Something about the correct angle of the light and refracting and . . . I don't know."

We watched for a while as the full sun drifted upward, turning into a sphere, dropping pieces of light onto the edge of the lake as it struggled to free itself from the horizon.

"Drink slowly," I warned him again.

It was one of the more special versions of a sunrise I'd ever seen from the top of Captain's Mountain. I felt really glad I'd figured this out for him. The family was sleeping below— everyone except Daddy.

When he finished, I took the bottle out of his hand and stowed it back in my daypack.

"Let's go up to the top of the parking lot and sit on the swings for a bit," I said. "Then we'll head home."

Robert followed slowly, walking backward, still watching the sun and the sky and the lake. I didn't say anything. No way was I going to ruin this event by talking about how problematic changing from a boy to a girl was. No way at all. The whole reason

I'd done this sunrise hike, though, was to make that issue seem kind of small. I think my intentions were accomplished that morning, but I still hadn't gotten the chance to state my case—if it even was a case. I mean, truthfully, who was I to tell a kid like him (or her) anything?

We sat on the swings up near the top of the lot for a while, watching the sun lift completely off the water and begin its normal drift above the earth. It had started as this little sparkling diamond and then morphed into a big ball, but as it rose higher it began turning into a flaming bubble, looking the way it always looks during the day. Overhead, the sky had wandered from a mashed lavender haze to an airy blue. Neither one of us said much. We drank a little more water, watching the sky, sitting in the cups of rubber swings, the slow squeak of metal chains mixing with the rush of wind in our ears.

14. Hope Off the Mountain

"On the way down the going is easier," I said. "At least it feels that way. You're using different muscles."

We moved somewhat slowly on the first steep part, descending to the three stairs and the switchback trail. I'd told Robert the hike would be easier, but I could hear him breathing heavily anyway.

"I'm so out of shape," he grumbled at one point

"It's not normal to hike on mountains. The altitude shift can get to you."

"It used to be normal for me."

"What do you mean?"

"I used to run cross-country. Three years."

"Really?"

"I quit about a year ago. I didn't like being . . . you know . . ."

"What?"

"One of the guys."

"Yeah, that would be a bit weird, I guess."

"But I was good."

"What do you mean *good*?"

We came out on the switchback trail and the going got easier.

"It was a running club," he said. "My dad made me start when I was ten. He said it would give me something to do that wasn't a girl thing or a guy thing. And that was true. But I hated it. Sort of, anyway. I mean, competition turns people into jerks."

"It can, I guess, but—"

"No. Listen. I'm just really sensitive to that kind of thing. I know when people are acting like jerks. But I won my first race. It was in the twelve-and-under group. Everyone was really impressed. Then I won another race. They got pretty excited. I mean, I was ten, and I wasn't very big, but I was beating these taller, longer-legged twelve-year-olds. So, they signed me and a couple other kids up for the SoCal Run. It's regional. I didn't win, but I came in seventh in a group of maybe two hundred kids."

"Impressive."

"I know, right? I sort of started to like it. Not because I was winning, really, but because people seemed to care about me. And I kept doing pretty well for the next couple of years. I actually placed third in the SoCal when I was twelve—a very close third to both second and first place. Pretty cool. I got a medal and my picture in the paper. Some of the schools started talking to my parents."

"Schools?"

"Colleges."

"Seriously? When you were twelve?"

He hesitated just a little. "I was really good, Ivy."

"Was? What happened? Did you get injured?"

"Nope. At thirteen they split everybody up. Boys and girls. I was in the boy group. I hated it."

"Geez, Robert."

"I know. Pretty stupid."

Stupid? How about you overthink things like no one else I've ever met.

"Actually, I take that back. It wasn't so stupid," he said. "I felt really uncomfortable. Like I was lying to people or faking, you know? I wanted to be running with the girls. It was horrible. And because I felt so crappy all of a sudden, it felt kind of good to lose. I didn't practice or train anymore. I'd tell my parents I was going for a run and I'd jog down the street, then catch a bus to the mall and go look at clothes."

"Clothes?"

"Right. Girl's stuff—skirts, blouses, shoes, bras, panties, you name it. I had just turned thirteen when I bought my first makeup kit. That was an interesting experience. It took me almost an hour at Macy's to get up the courage to face the person at the counter. They were watching me, I'm sure, thinking I was a shoplifter. I made up this whole story for the cashier about how it was a present for my older sister. After all that anxiety, it turned out she really didn't seem to care that I was buying makeup. But outside the store, bag in hand, I felt like a million dollars. It was amazing. I wanted to put it all on right then."

155

What could I say to that? I had never purchased makeup in my life.

He laughed in a hard, scary way, almost a cackle. "Back then I was like a teenage boy buying his first rubber. It was so stupid."

I didn't know how to respond to that either. I mean, he *was* a teenage boy. And I got the joke about the condom, but that made me feel uncomfortable.

"So, yeah, I quit running eventually. Telling my parents was pretty epic. They were obviously disappointed. I think they really thought they'd cured me."

"Cured you?"

"They never said anything to me about knowing what was going on and that I wanted to be treated like a girl, but it was so obvious."

"What did they think of the makeup?"

"Obviously, I didn't tell them a thing. I would put it on at night when they were asleep or maybe during the day in the bathroom behind the locked door and just stare at myself in the mirror."

It was getting warmer. We fell silent for a while and kept walking. It felt almost normal just walking together in silence. I was trying not to think about anything, but all of a sudden something was bothering me.

"Why didn't you just quit racing but keep running on your own?"

"Yeah, I know. I could have. But that's not the way my brain works. I wanted nothing to do with any of it anymore. The whole athlete thing made me feel slimy and gross. Pretending I enjoyed the competition thing made me hate myself. It's hard to explain."

"I like sports. And competition."

"I know you do. I think that's cool. But, Ivy, a lot of girls don't like sports at all."

"That's their loss."

"I suppose." We walked on in silence for a bit.

"It's funny," Robert said finally. "I kind of like not being in shape."

"Well, I sure don't."

"Well, of course, you wouldn't."

That really struck a nerve. I, too, had gotten out of breath as we were hiking up the mountain earlier. All of a sudden, I felt mad at myself and mad at my coaches and mad at my family for making me leave Philadelphia, not letting me play summer softball. I was never going to be good enough to make a Division I team anywhere.

"It's not about being an athlete," I said, and I hoped my voice sounded severe and cutting, because that's how I meant it. "You should have some self-respect. Who cares about competition and being an athlete? If you're good at something and it makes you happy, you should do it. I mean, it's just running. I'm terrible at running. My legs are short. I'm not built right for it. And so, it kind of hurts when I run. If I were you, if I were good at it, I'd just run to run."

He didn't say anything to that. I started walking a little faster.

"Sports isn't only something for boys," I told him. It came out like, *you're not just an ass-butt, you're stupid.* I

157

really felt like letting him have it. I also wanted to say, don't be a girl if you can't be what you want to be as a human. Don't be *anything*. He sighed. I could tell he was maybe mad now, too.

We had a view of the lake as we cut down off the trail. You could also see the roof of the little house farther down, way off in the distance. Then I recalled a question I had wanted to ask earlier.

"Hey," I said. "What's the deal with you and Del?"

At first, he didn't respond. But then after a few more beats he said, "What?"

"Sometimes you guys disappear. He does all the time, but I've seen you as well. Up the mountain a ways. Not this far, but far enough."

"Why don't you ask him?"

"Because if I ask a question like that, he'll be an ass-butt back."

He stopped and put his hands on his hips. "Ass-butt? *Ass-butt?* Ivy, what is your problem? Can't you say bad words? Is he an ass-butt or an ass *hole*?"

I felt my face getting hot.

"Seriously. You are such a goody two-shoes in so many ways. Such a perfect little . . ."

I thought, *don't you say it. Do not say what I think you're going to say.*

He stared at me with his hands on his hips still. Then he shook his head and gave in. "We come up here to smoke weed, okay? Not a lot. Not too much. We're not stoners. We're not drug addicts. But, yeah, we smoke weed some. I brought it from home."

He had a funny look on his face, like maybe he was worried I would hit him. Or maybe it was just that he thought I was going to cry or scream, because that's actually how I felt.

Some things you don't want to know. Why did I ask that question? I have no idea. We were standing a few feet apart on the trail. Both of us had our hands on our hips now. He was waiting for me to say something. I could see his chest pulsing under his sweatshirt. Was that his heartbeat? Was he scared? Mad? And how was I going to respond to this?

I'm not a goody two-shoes, really. At least I don't consider myself one. I know plenty of kids who do stuff like that and drink beer, smoke cigarettes, whatever. It's just that right then, all of a sudden, it was way too close. Also, he was talking about my older brother. Maybe it was stupid to feel like I did, but somehow it was like they'd let me down. I felt disappointed.

He was still staring at me, waiting. Finally, he said, "You heard me, right? I brought it from home. Your brother isn't—"

"That's cool," I blurted. "Really. It's cool." I raised my hands, palms out, then turned and started walking again. I figured maybe we'd just ignore the whole thing. Maybe I could just forget the entire conversation ever happened.

But some knowledge is just too much. My mind went on the fritz. It occurred to me that maybe Rita was smoking with Bailey, too. Bailey was older. It *was* possible he'd do something like that. I mean, I didn't really know him at all. And what was I doing, going out on a date with him today? Oh, my God, I was going on a date in, like, six or seven hours. I was going to be a mess with so little sleep.

I turned. He was still standing where I'd left him. "Come on," I yelled. "Hurry up."

He moved toward me reluctantly. When he was five yards away, he said, "Ivy, I'm sorry. I didn't mean to upset you."

I put up my hand. "I said it's cool. Forget it. Let's just get back."

We walked in silence after that until we reached the point where we needed to bushwhack down to the house. I felt like I'd been pulled into a whirlpool that I didn't know existed until just a few minutes earlier. And, no, I didn't like to use curse words. And, yes, I guess it's true: I *am* a goody two-shoes.

15. Getting Ready

We were exhausted when we returned to the little house. Del was still sleeping. I taped a sign on a kitchen cabinet door that read, *"Did the Captain's Sunrise. Do Not Wake Us."* He would understand what I meant.

Sleep did not come easily. I was worried about spending the afternoon with Bailey. What would I do if he wanted to smoke something? I was so tired! How would I say no? And what if he actually wasn't who I thought he was? My heart was beating like I was trapped at the very top of the huge sycamore tree in our backyard. I wanted to be on the ground, but I had no idea how to get there.

Out of nowhere, it seemed, I was alone in the backseat of a car, creeping uphill. There was no road. Out the window, trees, boulders, bushes, and cows popped up from nothing. The driver had on a hoodie. I couldn't tell who it was.

I wanted to say, "Look at me. Who are you?" but every time I opened my mouth, nothing came

161

out. We kept going up and up and up, through some woods, onto a beach with the blue edge of an enormous body of water sliding along next to us.

After a time, we were driving in slow motion through a series of fields that somehow I understood were part of a vast farm. Finally, we rolled silently into a suburban-like neighborhood with well-kept lawns and modern cream-colored houses trimmed in black around the windows, doors, and roof edges. Every street we turned down was empty—no cars, no kids, no parents. Our windows were down. We could hear music no one had ever heard before.

My name was called by a singsong kind of voice. The driver wasn't making a sound. I looked behind me, then out the open windows on both sides, even up towards the sky. I heard my name again. Louder. I glanced in every direction. One more time. Still no one.

Then I was shaking. Hard. I tumbled awake, blinking. Delmore's and Rita's faces hovered above me, laughing.

Rita said, "We don't want to be a sleepy mess when Bailey picks us up, do we?" The two of them laughed again. It sounded conspiratorial.

I sat up and stared at Rita. "Hey! What?"

I stopped myself. Had I dreamed that whole sunrise thing and climbing the Captain? This was Rita, not Robert. I searched her face. It was hard to read, but something seemed to be there acknowledging we had a secret.

Still, had we really gone up that mountain and seen the sunrise or not?

"What time is it?" I asked.

"Nearly 11:30," Del said. "Mom sent me to wake you both. I told her that you went up for the sunrise thing. It sort of weirded her out, but she seemed more excited about Bailey coming over than anything else."

I swiveled around and put my feet on the floor. "Why would going up the Captain weird her out?" I asked.

He tilted his head and squinted like I was stupid. "Because you went off and did something kind of dangerous in the dark? With no permission, and no one even knowing that you guys were gone?" He glanced at Rita. "I guess two girls hiking up the side of a mountain in the middle of the night is still something that moms can't handle."

I snorted. Then I leaned back to stretch. My legs and back were a bit stiff and sore. "Ugh. I don't think I can go on another walk with someone today."

"Oh, no you don't," said Rita. "No excuses."

I wriggled my shoulders. They hurt too. "It's not an excuse."

Delmore clucked his tongue. "You really are so full of kidney beans sometimes, Ivy. Come on, get up. Take a shower. Mom says she'll have toast and juice ready for you in ten minutes. He'll be here soon enough."

"Knowing Bailey," Rita said, "He'll be here early. You better hurry." They both started to leave the room.

163

It wasn't until I got the shower running that I realized I was mad at Rita again. Rita. Robert. Whoever! It had been weird up there on the mountain. But I'd actually started to feel okay with him. He was opening up. I was mostly dealing with Robert up there, but still.

And now, again, Rita was back.

I suppose I could have been hurt or sad that he'd made the decision to go back to her without talking to me. Rita probably hadn't told Delmore she'd transformed back into Robert, either. He'd said, "two girls" on the mountain. That ticked me off more. So much openness and honesty up there, then, *poof*. Back to hopeful thinking. After all, we'd done and been through in the middle of the night, she owed me an explanation. The thing was, I honestly didn't know if I wanted to hear what she had to say. Or even whether there was anything she *could* say that would make sense or be acceptable. And why was I such a truly dumb-ass fifteen-year-old know it all jerk when I really didn't need to be?

No time to think about the transgender puzzle now, though.

I broke the record for a quick shower where you wash yourself and shampoo your hair. I got in with the water still cool and started counting. I was out by the count of 97, feeling refreshed.

However, when I got back to my room I had a bit of a dilemma. How was I going to dress? It was an eerie feeling, and I didn't like it. I never, ever had to think about what to wear. That's when mind reader Rita knocked on my door. "I know it's none of my business, but what are you going to wear?"

"Just a minute," I said as I finished toweling off.

Given how I was feeling toward her right at that moment, I'm sure my tone of voice was kind of gruff when I added, "I don't know what I'm wearing, *Rita*." I put a lot of stress on those four letters when I said that name. "Maybe you can loan me one of your *blouses*. Have you got some *slacks* that would make my *ass* look nice?"

She didn't say anything at first. Maybe she'd silently just headed back to her room to actually get me some of her clothes. I pulled on some underwear and scanned the room for a clean bra.

"Very funny, Ivy," I finally heard. "My clothes wouldn't fit. I'm bigger than you."

Here's the thing: I was sliding on some cargo shorts when she said that, but I really was feeling kind of panicky about whether I knew how to dress myself properly for a date. It was truly a relief to have her there on the other side of the door. I quickly towel dried my hair and fluffed it out, put on a Red Sox T-shirt, and opened the door.

She was leaning up against the wall next to the door.

"Okay, I'm not going to wear this," I said, "but I honestly don't know what—"

"Stop," she said. "You look fine. I was teasing."

"What? A ratty old T-shirt and shorts?"

"Ivy? Seriously. First of all, we're talking Bailey Cooper here. He doesn't care what you wear. That's one reason why you like him so much. Second, you don't have much else other than tees and hoodies, right? And third, I knew you'd have this problem. That's why I'm here. Just be yourself. He likes *you* and doesn't care what you look like."

That wasn't meant as a dig, I was pretty sure, but it kind of felt like one.

"So, you think I'm ugly?"

She laughed. "You are so weird, sometimes."

"You said he doesn't care what I look like."

"I didn't mean it that way. I just meant he likes you as a person. He doesn't need you to make yourself look like some special girl."

"Special girl? That's funny coming out of your mouth."

"You need to chill."

"No, really." I was breathing hard and didn't know what I was going to do or say next.

She raised her hand and stepped toward me. "Ivy, seriously, calm down. I've seen this before. You're nervous because you're going out with a guy for the first time. I didn't mean anything by what I said except that you're fine just as you always are. Bailey's one of those good guys. He's real. He likes girls because they're great. No, wait. That's wrong. He likes girls like you because you're real. I have friends back home who would kill to go out with a guy like Bailey. Like you, they deserve to find someone like him. Just calm down."

"Yeah," I heard Del say from the kitchen. "You don't have time to be an ass-butt anyway, Ivy."

I was about to tell him to shut up, but I stopped myself.

Rita leaned in close to me. "It'll be fine. You look great. You look like you." She stepped back.

I took a deep breath. "Sorry," I whispered sheepishly. I still wanted to have that talk about what happened to Robert, but there wasn't time, so I sat down to put on my socks and Nikes.

She shook her head. "You know you're pretty anyway, right? I mean, no matter what you wear? I'm not saying that because I know you think that's dumb to worry about, but it's true. He knows it, too. Just be yourself."

That partly felt good to hear coming out of Rita's mouth, and partly seemed really freaky somehow, coming out of Robert's mouth in a girl voice. It also made me feel like an alien version of myself. Because, no, I do *not* want to care what I look like to boys or anyone else. It's one of the biggest problems with girls everywhere in the world. Worrying about what other people think about how you look can make life so hard. And here was my cousin, who didn't like the way she looked (as a boy, anyway), trying to make me feel good about how I look just as I am.

What a stupid kind of pressure. Just saying "you look pretty" created this horrible responsibility I didn't want.

But there wasn't any time to worry about all of that, so I just let it go. Rushing by her, I went back into the bathroom and brushed my teeth quickly, then put my flubby damp hair in a ponytail.

When I came out, she was right where I'd left her. I said, "I guess I'll go get some food before he gets here."

She shot this weird little smile at me. "Hurry up, then."

I went into the living room, took a blue Cliveden Friends Dragons hoodie off the hook in the hallway near the kitchen, gobbled down some juice and crackers, then headed for the front door.

"Have a good time, Sis." It was Delmore. I turned with the doorknob in my hand. He was sitting cross-legged on the floor with a video game controller in his lap. He, too, gave me the same weird smile that Rita had given me.

In September I realized that smile came from them being proud of me and happy for me, but a bit worried, too. Right there when it was all happening, though, it just seemed like this secret thing they were sharing that I didn't understand. I ignored it and went out the door without saying another word.

16. Which Way Are We Going?

Have you ever had a perfect day? I'd never really thought about that idea personally until I was in bed later that night. I didn't have a perfect day, but just as I was drifting into sleep, I knew I'd had a near miss. Maybe if I hadn't been so tired. I don't know.

It started as you would expect, with Bailey driving his old Camry and me sitting next to him. We mumbled things about the weather first (it wasn't going to rain on us, and would be warm enough for no sweatshirts, maybe). I asked if his parents had given him this car and he said nope he'd bought it with his own money, but they paid the insurance. Then we talked about baseball teams, but Bailey didn't have much to say, really (except to note that he didn't read the sports page and didn't like American League baseball much because someone hit for the pitcher). I decided I wouldn't tell him how much I loved the Red Sox. It was always fun to talk about that because then I could explain why I wasn't a Phillies fan even though I was from Philadelphia. He changed the subject to

Mom, actually, and what it would be like to work in a hospital every day (he said hospitals were so big and full of all these people doing weird things all the time).

After maybe five minutes we fell silent. I noticed my nervousness had faded. Then a yawn grabbed my entire face. It was one of those yawns that jerks your body in a spasm as it finishes.

"I should warn you, I might fall asleep at any minute," I said after I'd recovered.

"Am I really that boring?"

"Sorry. I'm just likely to conk out."

"Great. A narcoleptic. I should have known. I always choose friends who fall asleep at the drop of a hat."

"Very funny."

He pretended to look around. "Except we don't seem to have any hats with us."

I should have had a good comeback in me somewhere to that. You can see, I'm sure, that I was on my way to being a rather difficult person to date.

"No," I said just as we were turning into the parking lot. "My cousin and I went for an early morning hike up Captain's Mountain. Super early. I thought *she* should see the sunrise over the lake."

I wanted to explain that it hadn't actually been Rita, but that would make things hard right from the start. Not a good idea.

He pulled into a parking space. "You hiked up in the dark?"

I tilted my head and stared through the windshield in front of me at the path that led to the main trail. "You haven't done that?"

He shook his head and closed his eyes for a moment. "Can't say I have. That's a likely ankle sprain or encounter with a bear. Besides, I'm one of those beauty sleep guys. I hit the sack at 11:30 sharp and don't get up until 7:30."

"Sharp?"

"I'm sort of over-organized about things sometimes."

"Over-organized?"

"I like to have my life under control."

We were having this conversation with both of us staring out the windshield. Just quick glances in each other's direction.

"We gonna walk?" he asked, finally.

I nodded and we scrambled out of his car.

The trail had once been a railroad line. "The only thing about this trail that I don't like," Bailey said, "is that it's not a loop. You walk as far as you want on it, but then you have to walk back the same way you came. The walk back always makes me feel like I'm duplicating my efforts in an unnecessary way."

I laughed.

"You think that's funny, huh?" He was grinning at me.

I bobbled my head at him. "I never thought about hiking that way. Interesting."

"Okay, smarty pants. Deal with this: which way are we going to go? Left? Or right? East? Or west?"

I looked both ways. Then pointed to the right.

"East. Good choice."

"Why? What's west?"

"Everything we're not going to see today. And California."

We walked silently for a couple hundred yards and then he chuckled a little. I glanced over and he looked me right in the eyes. It felt very overwhelming to have Bailey Cooper look me in the eyes like that. After just a few beats I turned away.

"One of the girls at sailing camp asked Del about you once," he said. "In whispers."

"Hmm. She must have needed dirt."

He laughed. "No. She thought you were cool. We all did. I mean, I always did. But by the end of that summer, the others did, too. I felt like: 'the secret's out' now. I'm going to lose my chance."

"Lose your chance?"

He didn't reply at first. Our view of the lake was gone. Not even little sparkles through the branches.

"To ask you out."

Bailey Cooper had wanted to ask me out for a long time?

"That doesn't sound quite right, though," he added. "I didn't even really know what asking a girl out was back then. I was kind of scared of you, but I also knew I liked you. I didn't think about anyone else respecting you the way I did. And that's what it was. I certainly didn't know that feeling scared of you was actually just having respect for you. But I've known for a long time . . ."

I think he was ready to drop the conversation right there. Maybe I should have dropped it, too, but I was beginning to get warm in the face and my legs felt weightless. Also, my heart was beating up into my chin. I was embarrassed, I think, but there was something else that I didn't really understand.

"Wait," I said. "You've liked me for, what, a couple years?"

He nodded. "Yeah." He stopped walking. "But I didn't really want to."

He looked down at his feet. All at once his head jerked up. "Wait. I didn't mean that. Why do you make me say dumb things?"

"Maybe because I'm so scary?"

"You know what I mean."

><

So, maybe you have a crush on someone for a few years. Maybe it's just an attraction. Who knows? But then, all of a sudden you're alone with them, and talking to them, and everything is real. It's very unnerving to need to be honest about yourself with someone you care about. I knew what I wanted to say, but at the same time letting words like that come out of my mouth might create a big, empty, dangerous hole inside me. Saying things— for both of us—meant having to be brave. It was like we had to think the same way explorers had to think in the old days when they had no idea what was over the next hill or beyond the horizon at sea.

173

I tried to show I wasn't lost or scared or whatever. "I honestly can't remember *not* having a crush on you."

I looked up into his face. He gave his head a little shake and inhaled deeply. *See?* I thought, *that's why I was scared.*

"I can say the same thing," he said, letting out his breath.

We stopped walking and stood there in the sunshine with the wind blowing on us, looking into each other's eyes. I don't think I'd ever felt so serious and mature in my life.

That lasted about fifteen seconds. Then I started laughing. I couldn't help it. Bailey started laughing, too. I don't know which one of us moved first, but one moment we were laughing and looking at each other, and then we were hugging—still laughing, but hugging.

Somewhere above my head I heard Bailey say, "Well, I guess we got that out of the way. Now what?"

Yup, it was just a hug. But it was a hug between two people who had been interested in touching each other before they even knew what that kind of touching might feel like. It isn't such a big deal to a lot of people in this day and age, but it was a big deal to us. I forgot where we were. When we stepped back from each other, I looked from Bailey to the trees in the distance, and then down the long, straight trail in front of us receding all the way into a tiny black dot.

"Where are we?" I asked. It was meant as a joke.

"In the middle of somewhere," Bailey said. "I say we just keep walking in the direction we were heading."

We turned and looked back down the track. "We've come pretty far," I said.

He took my hand in his. "Forward?"

So, all of a sudden, we were walking, holding hands, not saying anything. Just walking and touching.

I kept my gaze way down the line at first. It seemed like you could see a mile, maybe more. But as our silence lingered, my eyes moved from the distant horizon to the ground just in front of our toes.

"You like music like the kind that Katy Perry sings?" I asked. I had to break the silence.

He didn't respond at first. "Not really," he finally said. "I mean, she's okay. But no. I have a favorite . . . group or person or songs. Some songs. Sort of."

"That's kind of mysterious."

"I'm not sure I'm ready to talk about my musical tastes with you. Tell me about softball. Del says you're pretty good."

"I don't know about good, but I really like it."

"Like it? That's important. Better than loving it, actually. Same with baseball, maybe, if you're a player. It's a nasty game. It can really get to you. Best not to love it."

"I never thought about it that way."

"You want to play in college, right?"

"That's the plan, at least *my* plan. My dad isn't so keen on it."

"How come?"

"I don't know. Maybe he doesn't think I'm good enough. Maybe it's sort of like you say. He doesn't want me to be disappointed . . ."

"Get your heart broken."

"Right. My heart." We kept walking. I wanted Bailey to say more about baseball, but he seemed to be waiting for me to go on.

Finally, I said, "I don't know how I'm going to make it anywhere if I keep coming up here every summer. Most of the good players in Philly play all summer on travel and tournament teams."

Bailey thought about that. "I'd tell you to play up here," he said, "but the team's pretty lousy. Most of them anyway. They usually can't start playing outdoors until late April or early May. Same with us guys."

"But *you're* good. Your whole team is good."

He didn't respond to that. We walked with the sound of our shoes crunching on the trail and the wind swishing in the grass and weeds around us.

"You don't really need to worry too much yet, anyway," he said after a bit. "It only gets important in your junior year. The main thing is to train and do strength and agility drills in your off-season time."

"I don't do that stuff enough."

"Well, it's not too late to get started. I assume you run."

Okay, feeling stupid. "I keep meaning to start."

"Been there. You need a partner. Have you asked your cousin?"

"Who? Rita? I don't think so."

"She used to run competitively."

"I've heard."

How was I going to explain Rita to Bailey? In a way, part of me felt kind of devious. I obviously didn't like feeling competitive with her. Part of me was also embarrassed by her. And, I have to say, in a puzzling way I also felt a little protective all of a sudden.

He moved his hand around in mine. "She told me she missed running."

"That's not what she told me," I said. "She said she hated it."

"She told me that, too."

I lifted my head and stared as far as I could down the trail. Little glints of sun flickered through the trees near the edge of the lake. I searched my mind for some way to tell him about Rita. It seemed impossible.

"Must be pretty weird," he said. I turned to check his expression. He glanced over at me. "There was this kid in our neighborhood when I was growing up. We were friends until third grade. That's when he changed. I didn't know what to do. First the older kids picked on him and made fun of him. Then the kids in our grade started following suit, even younger kids."

I thought I understood what he was talking about, but I wasn't completely sure. We walked in silence again. Just as I was about to say something, he went on. His voice was almost a whisper. "I stopped hanging out with him."

"What happened? What exactly do you mean by changed?"

"You know, he started kind of acting like a girl, I guess. He tried to hang out with them at recess. His hair got longer and longer and he used little bobby pins to push it back from his face, even hair clips. He snuck jewelry onto the bus and put it on every morning, then took it off before our stop going home—girl's jewelry, necklaces and bracelets mostly. He wore fancy shoes with pink lights on them and tassels. Remember when girls did that? He chose to read girl's books, too, during free reading period. It made me uncomfortable. It made a lot of people uncomfortable. He freaked everyone out."

We continued to walk. I have to say I was pretty relieved. Rita had told him. Or maybe Delmore had. Whatever. At least I didn't have to manage a conversation that I dreaded starting.

Bailey shook his head and sighed. "Thanks to him, I learned lots of nasty names that people use for gay people."

"Was he gay?"

"I don't think so. But back then we didn't know about transgender issues. It was third grade. This is Resonance Hills. You have no idea what this town is like once the tourists leave. It's staid old proper Yankee New England through and through. The closest we came to that kind of thing was dressing up in our moms'clothes for Halloween."

"What happened to him?"

"It got pretty bad, the name calling and stuff. Most people wanted nothing to do with his family. They lived down the street from us. My parents are pretty cool and accepting, you know? But even they didn't have anything to do with the Culligans after a while.

It went on for a few years. That poor kid and his family were ostracized. We're pretty good at that here. Then one Saturday morning when I was twelve, end of sixth grade, a big old moving van parked in front of their house. By lunchtime they were gone. I never saw Eugene again."

He breathed that last sentence very quietly.

I think I was drifting into a walking nap when he finally spoke again. His voice came out of nowhere, startling me.

"Rita said you don't like her much. She said she couldn't figure out if that was real or if you just didn't approve of her trans needs. She called them that—trans needs."

I knew what my real problem with her had been—like, *stupid competition over Bailey*—but there was no way I was going to talk to Bailey about that.

But did he sense that whole emotional mess? Because, next he said, "She told me I should ask you out."

Now that was interesting. And a bit humbling.

"I can totally relate to being weirded out by her, Ivy. But she's actually pretty cool."

I couldn't help myself. "So, you're telling me she knew you were going to ask me out?" I'm sure Bailey could hear a little bit of "Ivy the Butt Head" in my voice. He had to, because he just stopped walking and put his hand on his hip.

"You know," he said, "you're a pretty hard person. I mean, sometimes it really is scary to be around you."

He shook his head a few times and waited. He was right. I saw that, and it kind of scared me, too, all of a sudden. I was really tired, though. Plus, I understood that I just wanted to hold his hand and keep walking with him forever. It was too hard to talk about all of that Rita stuff right then. But he was still waiting for me to respond.

"You're right," I finally said, "I get it. I never until this summer really understood what an ass-butt I can be sometimes."

I watched as a smile half-formed on his lips. He tilted his head a little.

I said, "It's just that I really don't agree with what he's doing."

"He?"

"Robert. Rita. Whoever that person is."

"Robert!" He looked at me, then squinted up at the sky. "Robert! That's her old name? Robert?"

"Yup. You didn't know that?"

"She wouldn't tell me."

"Yeah, well, that's what I'm talking about here, see? I mean, that's his real name. That's who he is. He's not Rita Gomez. He made that name up. Just totally made it up. He's Robert Scattergood. And that's messed up in a lot of ways. He hasn't just changed his first name, he's dumped our family name, too. It's like he's ashamed of being related to us."

"Kid's got a lot going on."

"You don't know the half of it. *He* doesn't know the half of it either, apparently. His parents are getting divorced. There's a court order or something where a judge says by law he's not allowed to dress or act like a girl—even in private."

"Wow."

"Right. My parents haven't told him. They're kind of, I don't know, playing along, I guess— letting him work through things without having to deal with the real issue, which is his parents' marriage."

I explained how the whole thing started, with Robert walking right by us at the airport, fooling us, and my parents being my parents, and Daddy having some weird issue with his older brother, and how I was the only one in the family who welcomed Rita as Rita in the beginning. Then Daddy talking to his brother on the phone and finding out what was really going on. I also realized that I was the only person who had talked to Robert as Robert and it had been pretty awful and depressing in a lot of ways, but it had also been strangely real and honest and true.

"So why did she say her parents sent her out here to make up her mind about whether to transition or not?" Bailey asked.

"I don't know where she got that," I said. "But it sure beats saying you were sent away from home so your parents can end their marriage in peace. Divorce really sucks."

"It changes everything for everyone," he said. "Kids get totally screwed over. I see it with so many of my friends."

"It's pretty much everywhere."

"You're actually one of the few people I know who doesn't have to deal with that."

"Huh."

"But Rita has no idea about her parents? That doesn't seem like her. She's pretty sharp."

Finally, I said, "My parents are not happy with any of this. My uncle says Rita has to remain Robert and that we can't let him . . . her . . . know what's happening. She's said some things, though. I think she has a pretty good idea, somehow, that her parents are having issues."

"It sucks for that kid," he said. "I had no idea."

Somehow, we'd let go of each other's hand. I don't know what happened. I didn't like it.

I said, "I'd guess she's partly got to be affected by her parents' problems and doesn't even know it."

"That's all the more reason to get her to go running with you, then."

He was serious. But running with my cousin was certainly not a good idea for me. I felt competitive enough with her. I wasn't a runner and she was—or had been, regardless of the smoking. I really didn't need to put myself in that kind of situation.

"Got it," Bailey said. "Why don't we all three run together? Every morning. We'll start out small. Maybe we come out here and just take it slow 'n' easy while you two work your way into it."

I peered up at him. He had a big puppy-dog grin on his face, his eyebrows were raised in expectation, waiting for my response.

"I'm not sure if she'd be up for it, Bailey. I already tried to encourage her to run. Just this morning, in fact. She wasn't having it."

"I can handle your cousin," he offered.

I sighed. I had to. I understood the potential problems. I knew I'd feel I was competing with her for Bailey. But I also knew I was being kind of stupid and selfish. "Okay, then. You ask her. No matter what, I'll get in better shape. Maybe I'll be ready for fall softball."

"Great!" he said.

Out of the silence between us, Bailey turned to look back down the track. "Wanna head home?"

I squinted up at him, "I guess."

As we started walking, he said, "So I'm sorry if I was too forward."

"What are you talking about?"

He hesitated. "Holding hands."

There's a lot I could have said to that. Really. But I felt like I would burst into tears if I said much else that day. Instead, I took my hands out of my pockets, grabbed his right forearm and tugged his hand out of his pocket, then let my fingers nestle between his. I didn't say a word. We kept walking.

After a few minutes, he said, "I like our hands together."

We kept walking. You could smell so much of that summer on the wind.

"I like our hands, too, Bailey. I like them a lot."

17. A Luxurious Day and Endless Night

When we got back to *Casa Cielo*, I let Bailey tell Rita our plan. He talked to her outside while she was smoking. I sat in the living room, exhausted, watching them through the glass door. How could I possibly feel competitive about running with my stupid cousin the smoker? I laughed at myself. In the end, they decided on an eight o'clock pick-up time, and a simple thirty-minute easy jog to start for all of us.

Bailey came back in to say goodbye. Del had gone off somewhere. I had the feeling Bailey wanted to kiss me. When I stood to walk him to the door, he let his hand find mine. We said goodbye standing close to each other. He squeezed my fingers a little, then said, "See you in the morning."

I watched him pass Rita as he walked by her to his car. He may have said something, I don't know. She offered him a half smirk, then lit up another cigarette as he was pulling away. After Bailey's car dropped down the hill to the main driveway, I realized, Rita was staring up at me. She gave me a thumbs up sign with both hands, the cigarette dangling from her lips. I offered her a little nod back, then shrugged my shoulders and closed my eyes.

That's when it hit me: Bailey Cooper liked *me!* Bailey Cooper had had a crush on me for about as long as I'd had a crush on *him*. How was that possible? I wanted to tell someone. No I didn't. Yes I did. Wait.

"Relax Ivy Scattergood," I said to myself. "Don't get crazy. He doesn't know you. Not really."

I needed to stop thinking. I was so exhausted. It felt like I was going to burst into tears at any moment. Lying back on the couch, I fell asleep almost immediately. It was a nice three-hour nap until dinnertime. I don't know if I dreamed or not. I didn't need to, though, did I? I'd been living a dream in one way or another all day.

At the dinner table, I was listless and groggy, but I remember Rita telling everyone we were going to start training with Bailey in the morning. My head hit my pillow by nine.

There's no telling when Rita called it a night, but she was stretching with me out in front of the house before eight that next morning. A few minutes later, we heard the crackle of gravel from Bailey's tires coming up our drive.

In that first week, the plan was to keep things to half an hour of actual running with about fifteen minutes to stretch before and after. I expected my cousin to be hacking and coughing all over the place, but she ran with ease—beautifully, actually—her back straight, shoulders poised, legs striding like they were stepping on clouds. On that first morning, as Rita took off, gliding like some strange golden gazelle, putting distance between us with no effort at all, Bailey said, "Either she's showing off or she's really happy. Either way, you and I take it slow and easy, build up some resistance. Okay?"

I was already sucking wind and wheezing a little. Why, oh why, had I not been doing this all summer? Even just three times a week.

"It's fine," I managed. "Don't stay back with me."

He smacked my shoulder, kind of hard, with the back of his hand. "I'm doing this to help you." I thought about what that meant. Then he added, simply, "And to be with you."

"You'd get more out of this if you went at her pace."

"Ivy, chill out. I get plenty of a workout every night we play. Also, we practice a lot on non-game days, too. I'm fine. This is a perfect addition to everything else I've been doing."

We ran a minute or so more and then I really didn't care what he was thinking. I was dying. Rolling into a ball on the ground and sucking my thumb seemed like the best course of action.

But Bailey Cooper isn't Bailey Cooper because he's tall, dark, and intelligent—and a great athlete. Bailey Cooper is also aware of things most people find hard to figure out.

Watching me struggle, he didn't say anything. I probably would have. He just shortened his steps and slowed down to calm my efforts. It helped a little. Then he slowed down a bit more. Then a bit more. We could barely see Rita way down the trail. He probably could have simply walked next to my stubby-legged gait.

I let out a loud blast of laughter. I couldn't help it. Frustration, embarrassment, and relief. "Yagh!"

"You okay?"

"Out of shape."

"Gotta start somewhere."

He was right, of course. We kept moving. Slowly, I built up my wind and found my rhythm. Even so, I'm sure we looked hilarious—the short girl with the ponytail pushing hard and straining; the long, tall athletic super boy holding back, practically standing still.

A few minutes later, we caught up to Rita, stretching her legs and checking her watch. I expected a smug look and the usual chatter about slowpokes, etc. As we came up to her, though, she fell in stride with us. Her face was bright red and sweaty. I noticed her wig was a bit twisted and out of position. We all three ran side-by-side, silent, breathing together, our feet thudding in time (more or less) on the ground.

It wasn't a particularly nice morning. The sky was full of thick, dusty gray clouds. The air was dense, kind of hanging on your shoulders like warm, wet laundry. Rita kept checking her watch. Finally, she said, "We're at fourteen minutes. How 'bout we turn at fifteen?"

On the way back, my breathing was fine, but my legs were beginning to feel like stone clubs. At some point Rita sighed very audibly and said, "Remind me not to head out like that again. You guys had the right idea."

That's how our mornings went for the rest of July. We boosted the amount of time we would run by ten minutes each week. Afterward, Bailey dropped us at *Casa Cielo,* then went to work down at the boat club. On home game days he'd stop by after work and shower at the main house while I made him sandwiches and maybe a smoothie or a milkshake. He had to be at the field by five, so we'd sit on the back patio looking up Captain's Mountain for an hour or so. Sometimes we'd see Rita and Delmore in the trees. I didn't want to talk about what they were doing. I assumed Bailey didn't either.

On practice or away game days, he had to be at the field by three. We didn't see each other at first on those days until he started coming over at night after everything was done for him. Away games meant a late arrival for him, sometimes after midnight. We'd sit on the steps talking while Del and Rita made a ruckus inside playing video games. Rita had brought a few weird ones with her, including *Lollipop Chainsaw* and *Skullgirls.*

I guess you'd say Bailey and I talked about everything. I kept finding new ways to complain about my aching legs and feet, especially on the first few days after we'd extended our runs. Bailey liked to read, so we had good talks about books. He also admitted to me early on that he was a sucker for Julia Roberts,

Sandra Bullock, and Meg Ryan romantic comedies. I teased him about that. I'm more the Adam Sandler-Will Ferrell type. But one night he made all of us watch the Sandra Bullock movie, *Hope Floats*. It's a pretty emotional movie, not totally a comedy, but Bailey said it was great because it's about being uncompromising. It made me a little uncomfortable because the plot has a lot to do with divorce. I kept looking over at Rita when that issue came up. I think that's really why Bailey wanted us to watch it, because in the end, even though things get really sad, the mom and the daughter figure out how to go on living and loving. Which, I guess, is why the movie is called *Hope Floats*.

In some of our night talks, Bailey wondered out loud if there was something wrong with him for not feeling more political about life. He said it was weird to live in Maine, completely out of touch with so much of the rest of the country. He wanted to know what Philadelphia was like, and whether I had black friends. I said, yes, of course—and Jewish, Asian, and Hispanic. I reminded him that the Scattergoods were a mixture of a lot of things. He wondered if people were weird to us about that. I said, no, they're weird because of Daddy mostly.

Those were such sumptuous nights when I look back on them. Just sitting side-by-side, slapping at mosquitoes—and talking. Luscious. We laughed at each other—and ourselves as well. It was so easy for us to say things that we'd never said to anyone before. We talked about racism and prejudice, which felt very exciting to me since I wasn't worrying about that stuff much yet. We talked about pollution and how weird climate change is—so big and hard to understand, but so important and scary. We also talked about terrorism and wondered what the deal was with people being so intent on killing each other and hatred. So many conversations just went on and on—except when it came to talking about baseball—especially Bailey and baseball and college.

I knew he didn't really want me to come to his games. I went to a few anyway. He seemed, happy to see me and would wave sometimes. But there was some kind of uneasiness to the way he played. I figured it had to be hard for him with all the expectations people had for him. Maybe it even got boring listening to them go on and on about how great they thought he was, and how he was maybe going to become a major league player someday.

I wasn't driving, of course. Mom dropped me off with Rita and Delmore a few times. Once, I went with Zaxy. It usually got strange after the game because Bailey and I couldn't be alone together. We never talked about that, but it was an obvious issue. Hanging out with Rita and Del was fun enough, though. We'd all four drive to Greenville or Millinocket and get ice cream or sometimes stop in town for a trout burger and cheese fries.

The night Zaxy came with me, we went with Bailey, still in his uniform, to the Green Vegetable and had an authentic late-night vegetarian dinner. We shared broccoli lasagna, a roast vegetable medley, and mushroom risotto. Zax said he had decided being a vegetarian was the right choice for him. But the next day he wanted hot dogs for lunch. He also went crazy over the grilled ham steaks we had for dinner that night. I didn't have the heart to remind him of his declaration from the night before.

It was the part of the summer that just lies down and stretches out flat. All the days bunch together in your memory. I know I'm describing things like they're broken up and distinctive, but even now it all seems like one single, long, luxurious day connected to an endless night of unhurried talk and conversation. I'd never felt like I did for those few weeks. I'm sure Bailey, Del, and Rita would know exactly what I'm talking about. Maybe Zaxy, too.

Things changed as July came to an end, though. Nothing lasts forever, especially a single, almost infinite luxurious summer day connected to an endless night of conversation.

18. Even Starlight

Things changed the night we drove to Millinocket for Rita to buy beer after one of Bailey's games. He hadn't hit well and the Seals lost. Somehow, Rita and Del talked him into driving all that way for her to buy a six-pack using her fake I.D. card. I was not happy. We also discovered that Rita had been taking special driving lessons in San Diego. Bailey even let her drive the last mile to the beer store. That freaked me out even more since she was still under sixteen. Bailey tried to get me to relax by explaining you could get a learner's permit at fifteen in Maine. I pointed out if she didn't actually have a permit that meant she was still illegal.

After she bought cigarettes and beer at a gas station, we drove to the top of Captain's Mountain for my brother and cousin to drink their beer. They got out of the car pretty fast because they knew how ticked-off I was. I guess they figured Bailey had some explaining to do. They also obviously wanted to smoke.

Once we were alone, Bailey said, "I'm going to make this up to you."

"Don't worry about it," I said back. I mean, really, what could I say?

"I know you're mad, Ivy, and didn't want to do this. To be honest, I'm not sure why I did it. Maybe I was just frustrated because we lost the game tonight. Rita's been talking about doing this for a long time. I just wanted to help her out."

"You say that like you've known her for years."

"It's weird. I kinda feel I have. I like her, you know? She's pretty cool." Then he added something that startled me. "I wish I could be like her."

"What? You want to be something that everyone figures you're not?"

At first, he didn't seem to know how to take that. In truth, I didn't really know how I meant to say it. Then I heard my words still rolling around in my head. I had to laugh. He laughed, too. I felt his hand on top of mine.

"I like her confidence. She's comfortable with herself—including all her faults. I wish I could be the same way."

The smokers were yelling at us. They were holding up their bottles of beer and making pretend opening motions.

"They need an opener," he said. "I have one on my key ring. It's not for me. I promise. I just have it. Wanna get out with me? It'll be a bit chilly. But beautiful. They can drink their victory brew and we can appreciate the stars."

"Appreciate the victor, too?" I asked, meaning Rita who had just bought beer for the first time in her life with a stupid fake I.D.

"Yeah," he said. "That's been the idea the whole time. She's pretty happy with herself. She didn't just buy beer, she did it as a woman."

"I don't care if you have one, Bailey. Whatever."

"But *I* do. I told you. I like to be under control. Come on."

He let go of my hand and waited for me to open my door. As we both got out, the two idiots began clapping and cheering.

"We're gonna sit up-wind of you two stink clouds," Bailey told them as he handed over his keys with the opener attached.

"Wouldn't have it any other way," Rita said. "Really! I'm not sharing my cancer with anyone."

That was supposed to be funny, I guess. It wasn't.

I heard the beers being opened, bottle tops clinking on the cement at our feet. Del handed the keys back to Bailey who was waiting for me to choose a seat on the bench across the table behind Rita and Del. He sat down next to me with his leg touching mine, then found my hand again with his.

A breeze rustled away at our backs. The big black mirror of Resonance Lake extended out before us, reflecting drips of stars and an incandescent foggy clump of something about to rise at the edge of where the lake met the sky.

Delmore said, "Here's to ever more success in her life. To Rita Gomez!"

Rita clinked bottles with Del, then leaned back a little and burst into tears.

All three of us sat listening to Rita trying to get herself under control. There were moments of sniffling, then silence, then more sniffling. Her shoulders would start to shake, and her head would bob backward. Then the shaking would stop, and she'd blurt something through her sobs. She tried talking, maybe to explain herself, but every time she opened her mouth she burst into tears again. Bailey squeezed my hand. Our shoulders touched. He lifted our arms up and rested them on the tabletop behind Rita and Delmore.

I squeezed Bailey's hand back, probably too hard. Then he stood up, let go of me, moved around the table to the other side of Rita, and put his arm around her. She leaned her head against his shoulder, shuddering.

Alone behind them all, I finally stood and went to the other side of the bench. There wasn't room for me to get in on the hugging properly. I stood listening to Rita's messy breathing and didn't know what to do. Hugging from the front-and-center position didn't make sense. Not real elegant is how I thought of it—which was interesting, since I'm the least elegant teenager on the eastern side of the country. Finally, I sat down on the bench between Rita's knees. I felt useless and stupid, but it was the best I could do. She was wearing a dress.

Her legs were partially exposed. She had to be cold. I draped my arms across each bare knee, wrapping them down along her exposed calves.

Her sobbing was subsiding a bit, but she was still breathing with that sad desperation that comes at the tail end of a big cry.

I couldn't help it. I said, "This is why I don't wear dresses—ever. You don't know when you're going to find yourself on top of a mountain at midnight in the cold. Jeans beat dresses pretty much all the time."

She stopped in mid-breath. There was a moment of silence, then I heard her chuckle. Delmore smacked the top of my head. I'd know that smack anywhere. Rita's breathing started to catch up, finally.

She said, "I'm sorry. I'm so sorry." She snorfed a couple times. "I'm so, so sorry."

We all let her apology float in the darkness.

"A lot of stuff went through me there," she said. "The main thing, though, was that I realized we've been in cell range most of the night and I never once thought to use my phone or check Facebook, or anything."

It wasn't completely silent after she said that. The midnight wind on top of Captain's Mountain kept shifting from a mumble to a whistle, then back to a mumble again.

"Was that a joke?" Bailey asked out of the dark. "You were crying about your phone?"

Instead of directly replying, Rita squirmed around. We heard the muted flicking of a soft phone vibration buzz. "Sort of, I guess," she said.

Two things happened simultaneously for me right then. The first is that I got hit by this very strong curiosity about how the Red Sox had done that night. A win would give first place all to themselves. I also felt that a loss would be the end of their season. Yes, I know it wasn't even August. But I'm a true member of Red Sox Nation. We think the worst of our team in order to be pleasantly surprised every once in a while. And we are all aware that we're gluttons for punishment since we won the World Series in 2004 and 2007.

I fished in my pocket for my phone and took in the view of the sky in front of us. That bright white mist on the corner of things was now a strangely growing chip of moon bobbing right above the black mirror of water. It was kind of like seeing the corner of a smeary eye trying to blink.

That's the second thing that happened. You can even say it was a third thing, because the exact same distorted piece of eye began swimming across the dark water as a rippling reflection trying to dab itself more permanently into the sky.

"Look at that!" I said, pointing.

I don't know if Delmore or Rita paid any attention to that command, but Bailey responded. "Wow. I love how chunky it is when it first comes up. Even when it's just a dispersed piece of itself like tonight."

That's when my screen popped on. I immediately tapped up the Red Sox app. It took a few seconds to understand. I was looking at the cartoony Gameday simulation screen with a batter at the plate and the drawing of a baseball field and stadium all around him. It seemed like the game was still in progress even though it was past midnight. I tried to focus in the dark on the scoreboard window.

"Oh, my God," I said. "The Sox are still playing the Mariners. It's the fifteenth inning. Tied up. Four to four."

Of course, no one cared. I felt Bailey lean closer to me, though.

"Looks like they've got a chance right now," he said.

"Whoa, yeah. Bases loaded," I said. "But two outs. And Stephen Drew is up. He can't hit at all. He's just a glove."

"So . . . um . . . you guys are going to need to get off of me," Rita said. "I want another smoke. And I need that opener."

That didn't bother me one bit. I was too amazed by what my phone was telling me. I got up and so did Bailey. He handed over his keys and we sort of huddled to the right, upwind of the idiots.

"There's always a chance," Bailey said as he put a hand on my shoulder.

Right then the screen showed an arcing streak that was supposed to simulate a pitch coming in to a batter. A few seconds later, a blue dot showed up near home plate and the words "In play, runs" in a little white box. I didn't need anymore.

"They won! Stephen Drew gets a walk-off RBI. Impossible!"

I know I was more excited than I should have been. Maybe it was the moonlight squeezing its way out of the lake. Maybe it was Rita's emotional outburst transferring to me. I actually realized, very briefly in my victorious glee, that none of us had pressed her on the real reason for her tears. Her phone obviously had nothing to do with anything.

But the Red Sox had won. Maybe they had a chance in 2013, after all.

What I wanted was to go to the video section of the team website to check out the highlight clips. They would show Drew's final hit within minutes, and the runner scoring at home plate, with the whole team running onto the field like beastly wild boys. I wanted to see the fans. They were my people! It might be a Wednesday and past midnight, but I knew most everyone had stayed because they were Red Sox fans. The only time people left a game was when we were getting destroyed by the other team. But tonight, we'd won! We'd really won. Walk-off Stephen Drew!

I came back to earth very fast, though. Bailey's hand was still on my shoulder. His face was next to mine. With one very simple thumb press, I shut off the screen, then stuffed the phone back in my pocket.

Grabbing Bailey's hand and hugging it to my cheek, I said, "Sorry about that."

It felt like a very forward thing to do, being so affectionate with his hand, but I was so happy. I leaned up against him and, still holding that hand, rested my head against the soft part of his chest just below the shoulder.

Rita and Del were now deeply (and pathetically) engrossed in their phones. I guess you could say though that Bailey and I were deeply engrossed in each other, too. But not pathetically.

"Hey," I said out toward the stars and the moon and the speckly white reflections in the shimmering water below us. "Why were you crying?"

Rita's face glowed in the dim screen light of her phone. How did I see in that faint luminescent face hovering in the dark a shift from bland screen observation to razor-sharp focus?

"I don't know," she finally offered. "I guess I was feeling a kind of final loss. Maybe . . ."

"Loss?"

"Right. Loss. The end of little Bobby Scattergood. It's pretty clear. But I know, I need to make this decision as much for my parents as I do for myself."

Del had been staring at his screen while she explained herself. With that last statement, his head shot up. First, he stared out at the lake and the sky, then over toward Rita whose face was only a shadow now.

She took a drag on her cigarette. After a moment, she laughed and said, "I am so weird."

The moon had finally squirted up enough to light the sky more than the water. It was smaller, too, more what you'd call proper lunar size. But it still seemed like the corner of some lost eye, maybe an animal's that doesn't live on earth anymore.

"It always used to be a question of why I *wasn't* actually born in a girl body," Rita said. "Sometimes I'd really try to understand. You know? Really understand. I'd make two-column lists with Boy and Girl as the headings. Then I'd try super hard to come up with stuff. You get so tired of figuring and wondering."

She let out a few memory chuckles with that. The wind had totally relaxed. There was almost no sound. Just our breathing and our bodies shifting around a bit in the dark.

"The Boy column usually only had the name Robert in it and the fact that I had short hair, wore boy's clothes—and had a stupid penis, of course. Oh, and I also listed my parents' feelings. I tried desperately to come up with other stuff. Not because I wanted to change things, but because I knew I needed to try as hard as I could to be sure."

"So, now . . ." I started to say. But I stopped. I felt idiotic trying to respond or even ask a question. It really hit me how none of us had a clue what it was like to be Rita.

"Yes, so now," she said. "It's sad. I mean, I'm *actually* sad. I just realized I can't choose—not really, anyway. In fact, it's not a choice at all, is it? Never was. If you must make a choice about who you are, the resulting person can't be real. There can't be any choices. You are who you are—or you're just making yourself up. Then you're a fake."

None of us responded to that. We sat in silence for what seemed like a really long time. Finally, Del said, "Stars are never boring in Maine." We all sat in silence with that.

"Their light is clean, but it wobbles some, too," Rita said, finally. "It's light from the past. It's hundreds of years old."

"Millions of years, I think," said Bailey. "That's sort of the idea of light years. Light from a star that's a million light years away is a million years old."

"The wobbling isn't real?" Delmore asked.

"It's real," Rita said.

"Real enough," Bailey replied. "Kind of."

"But if it isn't happening now . . ."

"Well it is," Rita said. "We see it now, don't we? The source may be ancient, but it's just arriving. Now. So, it's, you know, approximately real."

"That's a bit too weird," Del said. "It's like there's more than just one kind of time. It's starlight from a different dimension. The approximate dimension."

Bailey pulled me in closer to him. It had to be getting really late, I thought. Probably nearing one o'clock.

"One more thing to make me sad," Del said finally.

"What?" Rita asked.

"Everything seems like it's just an approximation of what's supposed to be real. That's sad."

"What do you mean?" Bailey asked.

Delmore laughed. "I don't know what I mean." He laughed again. "Whatever. Stuff on TV. Movies. Even video games. None of it's real. We know that. It's fake. That's the whole point. But it's not actually fake, is it?

A painting? A photograph? They aren't real either. But at the same time, they are. They're out in the world, but they're in our heads, too. And now you're telling me even starlight is like that."

I thought I heard Rita breathe like she was laughing.

"I mean, not everything's like that." Del said. "Bailey's car isn't. This picnic table. Our clothes. Beer. But there's a lot of stuff in life that's not as real. Pretty hard to get at. I kind of get scared, though, when I think about it. Scared—and sad."

Both Bailey and Rita laughed out loud at that.

"Scared?" I asked.

"Yeah. Maybe that's why people don't think about it that much. Things that aren't real but are real at the same time. It's like they exist together on two different levels. And because of that we really don't have either one of them here with us. See? All just approximations. We're just suspending the truth and living like it doesn't matter that things aren't easy to understand and touch, or even see."

"I've felt like that my whole life," Rita said. "It's not the same thing exactly as what you're saying. All I've ever been is a totally limited approximation of who I'm supposed to be."

And what you don't know can't hurt you, I thought. *Or maybe it can—or will very soon.*

It was the last day of July. She'd be leaving for home in a few weeks. We all would, except Bailey. She'd find out about her parents soon enough.

When we got back to the house, Del and Rita said their goodnights and disappeared, leaving Bailey and me alone. For a while there we sat in silence. He kept letting his eyes drift up to the sky.

"Are you looking for something up there?" I asked.

He shook his head. "Just wondering. There's supposed to be an aurora setting in sometime soon. I'd like it to be here when I'm with you."

"Aurora?"

"Northern lights. They appear sometimes in the winter but are kind of unusual for the summer. But it doesn't matter tonight anyway because they don't seem like they're going to show up."

Somehow, we had managed to be sitting closer to each other by the end of that conversation. Our bodies were connected from our ankles to our hips to our shoulders.

Did we kiss? No we didn't. Maybe he felt pressured, or was worried, or thought I might not want him to be so assertive.

Did it drive me bonkers? Not really. Maybe I'm just a stupid goody two-shoes, but I assumed it would happen when the time was right. I also thought that maybe I was going to have to make the first move. Boys really do have a lot to deal with when it comes to first kissing— even now, here in the crazy modern world.

Bailey did, however, again promise to make it up to me for being forced to participate in Rita's beer buying delinquency. That didn't seem necessary, but I didn't tell him that.

After he drove away, I sat on the steps watching the moon trying to bounce itself up over the treetops. I'm sure I was smiling ear to ear, wondering, honestly, exactly what Bailey Cooper smelled like, when Rita came bounding through the front door and down the steps to sit with me. She had the last beer in her hand.

"It's time," she said, then took a big swig from her bottle.

"What?"

"I need to call and tell them. They will be so relieved. How about we borrow a car and drive back up the mountain so I can text them?"

"Um, how about no way."

"Come on, Ivy. They need to know, especially my mom. I'm ready. I'm Rita. She'll be able to relax, maybe."

"It can wait until tomorrow, Rita. Really. You've been enough of a bad girl for one night. Plus, I don't care if you know how to drive, you're still just fifteen and you've been drinking. You can't take a car and just head up Captain's Mountain in the middle of the night."

She sighed at me, mumbled to herself, then took another sip of beer.

"They need to know," she said quite solemnly. "I've caused a lot of difficulty. You don't know the half of it. But I can fix it all now if they just understand I've made up my mind and finally know who I am. Really."

It was my turn to sigh. If I'd told her everything I knew, everything would have turned out differently.

But I had no juice left to devote to this high-energy, boy-girl-whoever-whatever cousin of mine. So I just told her I was happy for her. She seemed only slightly disappointed when I patted her shoulder and said it was time for bed.

"Sure, Ivy, sure," she said. "Just gonna have one more smoke. Right behind you."

19. An Offer You Can't Refuse

We would have slept late that next morning, but at a little after nine I heard the front door slam open and then slam shut. Zaxy's breathless voice yelped from the living room, "Get up you guys! Get up now!"

I stared at the mattress and spring wires on the bed above me for about five seconds until that little punk began pounding on my door. "Ivy! Get up now. Ivy! Can I come in? Ivy? Get up! Get—"

I had slogged out of bed and opened my door angrily. He could tell I wanted to smother him with the pillow I was clutching to my T-shirt. As he put up his hand in a "stop-don't-do-it" way, I heard another door creak open as well. Del screamed, "Shut the hell up, you little idiot!"

I completely agreed with that sentiment. But there in front of us was that nutty little kid, hopping from one foot to the other—like he had to go to the bathroom. Except for the insanely happy expression on his face—his grin somehow wider than his whole head—I would have gladly thrown him off the porch.

"Dude," I said. "What *is* your problem?"

He closed his eyes and kept hopping around.

"Seriously," Rita said from behind Del. "What's the deal with you, Zax?"

His over-sized light blue eyes jerked from Del's face to Rita's, then to mine. "Mom said to come for breakfast."

Disgusted, all three of us blinked at each other.

"And a really awesome surprise!"

With that, he raced through the kitchen and living room, then out the door, yelling something like "Baby's here!" which made no sense. We watched him bolt across the parking area to the path, his arms swimming through the air as he streaked into the trees.

"Baby's here?" I repeated.

"I think he said Bailey," Rita mumbled.

><

We got dressed in a daze and headed out the door. My legs felt a bit rubbery under me as soon as I saw Bailey's Camry in the driveway. I heard Delmore and Rita jabbering at each other behind me as we stumbled down the path, but I had no idea what they were saying.

What was Bailey doing back so early? And hanging out with the parents? We'd only said goodnight to each other a few hours ago.

The four of them were sitting around the table in the kitchen when we came in. Zaxy still seemed out-of-his-mind-excited. Mom had a hand on his arm. It looked like she was keeping him from floating away. A pitcher of orange juice sat on the table, along with a large bowl of strawberries and peaches, and a bowl of plain yogurt next to that. Bailey was drinking a cup of coffee and eating a donut. As we all took seats, Daddy lifted a plate up from his lap.

"Yogurt and fruit, or donuts and muffins?" he asked as he slid the plate onto the table. Mom started pouring juices. It wasn't that uncommon for Daddy to get donuts on one of his early morning cigarette and newspaper runs, but I wondered if this was the reason for Zaxy's excitement anyway. Maybe he'd had too much sugar. I looked across the table at Bailey. He had a funny expression on his face.

Once I had my butt in a chair, I couldn't help myself. I didn't care. I looked across the table hoping Bailey would be able to catch my eyes for a second.

That's all I wanted.

But Bailey was sitting next to Zax, and that little kid was the one making eyes at him. They were being goofy and weird with each other, grinning back and forth like idiots.

Daddy cleared his throat. "Bailey has a proposition for you guys."

We all stared at Bailey, who was finishing a bite of donut. After a few chewing seconds, and a swallow, he said, "How 'bout we go to the Red Sox game tonight?"

Zaxy put himself into his frozen robot mode, only he had a ridiculous happier-than-a-pig-in-mud-and-

209

sugar-slop look on his face. When my eyes moved from him to the rest of the people around the table, I found them all staring at me.

"What?" That was the best I could do. "The game is in Boston."

"My aunt is getting us tickets," Bailey said.

"But it's a five-hour drive to Fenway Park," I said. "The game's at 7:05. And we'd have to drive home."

"Not if we go by jet," Bailey said in this very matter-of-fact tone of voice.

I was confused, but I could tell everyone at the table was a little disappointed that I wasn't in the middle of a happy dance yet.

Bailey smiled at me. "My dad is flying a business group back to Boston this afternoon. He said we can tag along. We're getting picked up at the airport, then delivered to Fenway. We watch the game and fly back with him once it's over." He shrugged his shoulders like it was no big deal.

I looked over at our father, then Mom. They had those sparkly eyes parents get sometimes. Both of them gave me a little head tilt nod.

"All of us?" I said.

Daddy made a strange sound.

"Just kids!" Zaxy blurted out.

"Well, no." Bailey said calmly, "You're all invited, of course . . ."

"Thank you so much for the invitation, Bailey, but Scat and I are staying home," Mom said. "So, yes, just kids."

"Wait . . ." It seemed like magic to me.

"Cool." That was Delmore.

I detected Rita squirming around in her seat, but I made a point of not paying her any attention.

"Wow," I finally said. "So, we just fly to Boston and go to a Red Sox game?"

"Yup," said Bailey. "If you want."

"Wow." He'd said he was going to "make it up" to me. Was this how he planned to do it? I searched his face. He nodded and smiled with that calm Bailey look he had.

"We . . . I mean, *you* can just do that?" I stammered.

"My dad asks that we be more or less under control on the trip down with his clients."

"Still, but . . . tickets? They're always sold out."

"My aunt sort of works for the Henry Family Foundation. John Henry—"

"Is the team owner, yes, I know. But really? Your aunt?" I think I was laughing right there.

"Yup. Her company helps them with fund raising and special events and stuff like that."

"Your aunt knows the owners of the Red Sox? And you never told me about that?"

"Never came up. But yeah, I'm not sure if she knows Mr. Henry himself, but she does a lot of work for him and his people. You know, the foundation."

Everyone around the table was smiling and chuckling—everyone except Rita. And of course, this wouldn't make her happy. She hated baseball and barely knew anything about it. And yet, pretty much everyone in my family didn't care about the game. Why would they be so happy, then? I looked across the table at Zaxy who seemed happier than anyone. He was bobbing his head up and down like he was listening to music.

"You're gonna get to see the Red Sox!" he yelled. "The. Red. Sox."

I let my eyes wander to Bailey's face, and this time our eyes met and held. I said in my head, *"Thank you."* Somehow, I knew he heard me

When I finally glanced at Rita, she had a funny expression in her eyes. She'd caught the connection between Bailey and me and raised her eyebrows, but then a cloudy darkness seemed to overtake her. With an angry shake of her head, she made her gaze shoot out the kitchen window.

20. Living Large

We cruised past the main airport parking area and down a road that ran along the side of what was maybe a runway until we got to a gatehouse thing. Bailey gave the guard his driver's license. The guard's name was Sonny. He and Bailey talked about our trip for a minute or so.

"You kids are living large," Sonny said as a motor opened the gate in front of us. Bailey drove out onto the runway, which was a bit freaky. After a few minutes, we came to a stop next to a cute little jet. It looked like a modern, super-megatron seagull. Mr. Cooper had on fancy dark slacks and a short-sleeved white shirt with black and gold epauletes on the shoulders. He was also wearing his aviator sunglasses. Us Scattergoods got out of the car in awed silence.

"Jeez, Dad, you didn't tell me they were giving you the G-650."

"Wanted to surprise you."

"It's amazing." Bailey turned to the four of us. "You all remember my dad, right?"

213

I stepped forward. "Hi, Mr. Cooper." I reached out to shake his hand.

"Call me Coop, Ivy." He took off his sunglasses. "If you're a friend of Bailey's, that's who I am and should always be to you."

Our eyes connected. He'd been so serious and sour when we'd met at the baseball field on the Fourth of July. Now he seemed happy and confident and much more interested in all of us. I realized as he stepped by me to shake hands with the rest of our crew, that he probably also knew about his son and me—whatever that meant.

Bailey started up the stairway into the plane and I followed. Behind us, I heard Zaxy ask, "Are you a real pilot?"

"Tell you what, Zaxy," said Coop. "Once we're airborne, I'll have my assistant bring you up to the cockpit. You want to help me fly this puppy?"

"I don't think that would be a good idea," Zaxy said solemnly.

"It's pretty easy."

"I don't know the first thing about flying a jet, Mr. Cooper."

"Maybe I can show you how I do it."

"I guess so. But don't ask for my help, okay? I wouldn't want to crash us."

We all laughed—everyone except Rita. What the heck was her problem?

The silence inside an airplane is always startling. It was even more startling inside a jet this compact. I was introduced to Janet, the flight assistant. She was a very friendly woman in her forties, maybe, wearing dark slacks and a short-sleeved shirt just like Coop's, only she didn't have any epaulettes. Bailey pulled me past her and introduced me to Charlie the co-pilot, a young guy around thirty.

The group we were flying with, three men and a woman, had gathered in the main cabin. They stood to shake our hands and seemed happy to have a crowd of teenagers on board with them. They worked for some big software company in the Boston suburbs and had been on a team building exercise, fishing and hiking for a week. Two of them knew Bailey from past trips and asked about how his baseball season was going.

My brothers and Rita came up behind us pushing Bailey and me to the back of the plane. We sat next to each other in two seats positioned at a large table that dropped down from the wall. I was amazed by everything we were surrounded by and felt out of place and clueless all at once. I'm sure I looked like an idiot.

Bailey leaned his shoulder into mine as we watched the software group in front laughing and joking with my brothers and Rita—especially, Rita. What was all that about? And she was all smiles and jokes.

Rita and Delmore sat on a big couch near us with Zaxy. They helped him with his seatbelt. We were all in a quiet daze for a few minutes until the plane began to move toward the runway.

Once we were in the air, Janet came back to get a very reluctant Zaxy.

"But, really, I don't even know how to drive a *boat* yet," he said. "I could really mess things up."

Janet smiled and laughed.

"You won't," Rita said. "Go, man. Tell them you're just there to observe. Check things out and report back to us."

Zaxy hesitated another moment, considering, then unbuckled his seatbelt.

As she led Zaxy up to the front of the cabin, Janet turned and gave Rita a wink.

When they were gone, Rita and Del came over and sat down opposite us at the table.

Delmore said, "Sometimes I don't know whether to laugh or cry with that kid."

"He's pretty funny," Bailey said. "I've always really liked him a lot."

"People pick on him at school," I said. "We pick on him at home sometimes." I caught my brother's eye.

"It's weird being picked on all your life," Rita said to us. "Boy, was that me. And it wasn't just older boys or the bullies in my classes. It was everyone—boys, girls, teachers, some of my babysitters, our neighbors. Even some of my parents' friends when my parents weren't around, which was a lot sometimes."

Delmore gave her a smirk. "You must have been kind of a weird kid to everybody growing up." He nudged her with his elbow and then patted her forearm. "And you're still quite a handful. Must have been really confusing when you were Robert."

Rita smiled at that and shook her head. "I thought that's how it was for everybody. Seriously. That's a problem when you're an only child. There's no one you can compare experiences with."

"There's friends," Bailey said.

"I didn't have any." She stared at the middle of the table. "I guess I was very weird. But I honestly didn't understand any of that. I mean, I didn't know."

"You acted like a girl?" Bailey asked. "And people picked on you?"

"No. I didn't *act* like a girl, I *was* a girl. It never occurred to me otherwise—at least up until I got to first grade."

"What happened in first grade?" I asked.

"I'd never gone to nursery school. I always had a nanny or a babysitter. I didn't go to kindergarten, either, because we were traveling. My dad had a sabbatical the year I would have started.

"It all gets slammed home in school. Boys and girls get separated and sorted out in every activity. Then there's the bathroom situation." She rolled her eyes. "I tried following girls in twice. The first time they dragged me out and put me in front of the boy's room and told me that it was for me. I knew it wasn't, so I just held it. A few hours later I tried to go back in the girl's room. I was desperate. That's when they went and got the teacher. Thank God I had time to pee first."

She looked up and smiled at all of us.

"Pretty wild," Bailey said.

"Yeah, I guess it was, but it was also confusing. I figured I didn't understand something that everyone else did."

"People had to set you straight," Del said.

"They were trying. But, really, it went over my head for a long time. I wanted to wear dresses. Just at home, you know? My parents wouldn't let me. They gave me no explanation, just 'You are not allowed.' I thought I had done something wrong and they were punishing me."

"Sounds like they knew what was going on," Bailey said. "Your parents, I mean."

"They sure did. But they never confronted me with any of it. Not once did they tell me I had to act like a boy. They just ignored it all, hoping it would go away."

"Kids at school didn't ignore it, though," Del said. "Right?"

"I came to expect people were going to pick on me and make fun of me. They called me all the names you'd expect—faggot, retard, sissy, idiot, baby, pervert, whore, pussy—"

"They called you a whore?" I asked.

"That and a lot of other stuff having to do with sex."

"That really makes me mad, Rita," I said. "I wish I'd been there."

They all laughed at that. I looked at Delmore, though, and said, "We stick up for Zaxy when we can. No one bugs him when we're around."

"It would have been interesting to have you guys around," Rita said thoughtfully. She was silent for a few moments, staring at the middle of the table again. "Over the years, I figured out how to survive. And I got by. I mean, I learned to play the game well enough. I kept my hair boy-short, wore fairly regular-looking boy clothes to school, even used the boy's room, although never a urinal. I understood my place, you know? But, honestly, I didn't fully get what was going on." She laughed. "I was a very pathetic, gullible, naive little transgender kid in training.

"I was also the smartest kid in the class—me and Ann Rogers. Then, when I started at the running club in like fourth grade, people stopped being total assholes. I mean, I still got picked on. Mostly by then it was the girls doing it—mean-girl syndrome, you know. The boys just tolerated me, but I wasn't trying to be friends with them. Fortunately, I was just one of several girls that got picked on.

"Then puberty hit. That's when I started to get it. The girls were developing breasts and hips and curves. They started wearing makeup. The boys began to treat them differently. I felt left out and super conscious of my confusion. It was devastating. Everyone was ignoring me."

"What did your parents have to say about all of this?" Bailey asked.

"I guess they tried talking to me, sort of. But I didn't know what to say to them. I mean, you have to understand, until I turned twelve I was pretty small and slight. My body could have been a girl's body. My face, too, in a lot of ways."

"Nothing's changed much there," Delmore said.

"Right," Rita went on. "If I'd just been a normal boy, you know . . . I didn't find out until recently that girls had crushes on me because they thought I was . . . cute. Cute and smart works, I guess."

Her hand was trembling a little. Glancing up at Delmore, I caught his eye. He nodded very gently.

"There's a lesson in all of this," Rita said.

"You like girls!" Del said, half joking but also half amazed. Rita's hand was shaking more. I wanted to punch my older brother. What is wrong with boys like Delmore?

Rita seemed to have lost her train of thought. She was staring a hole into the center of the table again. But then she said, "I guess I do . . . like girls, I mean. At least, these days. But that's not what I'm talking about . . . not yet, anyway."

She straightened up in her seat and took a deep breath. The rushing, rumbling sound of the jet was all we heard, the crazy roar of wild clouds bolting out of our way as we went screaming through the afternoon sky.

"They were leaving me alone all of a sudden. They didn't know which side of the fence to put me on. So, I was basically a nothing to them. That's the way it seemed, anyway. Just inconsequential. Nothing.

"I never blamed them or thought that they were being unfair or jerky assholes or whatever, because to me the feeling of being forgotten and left out seemed like it was actually *my* fault. In fact, I decided that the reason people had always been weird and mean and dismissive with me was because I didn't give them any other choice."

I dropped my eyes to check that shaky hand. It was fine now. When I looked up, she was smiling at me.

"You noticed the hand," she said.

"What?" That was the best I could do.

"It's fine, Ivy. My whole body starts shaking sometimes when I talk about this stuff. It's like I'm vibrating. My shrink tells me its adrenaline. She may be right. It comes and goes. But to me it's more like my body is trying to transmute itself, like on *Star Trek* or some other science fiction show. It wants to be a new creature. My mind knows things don't work that way. But the body's different. It just starts pulsing, trying to move into some other person. Pretty funny, huh?"

We all sat inside the sound of the jet engine. The passengers in front were talking and laughing in that way people do when being airborne has become familiar and somehow normal.

"Finally, I realized two things," Rita said. "One is that if you feel and act weird, people will definitely treat you weird."

She looked at each one of us and shrugged. "If you've never felt like a weirdo, maybe you don't get what that lesson means, but it's actually huge for people like me." She held out her left hand, spread her

221

fingers as wide as they would go, and just stared at them for a while.

Finally, she went on. "The other lesson is kind of the reverse. If you act like someone who has lots of friends, you actually end up having friends. And—"

Delmore interrupted her. "It took you six years of school? Seven? To figure that out?"

She laughed with the same tone as his in her voice. "That's what I'm saying. I really was clueless."

"Right," Delmore said. "If you have a penis, don't pretend you're a girl, pretend you have friends." He looked at Bailey and laughed in a way that sort of indicated he expected Bailey to join in.

"You're missing the point, Cuz." Rita smiled at each of us. "It was like threading a needle. I did my best to stay girlie enough. I wore skinny jeans and brightly colored Pumas and pastel-colored shirts. I didn't cut my hair for a long time. I got my ears pierced, wore jewelry. Whatever I wanted. And I made friends. With girls *and* with guys."

"Right, with the other outcasts." Del said. "I know that deal. So does Ivy."

Rita shook her head. "Nope. With a lot of people—nerds, hipsters, jocks, cheerleaders, a couple cool teachers, older kids in the neighborhood, a few dealers, you know. Everyone. It wasn't easy at first. I never really developed a 'best friend' relationship with anyone. But I do have good friends. I go to parties and birthdays and hang out—with guys and girls—doesn't matter.

"The hipsters and the musicians are my favorites, I guess. We work hard to find new music no one else has heard. It's fun. That's how I got a hold of that Lorde chick's bootleg from New Zealand. I also have a few friends who are gay. We don't talk about gender or sex stuff much— mostly we just talk about clothes and politics and music. I've gone to some LGBTQ meetings with them. Two girls, and a guy named Les."

"What are the girls' names?" I asked.

"What?"

"The girls? Their names?"

"Jenna and . . . um . . . Peggy."

There was something about the way she was brought up short by that question.

"And you're in love with Peggy," Del blurted out. "I can see it on your face. Am I right? Am I right? I am so right. Is she cute? Got a picture on your phone? Come on!" He punched her arm softly.

My brother had maybe come too far in his appreciation of All Things Rita Gomez. Six weeks earlier he was at first disgusted by her, then shot into a crazed freak-out because he realized he'd been attracted to her. Now, here he was teasing her about being attracted to another girl.

I gave Bailey a quick glance. When I let my eyes focus back across the table at Rita, her face had pinked up and her left cheek seemed to be twitching.

"Wait a minute," Bailey said. "I can see maybe you don't want to talk about this, and if you want to change the subject, that's fine, but is Del right?"

She put both her palms flat on the table, leaned back a bit, and spread those long fingers of hers wide. We all stared at her hands. Over the wind canyon moan of jet roar, I heard her take a deep breath.

"I've never talked about this to anyone. I mean, she's kind of a hipster Rastafarian type, but, yes, I guess that's what I'm saying." I tried to catch my cousin's eyes. I don't know why, but right then I really wanted her to just be speaking to me.

"There's a movie," she said. "I don't know which one anymore, but I'll always remember what this woman says to a friend. She says, 'We don't get to pick who we fall in love with.' I say that to myself sometimes."

She took her hands off the table, then looked at each of us as she went on. "I was thirteen when I first heard that. It really stuck with me. At the time, I wasn't so much concerned with love as who people thought I was supposed to be. That question was connected, though. Right? You can't choose who you fall in love with. You can't choose how you feel inside, in any way at all. Ever."

Just then, I looked up to see Zaxy wading around our traveling companions up front. They had all fallen asleep. Once he made it through that obstacle, he came jumping and skipping and flapping his arms at us.

"We're landing! We're landing! I saw cities and the ocean and little tiny cars like bugs, and they said I should think about being a pilot when I grow up. And I am. I am. I am, I am."

Rita got up and gave him a hug, then went to sit with him for our landing. As she helped buckle up his seatbelt, she glanced up and caught my eye. With a shrug and a head tilt, it seemed like she was saying to me, "See. *I'm not so bad. I can handle this. It makes me sad. But it's who I am. And who I want to be.*"

That's a lot to say with just a shrug and quick tilt of the head. But sometimes that's all people need to do, though.

21. Game Time at Fenway Park

Our car was big and black with tinted windows. It's what they call a town car. We had a chauffeur named Donna who wore a black vest with a red Boston "B" on her chest.

After a couple months in the woods and mountains, I felt out of sorts and disconnected in such a big city. But my excitement and anticipation overwhelmed any sense of disorientation. Light rain was predicted for later, but as we moved slowly through the beat-up streets of Boston, everything I looked at seemed to give off a special shimmer.

It took a long time to drive through Boston traffic. Fenway Park is plopped in the middle of what would be backstreets and a quaint neighborhood in most any city on the east coast. Donna dropped us at the media and employee entrance. She said we could take our time meeting up with her after the game because the traffic would be crazy. We entered through an old metal door and stood in line for a few minutes. They gave us each game passes on red and blue cords to hang around our necks and then told Bailey we should wait while an usher came to get us.

It was still fairly early, but there were plenty of people buzzing by, making loud noises, happy to be at a baseball game. Fenway's guts are so complicated and goofy under the stands. The ceiling is sharp angled with exposed steel girders held up by hundreds of concrete columns and posts. Shiny metal pipes run every which way along the slanted ceiling. The floor used to be pitted cement with stains and puddles and funny textured patches everywhere. Now most of it's covered in big, more or less uniform panels under the stands.

The stadium turned one hundred years old in 2012—last year—but it felt more like it was five hundred years old. It smelled that old too, with the scent of ten trillion french fries in the air, and billions of hot dogs. Beneath it all floated a kind of cooked sugar fragrance mixed with the pickled odor of stale beer and old soda, all rising out of the floor, I think.

I'd been to a few games with my family over the years and was worried when I heard they were thinking about modernizing Fenway. Those smells and the whole dingy grunge of the stadium were a huge part of its character. I can't say I hate the Philadelphia Phillies or their new stadium, but ever since I was a little girl Fenway and the whole Red Sox experience has been in my bones. Fortunately, there's no way to get that scent out of all the concrete, wood, and steel that makes up this old stadium. It's the smell of old-time baseball spirit.

Bailey kept his eye out for our usher. Zaxy's head toggled right and left over and over again in his usual possessed droid style. Delmore stared into the phone screen in his palm, smiling every few seconds. And Rita still looked perplexed.

"What is wrong with you?" I asked quietly.

She shrugged a little and looked into the distance.

I leaned in closer. "Just tell me."

Lifting her eyes, she pointed with her chin. I followed her gesture to find a sign posted on the pole next to us that said, "*Absolutely no smoking anywhere in or around Fenway Park. By order of the City of Boston.*"

Just then, our usher arrived. The boys began to move off with her. Rita and I straggled behind.

"I don't know if I can make it," she whispered to me.

"Sure you can," I said.

"You don't understand."

"Actually, I do. I'm Scat Scattergood's daughter."

"He'd go crazy here."

"Nope. He's weird, maybe, but he says real smokers are tough and know how to relax and wait. Notice how he didn't light up once when we were at the July Fourth picnic and game? He held off until we got out on the water in the boat."

"I'm not your dad."

"What if you chew gum or, maybe, eat lots of ballpark food?"

She shook her head as we went through the short tunnel between seating sections and came out to the field area. Bailey was following the usher down the stairs. He stopped and let my brothers wade by him. "You okay?" he mouthed at me. I nodded, shooing my hand at him. Rita and I leaned up against a railing. I watched the usher wipe seats off for Del and Zax. Bailey was a few steps above them.

"If I get up and wander around, don't be surprised," Rita said. "There has to be a place that people who need a smoke sneak off to."

"I know you don't want to hear this," I said, "but it breaks my heart that you're only fifteen and already desperately addicted to something. I mean, watching my dad . . ."

"You don't understand what it's like to be inside this body. *Or* inside this head for that matter. It takes so much effort not to lose my shit every day. Seriously."

"I just think you—"

"Don't. Just don't."

Why does having someone talk to you like that hurt? I stood there continuing to stare out at the field, watching the players finish warm-ups. We'd missed batting practice. They were packing up all the nets and ball baskets. The game would be starting soon enough.

It had become a rather ominous looking night. The sky was stuffed full of low-flying clouds. It was still fairly warm, but you could tell it was going to be dark sooner than usual, and maybe even a bit rainy. They'd turned the stadium lights on already, making the green field shimmer like a pond full of liquid gems. The white bases and lines were pulsing, and the red-brown dirt seemed like the skin of an exotic summer animal.

"What do you think of all this?" I asked.

"You know I don't care about baseball," Rita said.

"No. Just the field and the people and the lights and the colors."

Her eyes seemed shaded somehow, her thoughts turned inward more than usual. Still, she got my point because she turned to consider the scene in front of us.

"It *is* pretty amazing looking," she said, finally. "So much construction and spectacle just for a sports game."

Does it make sense to argue with someone when they can't see something so overwhelming and magnificent? I had learned years before with my family and their disinterest to just let it all go. There was no point. Still, it made me sad. I felt lonely, like when Rita and Delmore made fun of my music.

"Are you hungry?" I asked. "Or should we just sit?"

"Sit." She grabbed my arm and pulled me in the direction of our seats.

><

The first inning was pretty nerve-wracking. Boston had Ryan Dempster pitching for them. He was an experienced, veteran pitcher. Not quite a superstar, but pretty close. He gave up a triple to the first Mariners' batter, but then quickly struck out the next guy. After a few more batters, the Sox were down a run and still only had one out against the Mariners. What a discouraging way to start a baseball game.

When the inning was finally over, my brothers stood and sidled by us. "We're going to the bathroom," Delmore said. "And then getting some food."

As they started up the stairs, I realized Rita was already missing. I didn't say a thing. I just wagged my head and made a disgusted sound.

"Let it go," Bailey said as he eyed her empty seat. "Seriously. I'm here. You're here. We're watching a Red Sox game. It's a beautiful night. Well, maybe it's not exactly beautiful, but it's nice enough. Whatever she's up to, let it be."

I could have said so much to that. Instead, I sighed, and pulled his arm around me. "I can't argue with you," I said. "I'd like to, but I can't."

The Mariners scored again in the third inning. I'd forgotten about Rita by then. Darkness creeps in so quietly at summer games. It felt like the only things in the world that mattered anymore were the field out there, and the players with their bats and mitts and helmets, and the umpires. And, of course, that little white ball people chased and hit and threw. Under the dome of darkness, the stadium lights made everything glisten with importance and consequence. You could hear that glistening crackle and pop all over the field. The huge left field wall that they call the Green Monster was so close to us in that light. It almost seemed to be breathing. I could see why they called it a monster.

We finally scored in our half of the third, but as the runner crossed the plate, the Mariners threw out Dustin Pedroia as he attempted to advance to second base. That ended the inning. I had a bag of pretzels in my backpack. I pulled the pack out from under my seat and plopped it in Rita's empty space to rummage through. Turning, I asked, "Anyone think we're ever going to see Rita again?"

Del gave me a weird look. Zaxy said, "She's been funny all day. It's like she's sneaking."

All three of us older kids just stared at him. Would it be so bad to tell him what her problem was? I took out a few pretzels and offered the bag to Bailey. "Pass it down," I said.

The score was 2-1 in the fifth inning when Rita finally came back.

"Where have you been?" I asked.

I could tell something was wrong as she took her seat.

"What's the problem?" I asked. "What happened?"

She closed her eyes and chewed on her lower lip a little. Staring blankly into some opening out in the field that I couldn't see, she muttered, "I'm fine."

"What, Rita? What happened?"

"I don't want to talk about it."

I squinted at her, trying to find some way of understanding what had happened without her telling me. Bailey put his hand on my left shoulder.

"Just tell me if you're okay," I whispered.

She turned and looked me in the eyes. It was quite obvious she'd been crying. Also quite obvious, from how she smelled, that she'd been smoking up a storm.

"Phone reception sucks here."

"Come on, Rita . . ."

She shrugged. "It'll have to do, Ivy. I don't want to talk about anything right now." She put her elbows on her knees and looked out at the field.

"Okay then. Have you been watching the game? Do you know the score?"

She glanced at the scoreboard. "Two to one, Mariners. Fifth inning. Shut up, Ivy. Watch the game."

That fifth inning was pretty painful. By the time it was over we were losing 7-1. Bases loaded, the Mariners' Henry Blanco had smacked a grand slam home run on the first pitch he saw. It hardly mattered that the next batter struck out. Ryan Dempster was well-cooked and beginning to burn around the edges. I wasn't happy to see him jog back out to the mound for the next inning. That's when I noticed Rita was gone again.

"I need to use the bathroom," I told Bailey. "I'll be back in a few minutes."

The bathroom really was my intention. But it didn't work out that way. Although, I did go pee first.

When I came out of the restroom, I turned to the right instead of the left. There had to be an obvious place to find her if I just thought about it hard enough.

22. Face Off

I envisioned an out-of-the-way corridor—wind-blown, poorly lit, ten or fifteen sad loser types leaning against the wall, smoking. They'd be texting friends and family, a few, perhaps, playing some dumb video game like Angry Birds. That's not what I found, though.

It took a bit of luck, but I'd turned on my radar for things that didn't seem quite right. About halfway around the outfield concourse, a little old man in a red safety vest was sitting in a chair next to an unmarked door. Hardly anyone was in the vicinity or passing by. The food vending areas and restrooms were located more in either corner of the outfield. This old guy was sitting in a little metal foldout chair with a walkie-talkie on his hip, leaning back, looking up at a monitor, watching the game.

"Excuse me," I said. "This is going to sound kind of dumb. I know you're not supposed to smoke here at Fenway, but if someone was really desperate, what would they do?"

He squinted at me with raised eyebrows a pretty long time. Finally, he noticed the pass dangling from my neck. He said, "You don't seem like a cigarette type of girl, missy."

"Oh, no. Definitely not. I'm looking for my cousin. She's the cigarette girl."

He glanced at my pass again, but didn't say anything for a long moment. "You talking about Rita?"

Whoa. That was a bit direct. "Yeah. Yeah, I am."

He pointed his thumb at the door behind him. "Through that."

I thanked him and started to head for the door. "Sorry, missy." He held out his hand.

"What?"

"You don't think you get into a secret part of the stadium for free, do you?" He squinted at me and rubbed his fingers together close to his chest. "Twenty bucks."

I took my wallet out of my left front pocket. "I'm not a smoker. I just need to find my cousin."

"Right. I got that. It's just that, you don't budge from your rules at my age."

I handed him a twenty-dollar bill, mumbled something at the floor, and stepped past him. Opening the door, I was surprised to find myself outside the stadium in a dimly lit, fenced-in storage area. Sounds of the city mixed with the deep hum of the crowd inside. It looked like the soda and beer delivery area. At the far end of the fence was a locked gate wide enough for a truck to back through.

Rita was nowhere to be found.

"Hello?"

I got no answer. I took a few steps forward. Then a few more to a gap in the beverage stacks. I peered around the corner of the gap and there she was, sitting in a mix of stadium and street lighting on a little foldout chair with a big outdoor ashtray pulled up next to her.

Her hair dangled across her face. She was hunched over her phone, moving her thumb at high speed on the keyboard. Her thumb seemed desperate, hyper, manic. I noticed her hand tremor a little as well.

"Can I ask what you're always so insanely engrossed in on your cell phone?"

Great way to start a conversation, huh? I was still pretty annoyed deep down inside that she couldn't just chill out and simply hang out watching a baseball game.

She didn't look up. She also didn't seem startled or surprised. Maybe she'd heard my initial hello. She finished texting, sat up straighter, took a drag from her cigarette, and exhaled. Then she just sat there looking at me for a long time.

Finally, she tipped her head to one side and said, "Do you realize that I don't actually know one transgender person? I mean, face-to-face? And yet I probably know fifty or sixty of them around the world through this little gadget here."

"So . . . what? You're texting strangers?"

She pursed her lips, nodded, took another drag on her cigarette, and stabbed it out in the ashtray. "Those strangers helped me through a lot in the beginning. Now they're helping me through a lot more."

"What do you mean?"

She took a deep breath and leaned back in her chair. Several other chairs were scattered around near her. Her hands jittered. I think I took a deep breath, too.

"I got harassed about an hour ago. It was pretty scary."

"What do you mean?"

"Harassed. Accosted. Attacked."

"Someone attacked you?"

"I'm kind of new to all this. But apparently it's supposed to happen."

"Wait. What happened?"

"I went to the bathroom. The women's room. I was washing my hands afterwards. These two girls, maybe early twenties, were touching up their makeup and jabbering away. They both had beers with them. I'm washing my hands and they just stop talking. I keep my head down and act like nothing's wrong. I can feel them staring at me. I know they've figured me out.

"I take a long time to wash my hands. When I stand up they're gone. It was uncomfortable, but I figure it's all over, right? When I leave through the exit, though, it's not all over. I was looking in my purse for my lighter, and all of a sudden I feel a hand on my wrist. Another

237

hand slams into my chest. Two guys push me up against the wall. No one's around. It's not well lit there. And the girls are standing behind the two guys. They all call me names. Every time I try to move, the bigger guy pushes me in the chest. Harder every time.

"Eventually, he slams me back against the wall really hard. They're threatening me. They claim they're going to call security. Say I'm a pervert for going into the women's room, spying on women. I try to move again. This time the smaller guy steps in front of me and mashes both his palms into my breasts.

"I don't feel like they're going to be finished with me until people come along. But no one's coming along. I can smell beer on them, hot pickled breath. They're laughing at me. It seems like maybe they're about to finally let me go, when one of the girls says hold *"it"* against the wall. Both guys pin my shoulders back. She steps close to me and acts like she's going to kiss me. I smell hot dog and mustard on her breath, along with alcohol. Her mouth is less than three inches from mine. Then she sneers, spits in my face and—"

Rita breaks down. All the shaking her hands have been doing spreads to her shoulders and chest and neck. She's sobbing spasmodically. But she's not letting a sound out.

"She knees me. In the crotch. Hard. Then slaps my face."

I wait. I'm feeling so angry, I don't think I can speak. I'm in such pain. Why do people have to be that way? Every jerk in the world!

"*Then* they leave."

She puts her head down. I can hear pain blurting out of her words even though, still, she clearly won't let herself cry. We hear the crowd murmur a little, then some quiet booing.

"Do you know what the worst part of it all was? They just walked away laughing. Just laughing. Like they do that kind of thing for amusement every night."

"Did you report them?"

She shook her head. "What good would it do? Look at me. What do I say when they ask why I was attacked? Because I'm transgender? Because I was in the women's room?"

"They physically abused you. You have every right to—"

"Ivy! Shut up. Are you that stupid? My God. You're so prim and proper, and you think everything's above board and simple and glorious. Well, maybe it is in your world. But in mine it's pretty weird and sometimes pretty scary and pretty sad."

I felt like walking away, escaping back to the game. Instead, I grabbed one of the folding chairs, slid it in front of her, and sat down.

"You know what?" I started, "it really sucks that people are mean to you and that people have problems with your decision, but it also really sucks to see you doing this to yourself. I've kept my mouth shut about it all ever since you got here. I like you as Rita. I like you as Rita a lot. But it also feels like *you're* the

239

one in La-La Land. You really need to face some serious facts if you're going to do this."

She was sitting up straight, studying me. I could tell she was about to speak, but I held up my hand. She shrugged, took another cigarette out, and lit it.

I wasn't going to let her smoke bother me.

"You need to understand some things about this supposed choice you're making." I looked straight into her eyes and went on. "You pass with most people. But you won't with everyone. Some are going to be offended. They shouldn't be, but it's what's going to happen. You know that. You're pretty good at dealing with it, I think, but every once in a while you're going to get in trouble like tonight.

"Maybe it will get easier over time. Maybe you can have operations and get real breasts and, you know, the other part. Maybe you can take drugs to change your body chemistry. Maybe you can have plastic surgery, too, and let them operate on your Adam's apple. I get that. I understand it's possible."

We heard the crowd again. They sure weren't being very loud. I wondered what was going on in the game, but I didn't care right then. It seemed like things had been much more straightforward earlier in the summer when I was so mad at her.

"It's really weird, you know? I mean, why can't you be Rita, but not so much Rita that you have to actually turn into a girl? I don't get that. There's so many things about girls that I hate and I think are stupid, but I would never, ever want to be a boy. Yuck!

240

"Do you see what I'm saying? No matter what, it just seems like there's something that's not right about caring what other people see when they look at you. This transgender stuff totally shakes up the idea of being male or female. But if all you want is for people to treat you like a girl, then just be a girl. Who cares what's under your clothes?"

She was staring back at me very pointedly. Almost desperately. I wanted to go on, but I'd run out of words.

"In the end," she said quietly, "the whole idea of gender being these very defined and stereotyped categories is going to get thrown out the window, Ivy. I know that. That's what people like me are doing."

"But if you change into—"

"You mean my body? If I change into a girl? What? If I do everything right, and I become a beautiful flower in the world, just like you? You don't get it. That is *all* I want. Then I want to go forward and live my life. Got that? I just want to live my life like everyone else."

"But you won't really be a girl."

"What does that mean? Are you really a girl? Seriously. I can be whatever I want. I will be whatever I want."

"No. I'm sorry. I've been thinking about it all summer. First of all, you won't have a period every month." I wince-laughed. "You can't get pregnant, either. And you're going to have to tell whoever your boyfriends—"

"Girlfriends? Maybe."

241

"Right. Whatever. You're going to have to tell people you love. I mean, where you came from."

"So what? They're going to have to tell me where they came from, too. Maybe they'll be trans as well. That's a thing, you know."

I squinted at her questioningly.

"A thing. Trans girl and trans boy. It's a thing."

"Oh."

"Right. Oh. And it solves the pregnancy problem."

"I suppose. But do you see what I'm saying?"

"I do, trust me. But it's so much more complicated than your little simple-minded, proper, Ivy perspective thinks it is."

"How about stuff like what just happened? I mean, that could go on your whole life."

"Maybe it will. Maybe I need to take up Brazilian jiu-jitsu or boxing."

She lit another cigarette, her hand still shaking. I wondered where things were in the game. Red Sox crowds can get awfully quiet when they're losing.

"What about your parents?"

She looked very uncomfortable all of a sudden. "What about my parents?"

"They want you to be a boy, Rita. That's what they thought they were raising. You're going to kill them when you come home."

"Right, and the whole gender thing was killing me, too, until I came out here to the other side of the planet and turned into . . . until I became . . ."

"Rita?"

"Right. Rita. Me. I am *so* her!"

"Yeah, but you're Robert, too. I met Robert. Remember? Robert's pretty messed up. Pretty depressed. Nobody knows about that."

"Robert's been killing me."

"Killing Rita? Or killing Robert?"

She didn't respond at first. We heard the sound of a ball being hit. There wasn't much crowd response. I figured it had to be maybe the top of the eighth inning and the Mariners were up— still destroying us.

"Me, Ivy. I'm killing *me*."

"But who are *you*? Rita? Robert? Someone else? I mean, you like being Rita. I see that. I like Rita, too. Everyone does. But are you actually Rita, or are you *pretending* to be her? And how would your parents react if they were here and they had to see their kid, the kid they raised—definitely an interesting kid and a half, but still, *their* kid. How would they react if they met Rita?"

She shook her head and shrugged. I was starting to feel a little nauseous from breathing in all that second-hand smoke. Earlier in the summer, I would have gotten disgusted and simply left. Right then I was willing to suck it up in order to have this conversation.

"My parents have always said they just want me to be happy. My dad has, anyway. My mom, you know, I just figure she feels the same way even though she's so busy being a diva. They let me know, *we want you to be happy* all the time. Even when we're arguing about things. And— except stuff like those four ass-holes who attacked me—I've been happy most of the time up here. Besides that one night."

"The night of Robert crying in the shower."

"Yes. The night of feeling sorry for myself. But I'm done with that now. You can't go through life feeling sorry for yourself. That's how you fail at everything. Might as well put a big F on your forehead. F for Fail."

That got me exasperated. Honestly, I don't know what I expected. I didn't have a right to argue with her. I get that! Hopefully, you understand by now that I really did not want anything horrible to happen that night—or any other night. Still, I said it anyway.

"Your parents did not send you out here to decide whether you really want to be a girl."

She gave me a funny look. The fingers that held the last remnants of her cigarette seemed even more unsteady. "What do you mean? Of course they did."

I shook my head. "Daddy talked to your dad that first day after you arrived. Your dad said that we weren't allowed to let you be a girl. There's a court order from a judge in San Diego requiring you to remain a boy."

"What are you talking about? A court order? You can't have a court order for something like that. Why would anyone think that?"

"It's true. You can ask good old Uncle Scat."

"Well if there's a court order, why didn't anyone tell me?"

"Because no one tells Rikely and Scat Scatter-good what to do. Ever. Especially, apparently, your mom and dad—or some ass-butt judge. And I don't think they wanted to tell you what to do anyway."

"But why didn't someone else tell me?" She meant me, of course.

"Why? Yes, well, that's exactly why I haven't told you about this."

I saw her swallow. It's funny. I hadn't really noticed that Adam's apple until right then. That's what those girls clued into—and those jerks at the coffee shop.

She looked mad now. I don't think I'd ever really seen her look mad. "What the hell are you saying, Ivy?"

"Your parents," I sighed. "They're getting a divorce."

You don't ever want to say those words to a kid. I didn't realize that until it was coming out of my mouth. It's like shooting their dog in a little tiny room. You're telling them that the one thing they could count on in life has now been destroyed, and they're going to be locked in that room forever with their dead pet.

She should have been in shock. But somehow she wasn't. She calmed herself almost immediately and became focused instead. We heard another ball being hit by a wooden bat.

"It's me," she finally said. "I did it to them."

"Now, wait a minute—"

"You don't understand. We had a lot of conversations. I dressed up at home sometimes. They'd catch me. We had some arguments. All of us. Before I left.

245

I couldn't actually come out and tell them what I really wanted. So the whole discussion happened with me saying it was something I was working through. I needed time. They had to be patient. I didn't know for sure."

"But you did know. You've known for a long time."

"Of course. I mean, not totally, but I had a pretty good idea. I was telling the truth, though, up there on the mountain with all you guys. That's when it became crystal clear."

"And that's why you were so excited about telling them? The other night? Last night? Was that last night?"

"Yeah," she said uneasily. "It was last night."

"There's more to parents getting a divorce than a single thing, Rita."

"No. It's me. You had to be there. They'd catch me in a dress or with makeup on. We'd go around and around. I'd stomp out or leave them in a haze. Totally confused. And then, from up in my room, I'd hear them downstairs arguing. I would put on headphones and turn up the volume."

"Are you sure they were arguing about you?"

"Oh, yeah. No. I did this."

"Well, maybe they'll work it out. There's still time. There's always time."

"I just thought, you know, they disagreed. I mean, my mom is pretty nutty. She can get very passionate. That's the Latin side of her maybe. It's always the Latin side."

"I think you need to maybe talk to my parents. I shouldn't have told you any of this. I wasn't supposed to, anyway. But my parents can maybe help."

"Oh, Ivy. You don't really mean that, do you? Your parents are great and they're pretty damned cool, especially your mom, but they've got their own problems."

Her cigarette smoke had dissipated into the night air, but I'd been inhaling it so long my throat was sore, and I felt slightly oxygen deprived. I wondered, maybe for the first time in my life, how my mother could stand living with someone who smoked so much and drank so much and was always making a big thing out of everything.

"Okay, well, we're done here," I said tersely. "I tried to let you know what I think, and I told you things maybe I shouldn't have. And now you're turning it all back on me."

I rose from my chair and crossed my arms. "I was worried about you. Apparently, I had good reason. I hoped I could get you to come back to the game and have some fun with us. But it doesn't matter now anyway because the Red Sox suck tonight. Just make sure you're paying attention enough to know when the game ends so you can fly back with us. Okay? Wouldn't want to leave you here all by yourself in Boston."

I didn't wait for her to respond. I turned and left the little cubby area, then went back through the door into the stadium. The little old guy was sitting in the same chair, staring up at the screen, watching the game. I stopped next to him.

"What inning?"

"Top of the ninth."

I sighed.

"It ain't over until the fat lady sings, kid."

"I know that," I said. "But when it's seven to one . . ."

He shook his head. "You missed it. Victorino hit a big one over the fence. Home run! It's seven to two now. We're gaining on 'em."

My eyes roamed from the screen near the ceiling down to the little old guy in his chair. He was laughing silently in a strange way. I couldn't tell if he was being sarcastic, or if he was serious and maybe laughing at me for having a loser's attitude.

23. People Change

The final inning was just beginning when I got back to my seat. I sat down next to Bailey and tried to focus on the game. But Rita had really depressed me.

Zaxy leaned across Bailey. "Did you find her? Where is she? What's she been doing? Did you see Victorino hit his home run? I wish he was still with the Phillies. Did you find Rita?"

I glanced at Delmore. He pointed at the giant plastic soda cup in the holder next to our little brother's elbow.

"Whoa. Did you drink that entire thing?" I asked.

Zaxy was leaning on Bailey's legs, his little face beaming at me. Bailey said, "My fault. He said he was thirsty. I forgot what soda can do to little guys."

I couldn't help chuckling a little, then leaning against his shoulder. "Did Shane Victorino really hit a home run?" I asked.

"He did. He really did," said Zaxy. "He was first up in the eighth and hit the second pitch out of the park right there in left field." He pointed in the direction of the foul pole.

"I probably had too much soda," he said to all of us. "I really gotta go bathroom."

Bailey shifted in his seat and said, "I'll take him."

"No, Delmore should," I said. "He knew better on the soda thing." I gave my older brother a cold look.

But Bailey wasn't having any of it. He stood up and stretched, then said, "Come on, little guy, let's go hit the head. I've been holding it too long myself."

Once they'd gone, I moved over next to Delmore.

"I think I really messed up," I said.

"What? How? Did you find Rita?"

"I kind of gave her an earful about everything."

"What do you mean?"

"Her trans deal . . . and other stuff."

"Other stuff?"

"Yeah. Stuff Daddy didn't want me to tell anyone. Especially not Rita."

"What, the whole thing about the court order and her parents?"

"Wait a minute. You *know* about that? Daddy told me not to tell anyone."

"He told me the same thing. I figured you knew, though, just by the look in your eyes sometimes."

"Yeah, well, I told her all about it."

He took a deep breath, then puffed his lips out and exhaled.

"Probably for the best," he said as he scratched the top of his head. "It's been weird to hear her so happy and confident when we know what the real situation is."

"She didn't take it too well," I said. "She blamed herself for their problems. Said they had a lot of arguments."

"That's probably true. That kid is totally messing with everyone's head. And she doesn't seem to get it. I mean, the weirdest thing about all this is that listening to her all summer has made me aware of how selfish I actually am sometimes. And I don't like that."

Was that the reason he'd calmed down so much and had actually become almost likable?

><

The ninth and last inning was going on in front of us, but I didn't care. The Mariners had a man on first with no outs. Everything felt so out of synch and lost.

I felt so bad for Bailey. He'd done this amazing thing setting up the game, and here were the Red Sox tanking, and Rita being impossible. Well over half the fans had gone home. It seemed like maybe I should suggest we be on our way, too. Why put people who really don't care about baseball through the final inning of a losing proposition? It was painful and frustrating enough for me to be losing. Why force that on others?

But it wouldn't really make a difference. The limo driver had said to take our time because of the congestion—which meant she probably wasn't even there waiting for us yet. I wondered if Bailey had a phone number for her and could call.

Just then, the Mariners' hitter slapped a ball all the way into left field off the wall. The runner on first was rounding second heading to third as the left fielder made his throw. Maybe, just maybe, I thought, we'll get this stupid Mariner at the base. Sure enough, that's what happened. He slid. The ball arrived and the third baseman put the tag on him right before the runner's foot hit the bag.

I wanted to clap. But, to be honest, even though the meager, deflated crowd made a fair amount of happy fan noise, it just felt wrong.

Bailey and Zaxy came back as the runner jogged back to the Mariners' dugout.

"Did you see that play? Did you see that?" Zaxy was still a bit more excitable than I would want him to be around our parents. If we brought him home like that, we'd get a good amount of flack.

From behind my right ear, I heard a voice that I recognized all too well. "Pretty cool." It was the same timbre and tone, only deeper. I spun my head around quickly.

"Hey," he said, eyebrows raised.

I turned back the other way and caught a glimpse of Bailey and Zaxy. Bailey was squinting. Zaxy's mouth had dropped to his chest, eyes bulging out of his head. Del still stared vacantly out into the field.

Robert was sitting in the empty row behind us. This time he didn't look depressed or defeated the way he had in the shower the night we'd climbed the Captain. He'd washed his face. His hair was a bit damp, and even though it was pretty short, he'd swept it back. Along with the clothing he'd come to the game in, the wig and earrings were gone, probably stuffed in his backpack. He was wearing a brand-new, over-sized long-sleeve Red Sox tee that he'd most likely bought from a ballpark vender. The only thing feminine I noticed was his fingernails. They were still painted purple. When he saw me glance at them, he moved his hands out of sight.

Bailey reached past me, "Hey. Pleased to meet you. Name's Cooper. Bailey Cooper. You're Robert, right?"

What else are you supposed to do in a situation like that? I caught a quick movement out of the corner of my eye and heard Delmore say, "Oh, shit! For real?"

Zaxy was locked into his open-mouth position, but his eyes still seemed to be working. They traveled all over Robert's face and torso.

"Dude," I said, leaning across Bailey to smack the top of Zaxy's head. "Stop."

He didn't seem to feel the smack or hear my voice. I turned to Robert again. He smiled. First at Zaxy and Delmore and Bailey, then at me. "Who's winning?"

That brought the little kid out of his stupor, although he still seemed somewhat stunned. "The Red Sox suck. I'm going to call them the Red Sucks from now on. Are you Robert?"

Our cousin closed his eyes and nodded silently.

"I don't get any of this," Zaxy said. "I just don't understand."

"Me either, kid," Robert said.

I was about to say something to Zaxy when another Mariners' ball got walloped really hard and went screaming into left field again. I had this sinking feeling in my legs. But then, Jonny Gomes, the left fielder, went flailing toward the base of the Green Monster. He sent himself swimming through the air, somehow catching the ball just before slamming into the wall. *Surely he's going to drop it*, I thought. But he didn't. He did an awkward backward somersault with the ball safe in his mitt—the third out in the Mariners' part of the inning.

Mercifully, we just had to suffer through the bottom of the ninth. The game would be over and we could head home. Maybe all of this crud, I thought, with Rita (and now Robert) was a result of being sleep deprived. Maybe it was some weird effect of flying on a small jet. Maybe it was all a dream. I was good at dreaming. Shoot, that's what it had to be. Because the alternative was far too horrendous.

Delmore looked like he'd been slapped in the face. He said, "You seem like you're cool, Robert. But I miss Rita. I mean, where is she? Pretty strange trick, that!"

24. Last Ups

The last half inning of the game began with the Mariners bringing in their closer, Tom Wilhelmsen, to shut the door on the Red Sox. What an amazing job to have. All he had to do was pitch one inning and get three outs. Of course, the hardest part of any baseball game is finishing the last inning with a win.

Wilhelmsen walked Daniel Nava on four straight pitches. Some in the crowd clapped and muttered a few cheers, but it was more sarcastic than hopeful. The next hitter was Ryan Lavarnway, our catcher. I looked across the field. Big chunks of the stands were now empty.

One of the cool things people don't think about is that when a lopsided game is nearly over, the crowd that's left tends to be a bit more vocal, even when they know there's not much chance of a win. People who stay for a losing team are a special kind of sports fan. When Lavarnway got the first strike called against him, we started clapping in unison to encourage him. I wondered if maybe it was okay to just let go and be a goofy fan, so I clapped along and nudged Bailey to do the same.

It was a long at-bat, but we were finally rewarded when Lavarnway shot a hard line drive almost through the pitcher's chest into center field. The runner on first advanced to second.

"Perfect setup for a double play at any base," I said to Bailey.

"At the same time, that guy on second base is in scoring position," he said back.

Right after he said that, the young Red Sox infielder, Brock Holt, sliced a double down the right field line, scoring Nava.

I can't say the fans went wild, but there was a bit more cheering and clapping. A walk and two straight hits off a closer? It was 7-3 and still no outs.

I turned to see if Robert was behind us. He looked down at me and raised his eyebrows. "Fun," he said. "Baseball. Ivy's favorite."

The Mariners' pitching coach came out to chat with his relief pitcher and catcher. Jacoby Ellsbury, the leadoff hitter for the Sox, stood in the batter's box waiting for his turn. Our best hitters were coming up.

Within a minute, Ellsbury had a three-ball, no-strike count. I said, "Pitcher's looking pregnant," out toward the field. A little tingle of hope popped up inside me; it wasn't so hard to fight it off, though.

Wilhelmsen managed to throw a strike after I made my pregnancy statement to the field, but then he walked Ellsbury on the next pitch to load the bases. The Mariners decided it was time to change relievers.

I heard Robert say behind me, "You know, the next batter can tie the game with a home run."

I turned around. "You bet."

Something interesting happened on the field at that point. The manager had come out and raised his left arm towards the bullpen, meaning he wanted the left-hander warming up to come in. But then he realized he'd made a mistake, and raised his right arm, pointing to it emphatically. He had wanted the right-handed relief pitcher instead.

We watched as the righty started running in towards the infield, but an umpire stopped him and said something. The righty turned and jogged back to the bullpen.

"What's happening?" Zaxy said.

"That's interesting," I said to everyone. "The manager made a mistake. He called for the lefty first. The rule is he has to bring him in for at least one batter if that's who he indicated first."

"Really? There's a rule for that?" This was Robert behind me.

"There's a rule for everything," Bailey said.

"That's why it's such an interesting game," I said.

"Of course," said Robert. "That makes total sense."

"What's that supposed to mean?"

"You kind of like rules."

Bailey put his arm around me and pulled me close. I didn't need him to say anything.

The Mariners' lefty, Oliver Perez, came in to face Shane Victorino. On the second pitch, Victorino slashed a single past the second baseman, scoring two runners just thirty seconds after the new pitcher had started pitching. It was 7-5.

My face felt like sparks were shooting around it. This time I couldn't hold back. There were still two men on base and no outs. I was going to be a serious fan, hoping against hope. The Red Sox best hitter, Dustin Pedroia was up.

"Wow, this is actually a good game," I heard Robert say behind me. "Interesting."

Bailey patted my shoulder as Perez began his windup to Pedroia. The first pitch was a ball. A lot of fans were standing and cheering now. I stood with Bailey. Glancing behind us, and before I said a thing, I saw that Robert was also up clapping and hooting like everyone else.

On the second pitch, Pedroia drove the ball into left field for a hit. Ellsbury came in to score because of a late throw from the outfield. I thought about all those idiots who had left. 7-6!

Then the greatest clutch hitter of our lifetime stepped to the plate. Big Papi, David Ortiz. All two hundred and eighty pounds of him.

The fans were really loud now. Zaxy was jumping up and down next to Delmore. I couldn't hear him, but he seemed to be chanting "Papi" over and over again. Perez struck him out on three straight pitches.

One out, but still two men on base. The Mariners decided to change pitchers again. But it was 7-6. We still had a chance.

As we watched the new pitcher warm up—Yoervis Medina, the one who had tried to come in earlier but got sent back—Delmore said to all of us, "I have to say, I've never been to a better game in my life." He waved his hand at the field. "This is what you read about and what they make movies about. I never imagined . . ."

I nodded and thought, *"Well, yes and no, big brother. More often than not, things get to this point and then, at the last moment, all your hopes and happiness get dashed."*

Jonny Gomes stood poised at the plate for the Sox. The first pitch came in—a perfect pitch to hit for a home run, right down the middle and just above the belt. But Gomes didn't swing. Strike one. The next pitch was a nasty, high, inside pitch for strike two. I thought, "Still only one out. He can strike out or whatever here and we still have one more chance."

The next pitch was a ball. And the pitch after that was, too.

"It must be really hard for the pitcher in a situation like this," Robert said.

I started to say something. Gomes hit a foul ball.

"It's one reason why they get paid so much money," Bailey said. "That, plus the TV and advertising dollars." He made his eyes really big for me, then turned back to game. I noticed that Stephen Drew was on deck.

The count was tight, two balls, two strikes. Everyone was standing now, cheering and clapping. The pitch came in. Gomes laid off it, and the ump called a ball. Now we were at the old full count—three balls and two strikes. Game on the line.

Medina looked in for the sign from his catcher and shook his head several times before finally getting set to pitch. The ball came in, and Jonny Gomes lined it straight up the middle for a single. Victorino came bolting around third and scored easily. Game tied 7-7.

"Holy shit," I heard just behind me above the cheering and stomping.

And now Stephen Drew—the glove—was at the plate. He swung at the first pitch for a strike. And then fouled the next one off for strike two. I tried not to think about how long people had been there the night before in a fifteen-inning tie game.

Drew let the next one go for a ball. Way outside. The next pitch was a hard inside fastball that the catcher dropped but kept in front of himself. Ball two.

All the players for both teams were up at their dugout fences. Medina threw another pitch too far inside, so all of a sudden we had another full count. Then he tried for another insider, maybe trying to get a swing for strike three. But he missed. So Drew walked to load the bases once again.

The pitching coach came out to talk to his pitcher. All the players in the infield came to the mound as well.

No one in our group said a thing. I'm sure most other fans were feeling the same way. I'm pretty sure everyone had forgotten how to breathe right then. We stood and bounced on our feet, waiting. Daniel Nava had started the inning with a walk, and now he was back at the plate.

On the first pitch, Nava swung hard and drove the ball deep to the center field wall. Dustin Pedroia came around to score the winning run. Red Sox players rushed onto the field and attacked Nava the way ballplayers will. For some reason these days they strip the jersey off the player who got the hit. Another walk-off win! It ain't over until the fat lady sings! Where was that little old man?

Bailey was hugging me. "You know, they're being really rough in that scrum, punching him, really pounding his back. It's gotta be painful."

I looked over at my two brothers. They both had their hands on their heads and were grinning ear to ear. From behind, Robert's hands squeezed my shoulders. "That was amazing," he said. "Just amazing. I loved it. Totally!"

Every bit of that moment made me happy, of course. Elated, even. A lot of fans stayed. Just standing there, gulping in that feeling of wonder and surprise. Jonny Gomes spoke in a TV interview that was broadcast to the whole stadium. The stands felt crowded around us because so many fans had come down to the lower level where we were sitting. It was starting to rain.

I turned to Bailey. "I am so tired all of a sudden. I mean, I'm happy, but I'm exhausted."

"Me too," he said. "We can sleep on the plane."

I looked up at him. "I am so grateful and amazed that you took us to do this. It is the coolest thing I've ever done in my life. I just really . . ." I was staring up at him and he was looking down at me, our eyes locked. It was time, I thought. I figured. I hoped. I worried.

We might have kissed there. Except Zaxy tugged on Bailey's shirt from behind. "Hey, are we really *flying* home?"

Bailey turned. "Yup, we are, little man. You ready to take the helm?"

"That's not funny."

Bailey cocked his head. "It is, a bit, kinda."

Zaxy looked up at me, then back higher at Bailey. "Well, maybe. But I just wanted to know because it seems weird that we're going to be flying in the dark."

That's what we did, though. And flying in the dark is a pretty cool thing, as Zaxy found out up front with Coop and Charlie.

I figured we'd all pass out as soon as we were in the air, but that's not what happened.

25. Arrivals

The flight home began with both Delmore and Robert buckled in and next to Zaxy on the couch. Robert seemed equally as attentive to our little brother as Rita had been on the way in to Boston. All three were chattering away as we took off from Logan International Airport.

Once we hit cruising altitude, Janet came back to tell Zaxy he was free to come up to the cockpit if he wanted. He hadn't gone to bed super late the night before, so he hopped right up, possibly still wired on soda sugar and caffeine. He asked Janet whether she knew anything about pilot schools. And then they were heading up to the cockpit, Zaxy explaining he probably would drive but wanted to watch so he could learn stuff.

Bailey and I tilted our seats back, not saying much because we were so tired. However within a minute Robert plopped down on the other side of the table.

"Come on. Over here. Del," he said. "You should hear this, too."

Oh boy. I stole a glance at Bailey. We both let our seats come back up. I truly just wanted to conk out until at least Thanksgiving.

Robert said, "None of you asked."

"Asked what?" Delmore said.

"Why I changed back."

"Oh, well, maybe because we've all learned it's none of our business."

"Right, well, it sort of is . . . Your business, I mean. Ivy told me about my parents. I know about it *all* now. They're supposed to be getting a divorce while I'm gone. And I also know that the reason they're having problems is specifically because of me." Before any of us could argue, he raised his hand to make sure we'd let him finish. "I've been fighting with them and definitely making them fight with each other for about two years now," he said slowly. "It's got to be my fault, plain and simple."

"So . . . what?" Delmore asked. "You think you have to follow some dumb judge's order to be a boy? Robert's going to save the day, and get his parents back together?"

"I don't know," he replied carefully. "I don't know anything anymore."

Bailey leaned forward. "If you feel you need to do this, then fine. No big deal. We just, well, we're all supportive of whoever you are. But, seriously, dude. It surprised the crap out of us when you showed up like that in the middle of the game. It will probably also be weird for Scat and Rikely when they see you tomorrow morning."

"Fine. I get that. Great. Weird. But there's something else."

The three of us exchanged glances.

"Ivy, you know how I said I wanted to drive up the mountain last night? To call my parents?"

"Yeah. You'd had a bit too much to drink, I'd say."

"Well, I ended up doing that. By myself."

"You what? You took the car?" I was so exhausted I don't think my voice sounded very upset.

"Dude, wait," said Del. "You'd been drinking, and then you took the van up the mountain by yourself? Just like that?"

Robert nodded.

"That is messed up. You are officially psycho."

Robert leaned back in his seat and tilted his head to stare at the ceiling.

"You really are a problem child," Delmore finally said in disgust. "I mean, even *I* know that's a shithead thing to do."

Robert dropped his face back to our level and shrugged. "I know. I know. I shouldn't have done it. But I did. I *had* to call them."

"And I'm sure your parents were happy to hear Rita's voice on the other end of the line," Del said.

Robert looked down at the middle of the table again. "No. No they weren't happy at all. At least my dad wasn't. I didn't talk to my mom."

"What did he say?"

"It was a short conversation. He got my basic message. I used Rita's voice, too, of course. I told him

265

it was all clear to me. I think I said about eight times in one sentence that I'd finally figured it out. He didn't say anything for a minute. Just silence. Then he told me he was flying out."

"Flying out?" I said. "You mean here?"

"Yup."

"You've known all day long and you didn't tell us?"

"I wanted to say something, but I didn't want to tell you about the car."

"Yeah, well, it's a good thing you didn't," I said. "When's he coming?"

"I don't know. He may be here already."

"Seriously?" Delmore asked, then looked away.

"And *that's* why you changed back in the middle of the game," I said. "You think your dad is going to be at the main house when Bailey drops us off."

He cocked his head. "I don't know. Maybe."

The lights were still on when we came up the drive. We had no way of knowing whether or not Uncle Edward was inside.

"We're not just dropping Zaxy and running," I said to my cousin. "If he's in there, you need to face him right now."

"What are you talking about?" Zaxy asked.

"Uncle Edward."

"Uncle Edward's here?"

"He might be," Delmore said.

"Oh, this is weird," our little brother said to no one. "I get it. But it's weird."

"You don't get it at all," Delmore said.

"I do too!"

><

They were sitting around the dining room table with several kerosene lamps creating the only light in the room. Mom was saying something when we all came through the door. She stopped and raised her arms to all of us.

"They're home! Our jet-setting children have returned!"

"Oh." She was staring at Robert.

Daddy and Uncle Edward had their backs to us. Edward was bald and more heavyset than I remembered. But he had Daddy's basic shape. You could tell they were brothers. As he turned, he put on his glasses.

We were standing together on the edge of the lamplight. A quick expression of what seemed like disappointment crossed our uncle's face.

"Hi, Dad," Robert said feebly.

Until that moment, I'd forgotten how uncomfortable Uncle Edward could make everyone around him. My parents talked about that a lot when they didn't think we were listening, but I had mostly let it go in one of my ears and out the other. Now, though, I understood.

"Hello? Son?"

Where was the acknowledgment of the rest of us—his niece and nephews? His brother's children?

Where was standing up to at least shake hands?
Where was hugging his son who he hadn't seen in
well over a month? I let my eyes move to my father.
His head was almost imperceptibly sliding back and
forth. His forehead had just slightly, somehow, tight-
ened up.

Mom passed a plate of cookies toward Robert. "It's been a long day," she said. "Everyone have
a cookie. Maybe we can wind down the way people
should wind down at this time of night—especially after all this special air travel. It will be easier to talk in
the morning."

"Wait. I came all this way," Uncle Edward finally
said, "to see this Rita person I've been hearing about.
That's who you've been, right? And you basically told
me on the phone you'd made a decision?" He turned
to Mom and seemed to wait for her to explain.

Most of us were munching on cookies. Robert
stopped chewing until Mom said, I think to all of us,
"We've been talking about Rita all night long. Then
you all come home . . . without her."

She let that sit in the air. I looked over at Bailey. I
could tell he felt like he should leave. I smiled at him
for a second, then shook my head and put my hand up
as subtly as possible. He looked puzzled.

Robert had finished chewing. With a half-eaten
cookie in his hand, he said, "Sorry, Dad. I didn't know
what I was doing. It's okay now."

"I think you did," Edward said. "I think you knew
exactly what you were doing."

"No one told me there was some judge . . ."

"Oh, yes, I understand that. I half-expected it. I know your Uncle Scat fairly well, even if I am his asshole big brother. No one tells him what to do." He turned to Mom. "I also know your aunt here, Robert. I'm not sure what I expected of you, because, quite honestly, I don't know you very well. *You*, I mean. Not Robert. But *you*. In there." He pointed at Robert's chest.

Our cousin let his eyes drop quickly to the piece of cookie still in his hand, then said, "If I'd known about the court order I wouldn't have done it. Any of it."

I flicked my eyes over to Bailey again. He was grinning, almost like he was holding back a laugh.

"Wait a minute here," Delmore said, holding his hand up in Uncle Edward's direction. "You came out here to see Rita, Uncle Edward? Is that what you're saying?"

Bailey leaned forward and snuck another cookie.

"Not completely," Edward said. "But after listening to your parents all during dinner, I realized that maybe I was curious to . . . to meet this new person you claimed to be. As curious, maybe, as I was worried."

Delmore laughed the way Daddy can laugh, partly like he's amazed at the human race and partly like he's having fun on a merry-go-round.

Out of the darkness behind everyone, came Zaxy's voice. "Why does something so complicated for one person have to be such a problem for everybody?"

Mom extended her arm and Zaxy rushed to her. His expression said he was feeling what I knew was one of the best feelings you can have as a ten-year-old. She pulled him close and kissed the top of his head three times.

"Life is complicated, sweetie. Get used to it."

"I miss Rita," he said. "But I don't ever want to be a girl."

Mom hugged him again. "It's late, everyone," she said. "Maybe we need to all get some sleep and see how things go tomorrow."

Uncle Edward closed his eyes, giving in. "Probably a good idea. We need to be on the road by nine."

"What? Why?" Robert asked quietly.

"We didn't tell you yet."

"Tell me what?"

"Your mother's flying in tomorrow."

"She is?"

"Right. Landing around 11:15."

We all watched as the two of them made eye contact for the first time since they'd seen each other. It was hard to tell what went back and forth between them, but they didn't look very happy.

><

When Aunt Samantha opened the van's door and stepped into the sunshine and breeze early that next afternoon, she looked stunning. I'd forgotten how glamorous she was, and how tall she seemed. She had on black stiletto heels and skinny jeans, along with a cream-colored, silk wrap blouse and a lightweight black cardigan. I'd also forgotten how full her figure was.

Standing there next to me, I heard Bailey mumble, "I should have realized."

And that beautiful Latina face. There was no question where Rita got her looks—the high cheekbones, full lips, delicate nose, and the deep, wide-set, cat-like eyes.

Uncle Edward was obviously stressed out and perplexed. Samantha, on the other hand, was bouncy and chipper and—can I say it?—vivacious.

As soon as she saw me on the porch standing next to Bailey she raised both her arms and almost squealed my name in delight. I don't know why, but I let myself skip down the steps and rush to hug her. She smelled of lilac with a hint of cinnamon.

"Who is he? That boy?" she chirped in my ear.

"My friend, Bailey."

She was about to say something but stopped herself and looked back up to the porch. Mom, Delmore, and Zaxy had made their way out the front door. Samantha still had an arm around my shoulder as we moved in tiny steps across the gravel drive. I caught the look on her face for just a flash of a moment. She was wondering where Robert was. I could just see his shadow inside the screen door.

Everyone came down from the porch into the parking area to have her make a fuss over them.

Delmore and Zaxy seemed a bit overwhelmed by all the sounds she was coming up with and the way she moved among us. She had bracelets on both arms that jangled together, several necklaces dangling around her neck, and long earrings in the shape of children holding hands. It was hard to imagine her as a professor of neuroscience. It wasn't hard, though, to imagine she was somehow a role model for Rita (and Robert).

"And where is he?" she said to Mom. "Where is the son I haven't seen in six weeks? I—"

She stopped because the screen door had squeaked open. We all turned toward the house. Robert stepped out onto the porch looking down at each of us—especially his mother.

"Roberto, Roberto," she shook her head. "Roberto!"

How you prance gracefully across gravel in four-inch heels is beyond me, but she was doing it—quite expertly. Bailey stepped up behind me and put his hands on my shoulders. We all watched this woman moving eagerly toward her son.

There was no time to turn and check how the rest of the family was observing this scene. All I knew was that we were watching something significant, some key to the puzzle of Robert and Rita.

"You didn't need to come here, Mother." Robert was standing at the top of the steps, his fists on his hips.

"But I," Samantha said, and she paused for just a few beats, "*we* missed you."

"I head home in ten days."

"Too long. We wanted to see you here, now, today. And tomorrow."

Robert let his eyes trail from his mom at the bottom of the stairs to the rest of us struck frozen and mute in the driveway. His eyes seemed to lock on his father for a few moments.

"We? You still speak for both of you?" Robert shook his head and sneered with disgust. "I just learned last night what's really going on with you two. There's no 'we' anymore . . . Mother."

Samantha's left foot took half a step back. I wanted to check how my uncle was handling this scene, but he was behind me and to my right.

"Don't talk like that, Berto," she said slowly. "We . . . *I* did come to see you. I was worried."

"You were worried?"

Now it was her turn to put fists to hips. She spun her head around to glance at all of us standing behind her. It was hard to tell whether she was feeling awkward or threatened or even angry.

"I don't know what you've heard," she said, "but now is not the time. Everything is complicated. We will talk later. Right now, I just want a hug from my sweet boy."

I heard Zaxy whisper something, then snicker a little. I don't know what that was about, but they did look pretty funny—Robert standing at the top of the steps with his elbows sticking out and hands on his hips, his mother standing below him with nearly the same posture and staring up at him.

"Just a hug?" she asked. She raised her arms toward him. "For now?"

Robert didn't move. "For now?" he asked. "I don't want any more secret, private talks with you. I want the truth. I want everyone to hear. I'm tired of wondering if you're hiding something. I know what that feeling was now, and I don't like it."

He turned and stalked back inside. The screen door banged behind him.

For just a moment Samantha let her head and shoulders droop. But by the time she turned around, the tigress had returned to her eyes.

"Samantha," I heard Uncle Edward say, "I explained. He needs time."

She waded through everyone, and said with her back to us, "I get that, Eddie. I get that." Then she stopped, turned, and looked out beyond the trees at the lake and the sky. "It is so beautiful here. Especially out there on the water. I forgot. So endless and serene. Why does that feel like such a trap?"

Then she headed straight toward her rather large suitcase, and without a word began to wrestle with it, trying desperately to haul it toward the porch. Bailey broke away from me. Del was right behind him. Somehow, the two of them managed to heave that giant piece of luggage all the way up the steps. Samantha followed right behind. Tilting the case back onto its wheels, she entered the house while Delmore held the door for her. She didn't offer a whit of appreciation.

I turned. My parents stood arm in arm. Zaxy and Uncle Edward were staring at me, like they were waiting for me to say something important. All I could do was let my head swivel back and forth while rapidly blinking my eyes.

"Brace yourselves, everyone," Daddy said. "Samantha Scattergood has returned to *Casa Cielo*. You all head in or whatever. I need to have a smoke and think about all of this."

Lunch was not completely uncomfortable. But I do think we were all a little too aware of Edward and Samantha in our midst. And all their issues. They sat at opposite sides of the table—Samantha near Daddy, Edward to Mom's right next to Delmore. Rita sat next to me on the other side, with her mom on her left (Whoops. I mean Robert!).

Mom had made an assortment of her special sandwiches. We passed around a big bowl of strawberries and blueberries. Bailey sat up near Daddy, too, next to Zaxy. Obviously, I wished Bailey had taken Robert's place next to me.

"This all looks so delicious," Samantha said. "If only I could have been a better example in the kitchen for Roberto."

"Oh, well, he's been helping out in the kitchen here all summer," Mom said. "But, really, Samantha, I remember you and your Honduran kitchen wisdom."

Aunt Samantha held up a hand. "That was a long, long time ago, Rikely. I have my work now. There is

275

never time to cook. I packed all that wisdom away in a box that disappeared when my mother died."

"She hasn't cooked a meal that I can remember, ever," Robert said with a sneer. "She's very proud of that. We go out to dinner, a lot. Or eat in. Well, at least I do."

Uncle Edward made a noise in his throat. "Robbie," he said, "you don't have to be that way. Every family is different. Your mother works a lot. Both of us do. You know that."

The wind swished in slowly through the screens in the back of the house, then gently hissed out the front windows toward the lake.

From the other side of the table, Zaxy said, loudly, "How come they call you Robbie and Roberto when your real name is supposed to be Robert?"

"How come they call you Zaxy?" Delmore said quickly. "Your real name is Zachary."

"I'm not supposed to be called Zachary."

"Yes you are."

"Only Mom calls me that."

Delmore shook his head and reached for another sandwich triangle.

"I don't know why people call me anything," Robert said quietly.

"Stop it with the sadness," said his mother. She put her hand on his shoulder, then said to Zaxy, "Names we use for people we love are like hugs and kisses."

"Really?"

She smiled. "Everyone in the family knows your real name, right? But when you were a baby, your sister had trouble with the "K" sound. So your name kept coming out of her mouth as Zaxory. And then everyone shortened it to Zaxy. Your big brother began to call you Zax. And it stuck."

"I know all of that story," Zaxy said.

"Yes, well, did you know whenever someone in the family called you Zaxy, it sounded like they were hugging you? And when people called you Zax, it sounded like they were kissing you on the nose?"

"You're making that up."

Samantha smiled at Mom. "Not really. Do you remember Rikely? I told you that the last time we were here?"

"I do," Mom said. "Nearly ten years ago."

"Wait. We've been here before?" Robert asked.

The adults all remained quiet for a while.

"Seriously. I was here before?"

Samantha and Mom raised their eyebrows at each other.

"We stopped on our way home from a conference in Switzerland," our aunt finally said. "You were home with . . . with . . ."

"The Russian one," Uncle Edward said. "Svet something. Svetlanka? Something like that."

"Svetlana," Robert said. "She was strict and kind of lazy."

It seemed like he was trying to figure something out. But Zaxy blurted, "And Berto too! You have too many names. I bet people also call you Bob."

"Or Bobby," Delmore added.

Robert blinked out of whatever he was thinking about. "I hate Bob. And Bobby. Don't ever call me either one of those names."

"You don't mind Rita, though," said Delmore. "What's up with that?"

And there it was. Thanks to my rhino-butt older brother, the whole room got very tiny for all of us. It felt like we had just arrived at a line that was shrinking right before our eyes. Crossing it would maybe kill us all. We'd smother each other. We'd all be dead. Not just Robert and his parents, but all of us. Dead. Even Bailey. Dead. Dead. Dead.

"Who wants cookies and tea?" Mom said. She turned to Uncle Edward. "I baked my sugar cookies just for you."

Aunt Samantha slapped the table and laughed. "The famous Norwegian Secret Recipe sugar cookies? I forgot about them!"

Mom scooted her chair back. "Zachary Dean Scattergood, I'd like you to clear the table. Bailey Cooper, could you please help him? Tea and cookies for lunch desert coming up."

"Lunch desert!" said Zaxy. He threw his arms in the air.

Uncle Edward poured himself a beer from the bar refrigerator near the table. All of a sudden, Delmore and I were stuck alone at the table with Samantha. She asked about our plans for the upcoming school year. Then she asked Delmore about college. She said she'd gone to Pomona in California and suggested to Del that college in California might be a wonderful experience. He leaned back in his chair listening to her, pushing away from the table a little bit. I'm sure she would have gotten around to me and my college plans, but Mom arrived with a huge pot of tea and then took cups out of the china cabinet. Uncle Edward came back to the table and sat down with his beer. I could see Bailey and Zaxy in the kitchen, chatting while they worked on dishes in the sink.

Finally, Daddy returned and said, "I've decided. We're going for a cruise."

"He means he wants to show off the boat," Delmore said.

Everyone started talking together about the new super boat. We had tea along with Mom's Norwegian sugar cookies. The only happy moment we got out of Robert that whole meal came when he'd finished his first cookie.

"My God, Aunt Rikely, these are amazing."

"Magic," said Daddy.

"No, seriously," Robert said enthusiastically. He helped himself to another. "I want to know how to make these."

"It's a secret recipe, dude," Delmore said. "Even my sister doesn't know it."

The adults kind of laughed at that.

"But they're so amazing," Robert said as he chewed away. He reached for another. "Does anyone else know the recipe? Because if Rikely died tonight

. . ." He took a bite then pointed at Mom. "The world would be out of the best cookies ever. And the maker of the best cookies, too."

"She's not dying," Zaxy said emphatically. "She's my mom!"

Robert reached for another. But his mother moved the plate away from him.

"Slow down, Robert. Too much sugar is not good for anyone."

My cousin closed his eyes, still chewing like a fool. Then he slumped in his chair. The air in the room got warm and awkward. I saw Bailey and Delmore sneak a headshake at each other with big wide eyes.

"Who is going for a cruise with me?" Daddy asked.

><

In the end, the adults all left for the afternoon and the kids stayed home. Robert and Delmore disappeared as usual. Bailey and I hung out with Zaxy, playing video games. They let me connect my phone to the stereo to listen to my Johnnyswim album.

Bailey stayed for dinner. It's a good thing he did, too. The adults came back from their boat ride just after five o'clock a bit sun-colored and tiredish. Mom asked for volunteers to help with dinner. But Bailey and I had been thinking about a walk. Delmore and Robert were back from their alone time at the little house by then, but quite focused on playing some dumb little kid quest game called *Rainbow Mountain*.

With no response from any of us, Mom specifically requested help from Robert.

"Come on," she said, "you've accomplished a lot in the kitchen this summer. Show your parents what you can do."

His face went pretty sour when he heard that. Before he could respond, I stood up and said, "We'll help, Mom." I turned to Bailey. "Right?"

"Of course," he said. "Just tell me what to do."

As we passed the dining room table where Daddy, Samantha, and Edward sat reading sections of the paper, I glanced back into the great room. Zaxy was busy with his iPad, and Delmore, controller in his lap, had his face plugged into the big screen video, oblivious to everything. Robert, though, was watching as we stepped into the kitchen hallway. He seemed upset maybe, or worried. It was hard to tell.

26. Who's in the Audience?

Mom pulled a bag of green beans out of the refrigerator and said that they needed cleaning and stem top snapping. She showed Bailey what to do, then got me started on a giant baby greens salad, cutting scallions and strawberries. Placing a bowl of toasted walnuts on the counter next to the cutting board, she instructed me to finish the salad off by cutting little cubes of sharp cheddar cheese and spreading them along with the nuts on top. She began preparing a marinade for the chicken pieces she'd taken out of the fridge.

I asked, "Is that our Greek marinade, or the Italian?"

Mom looked up from whisking a bunch of the liquids she'd poured into a glass mixing bowl. She glanced quickly at Bailey who had his back to us, then said, "Italian for chicken. Greek for pork and beef."

"What's the difference between them again?" I asked. And, yes, I was trying to impress Bailey Cooper.

Robert's voice chimed up from the other side of the kitchen. "Lemon juice, mint, garlic, and olive oil in the Greek," he said to all of us. "Italian's red wine vinegar, tomato sauce, olive oil, a bit real wine, and grated onion."

Standing near the sink, sipping her wine with a lopsided smile on her face, Mom said, "A little fresh basil and oregano in the Italian too. But very good, Robert Scattergood."

"So, can I help after all?"

"Sure," Mom said. "Come pour this marinade on the meat, then flip each piece and make sure they're coated all over on both sides. Use this brush."

"That's a lot of meat."

"Breasts and thighs from Sickler Farms," Mom said. "I'm trying to impress my sister-in-law." Her eyes darted to me quickly.

Robert busied himself washing his hands. "Why would you want to impress that person?" he asked.

"I don't know what my problem is. I've always needed to impress her. Maybe I'm a bit competitive. Or insecure. She's such a wild card."

"Who would want to compete with that . . ." he whispered here, ". . . bitch?"

The B-word. It had been whispered so no one outside the room could hear. I waited for Mom to do her thing.

"You know, Roberto," she finally said, "your mother is an amazing woman. A highly successful, professional. I get you have issues with her, but she's extremely well respected in her field, like your dad. She gave up a lot to accomplish that. Maybe she's made some choices that don't meet other people's needs, yours especially. But you of all people should—"

"Me? Of all people?" Robert blurted as he dried his hands. "She's breaking up my family. She's trying to control me. And she's pretending she's doing nothing wrong."

Bailey stepped away from the sink. "It's working too. She's got you right where she wants you. As long as you stay mad at her, you're dead in the water. Stuck."

"I'm not stuck!"

"Yes you are. When you're mad at people—especially people you love—you feel bad about it, and guilty. You're stuck, dude."

"No, I'm not."

"Okay. Answer me this. Are you Rita or are you Robert?"

"I'm both, of course. Right now I just don't want to hurt them. I've done enough. I've—"

"But you haven't done enough," Bailey interrupted. "You've left them on the fence thinking *they* have a choice, that it's up to them to approve or disapprove— them and some stupid judge. Maybe you wanted it to go that way, I don't know. Better to feel it's all about them and their control of you than actually having to take some responsibility and be who *you* want to be. I get it. We all get it. But still, you're letting it be their choice. Trust me. I don't think you want to do that."

"Trust you? What do you know about it? Your parents are happy. You're a world-class cool dude.

The ultimate guy's guy. A stud athlete and a good all-around person who everyone loves and respects and listens to. Choices? You have no idea."

"Maybe you just need to talk to them," I offered. "You're so mad. But they're trying. They're here."

Robert seemed like he was about to say something. He was turning the meat over in the marinade that he'd poured. But Bailey said, "Remember, you told your dad already—on the phone. You said you'd made up your mind. I mean, you *told* him that, and now they're here because of what you said."

"Right, they're here to talk me out of it."

"But they don't have to," I said. "That's what Bailey's saying. Seems like you've already talked *yourself* out of it."

"You know, *Rita*," Mom said, "one of the weirdest things about being a parent is that it gets harder and harder to fake like you know what's right and wrong for your kids the older they get. Maybe, they're here so you can tell them what to do."

"Yeah, man," said Bailey. He put his hand on Robert's shoulder. "Save all that piss and vinegar for them. I don't know if they know it yet, but you really need to have *the talk* with them."

Robert stopped working on the meat and turned around. Crossing his arms, he leaned back against the counter. "I make myself so tired. It's too hard. Sometimes I just . . ."

We all let his silence expand out into the room. There were a lot of ways that sentence could be finished. Mom put down her wine and stepped by me to give my cousin a hug. Bailey and I watched for a few seconds, then caught each other's eyes. He raised his eyebrows at me, then put his palms up in the air.

Finally, Bailey said into the silence, "I'm pretty sure the aurora borealis is going to make an appearance tonight. My dad said things were getting interesting last night. More than just a normal glowing color in the distance. He saw the light moving around from the air right when we were flying in to Bangor, but you couldn't see it after we landed because of the cloud cover.

Mom let go of Robert. He wiped at his eyes with the back of his hand. "That's right," she said. "It was in the paper a few days ago. It's going to be one of those rare shows down this far in the summer."

Right then, Daddy appeared in the room. "I need to get the flames going outside. Jeez, that's a lot of meat to cook." He went to the refrigerator and pulled out a bottle of beer. As he twisted off the top, he said, "Robert, I don't know what you want out of life, but you need to come outside and talk about it with me. Your parents clearly need your help."

He started to leave the kitchen for the back door. "You coming?"

Robert went the other way, through the hallway to the dining table and the great room. I looked over at Daddy. He looked like he wasn't surprised. We heard the front screen door open, then partially slam.

Daddy said, "Oh boy." He looked at Mom, then headed toward the back. Mom went over to the half-marinated chicken to finish Robert's job.

No one said anything for a minute or so. Through the windows, I saw Daddy heading toward his cooking area. I wanted to go after my cousin and tell him what a baby he was being, but a thought came to me. "So, wait a minute," I said. "I think I get something here."

"What's that?" Mom asked.

"They needed *us*. They're bad at talking. They needed Robert to come here and now they're here because they don't know what to do."

"Families are audiences," Mom said. "At least, some families."

"Wow, you're right," said Bailey. "And I've got the same problem Robert does."

"I hope you don't," I said.

"No. I mean, I'm an only child, too. No audience. Just the actors. Mom, Dad, kid."

"Your family is fine," I pointed out.

"Not really," Bailey said. He had a distant look in his eyes. "No, we're pretty bad at talking, too. Trust me."

"You know, you don't have to say 'trust me' all the time," I said. "You're the most trustworthy person I know."

"I'm just good at faking it," Bailey said.

He looked over at Mom. She made a goofy face at him and tipped her head to the side. "If you want

287

to bring your parents over for dinner sometime," she finally said, "I'm sure the Scattergood mob can be a useful audience for you, too."

I looked through the back window. Daddy had just started the fire and was sitting with a cigarette in his mouth, taking off his shoes. I wondered if my cousin was coming back for dinner. It was possible he'd play some immature game with everyone and disappear. Why that thought occurred to me, I don't know, but it did—quite intensely, actually. I felt so sad and defeated by that kid, it made me want to smash something.

"I wonder if we'll ever see Robert again," I said out loud to no one. Really, I said it to no one.

27. Heroes and Villains

Bailey helped Mom bring out the food. Four wine glasses sat on the table, along with an open green bottle next to Mom's glass. As he placed the giant wooden salad bowl in the middle of the table next to a platter full of grilled chicken and a smaller one with bunned-up hamburgers and hot dogs on it, he said, "Robert's not coming, you think?" I shook my head.

"It's not the first time he's done this," I heard Aunt Samantha say loudly from the corner of the great room.

That was all I needed to hear. She was going to ignore her kid when she was needed the most? I wanted to go find Uncle Edward and see if that was his conclusion, too. You've always got two choices when people are being rhino-butts: you can go out of your way to make sure you heard them right, or you can take a deep breath and just let it all go. I wanted to let it go. I really did. A question came to me, though: *Were they not going off to find their kid because they*

*were disappointed and embarrassed by him, or be-
cause they were worried, even afraid, that they didn't
know how to handle the situation?* I wanted to think
about it, but there wasn't time. Everyone was coming
to the table. Dinner was starting. And at least for this
meal, I was going to make sure I sat next to Bailey.

><

Everything started out well enough. Daddy had put
on a nice jazz CD with soft piano and whatever that
xylophone-sounding instrument is that makes bell
noises. You could hear a muted bass and quiet drums
keeping perfect time.

As Daddy took his place at the table, Uncle Edward
asked, "Is this the Modern Jazz Quartet?"

"'Softly as in a Morning Sunrise,'" Daddy responded. "The song they're playing."

"We used to play backgammon and chess listening to this, didn't we? That one summer before I left
for MIT?"

"MJQ. The best," Daddy said. "Calm, intelligent, subtle. We thought, they're just like us." Daddy
laughed. Uncle Edward didn't seem to agree with the
joke.

"I can't believe you still listen to this. It's been,
what, at least thirty-five years?"

"It's a remastered CD. The vinyl version warped
out years ago."

"Still."

"I listen to everything."

"Yes, well, except what you don't listen to."

The Modern Jazz Quartet made it seem to me that everything on the table was linked together by threads of soft orange light. I'm not sure how music makes you think things like that, because we weren't really connected by anything so simple and beautiful—as we would all soon prove.

Bailey asked Edward about his work as a physicist. Sitting there at the table in his plaid madras button-down shirt—bright green, orange, neon pink checks with light blue and dark gray lines running between the plaid in the background—my uncle looked very pleased with himself and maybe a little relieved to address a topic he felt comfortable with.

"Our work is all about elementary physics. Trying to finish up what Einstein started, you know?"

Yeah. Blah, blah, blah. What an ugly, idiotic shirt. It was very hard to imagine such a frumpy bald guy with so little taste in charge of finding something as supposedly important as particles of energy that maybe created the universe.

He was talking about overseeing all "his" scientists. So full of himself! Everyone except Daddy seemed reverent and interested. I realized I could really enjoy hating Uncle Edward. So I interrupted him. He was using words like "foundation" and "principles" and "process method" and "thermo-electric." I just blurted it out. I wasn't really thinking.

"Wait. I don't get it. If you're trying to track all these mysterious energy particles, and it's such a big deal and supposedly so important, how come the only thing that happens every once in a while is that we see you on TV? Nothing ever really changes in the world. I mean—you say you're in search of the evidence of how the universe formed. But what does that really do?"

I let my eyes drift across the table. Aunt Samantha had a smirk on her face. Daddy's eyebrows were doing a scribbly thing. I couldn't tell if he was going to laugh or yell at me. Everyone else seemed worried—even Bailey.

Uncle Edward blinked a few times and cleared his throat. "Well, it's all just science, my dear. Not really something you . . . I mean, a lot of hard work by a lot of smart people all doing bits and pieces. Nothing terribly important the way normal people think things should be important. And I'm just a figurehead. You know, the person to explain it all to the common man. Incremental advancements. *We* don't talk about the origin of the universe ourselves when we're working. That's just for the reporters. Makes what we do easier to understand. But, yes, nothing significant changes, you're right, which is actually kind of the idea, maybe. Except, I suppose, if you really want to know how the universe came into existence . . ."

He let that last sentence dangle like it was a big joke everyone should laugh at. No one laughed, though. They were all more worried, I think, about the tone of voice I'd used.

"You're proving a theory," Bailey finally said.

"It's part of the last bit of the standard theory of particle physics. Yes, without it we couldn't really understand anything."

His tone of voice said it all to me. I didn't need anything else. Daddy's issues with his older brother made total sense. Uncle Edward was a pathetic assbutt know-it-all and a half.

I couldn't help myself. "Can your energy particle theory that helps you understand everything about the universe explain why your son Robert is actually a girl stuck in a boy's body, and why you've done nothing to help him, like right now?

"He's hiding from his parents, you know—convinced his transgender needs are the reason you're getting a divorce . . . and you're just leaving him up at the little house feeling miserable."

Zaxy put his fork down and lowered his hands to his lap. I heard Mom say my name quietly. Uncle Edward was on my side of the table, but down near Mom. I couldn't really see his expression. No one was saying a thing. I had to wonder right there whether the ability to make everyone silent and uncomfortable is a good kind of power to have or just a really obnoxious problem I was going to have for the rest of my life.

Bailey's hand squeezed my knee under the table. I knew it wanted to protect me somehow.

"You don't know what it's like," Samantha said out of the dead air around us. "Any of you."

"Neither do you," I said back quickly. "You don't know Rita at all."

"Oh, my God, Ivy." She paused to draw herself up in her seat. "He's a teenage boy."

"No, *she's* not," I said coldly. "And you just proved my point."

"This whole thing is a fad," my aunt said. "Don't you see that? Every generation has a different version of alienation and identity crisis. He just needs to understand it for what it is. It used to be transgender this, transgender that—just a year ago. Now they're saying gender fluid, intergender, asexual, gender queer, and God knows what else. It's a cult thing. But they're kids. Just kids. They don't even know it's a cult."

I laughed. I couldn't help it. I laughed and looked at her when I did it. What was happening to me? It was a mean-girl laugh. It was a *you are so stupid* laugh, the kind of laugh that had been sent in my direction all too often from fourth grade through eighth grade.

Mom said my name again. I turned to look at Daddy. He had a secret smile in his eyes just for me.

"You need to meet Rita," I said quietly. "She's up there." I pointed toward the little house.

"Obviously, he's embarrassed," I heard Uncle Edward say.

"I miss her," Zaxy said.

"When he wore my clothes, I never uttered a word," Samantha said. "All those years with mermaids and fairies. He could dress any way he wanted. I let him alone."

"She's not a *he*," Delmore said very simply.

"You don't understand," Samantha said again. "*He* doesn't understand."

"Samantha . . ." That was Mom. I placed my hand on Bailey's, under the table.

"No, Rikely," said Samantha. "Don't try to shut me down. I got that enough at home. I'm the mother. He came from me. I literally made him. Surely *you* understand that. I know what he is. Who he is. I understand what he needs.

"I should have said no a long time ago. This is my fault. I should have made him doubt himself more. Like everything in life with teenagers, he needs to learn the brain signals necessary for self-control. Everything starts with doubt."

I leaned over the table to look down at the other end. I wanted to see how my ass-butt uncle was taking all of this. He was shaking his head back and forth like he'd heard it all a million times. He was also spreading yellow hot dog mustard on a piece of roasted chicken. Who *does* that?

Right there it hit me. These two had gone around and around on the problem of their kid way too much. Their perfect little world was stricken by this completely irrational and unintelligible problem child. They'd been holding it all at bay for like twelve or thirteen years—the whole time not talking about it as real, but scared to death anyway. They were scientists and super-educated. They probably ran in high-powered circles with people whose kids were supposedly amazing and talented and fun to be with. And what did they have in their house? No wonder Robert was so messed up. Who wouldn't be?

But more importantly, no wonder *they* were so messed up as a couple. They'd been trying and failing to deal with their kid forever without really talking. Everything they might have said to each other was probably the same old stuff over and over again.

"Samantha's very dramatic about all of this," Uncle Edward said. "Too dramatic, maybe. Emotional. What's really at stake here is she's upset because she doesn't want to lose her son. Neither of us does. But it feels like he can't wait to disappear or something . . . forever . . . from us. No parent should have to deal with that. Samantha just doesn't want to lose him."

"If you say that one more time I will leave the table," Samantha said viciously.

"Whoa. Whoa, you two. Stop." That was Daddy.

My older brother was forking a big piece of chicken in his pie hole, trying hard not to laugh. But the whole situation was really eating at Zaxy. He looked like he was being sucked into his chair. His little shoulders were even trembling a bit. I knew that look on his face. I glanced down the table at Mom. She saw it, too.

"Zachary," she said. "If you'd like to be excused, you may go to your room or outside."

For a moment he looked surprised. He squinched up his eyes and seemed ready to say he was staying put.

But all of a sudden, he scooted his chair back, stood, dropped his napkin in his seat, and bolted from the table. Dashing through the great room, he shot out the front door. We saw him actually leap off the side of the porch next to the stairs, and then he was gone into the evening light.

Before anyone could laugh or comment, Daddy said to Samantha and Edward, "That's the effect all of this has on your kid."

No one said anything for a moment. The Modern Jazz Quartet was still playing in the background.

"Samantha's on the run, too, apparently," Edward said. He took a big gulp of wine.

"Oh, well said, Eddie. That's exactly why I'm right here, because I'm running away. Makes a lot of sense."

"You followed me here. That's pretty interesting."

"All right you two," Daddy said. "This statement is generally reserved for lovers, but I have to say it anyway. *Get a room!* You're both acting completely ridiculous. There's a lot I'd like to say to each one of you, by the way" (he looked right at me) "but I don't want to be part of this event. Any of it. So, again, if you want to talk to each other like that, get a room. Please!"

That actually shut the two of them up for a few seconds. But I was beginning to understand even more about Daddy's issues with his family. It occurs to me now that I also should have seen the connection to his drinking as well.

Who knows how many glasses of wine Samantha had consumed that night? It certainly didn't take long before she began speaking her mind again.

"There's no control over what's real anymore," she said. "Every kid who doesn't fit in can find solace in a fictional solution. All those stupid video games. Have you noticed? There are only two kinds of men in them. Heroes and villains. But they always have a wide variety of female characters—princesses, cute girls, sexpots, archers, sleek spies, magic warrior sidekicks, even villains. If you're a boy and don't feel comfortable as a hero or a villain, you have your choice of the type of girl you can be. That's really odd, wouldn't you say?"

"The virtual world?" Uncle Edward asked. "Social media? You're blaming this on computers? Machines?"

"There's no such thing as machines anymore," Samantha said with a really spooky tone of voice. It was like she was saying something she'd said a thousand times already to her husband. "They're part of us. Each one of us, whether we know it or not. And they're taking over how we think. Every last one of us. Facebook? They offer all these gender labels for profiles. It used to be there were two. Now there are like fifty-five . . . and counting. If you're a fifteen-year-old kid, confused about who you are, and all of a sudden you're confronted with over fifty choices about what to call yourself, how are you going to deal with that?"

She was right, of course. We all let that point hover above the table. No one said anything, and that stupid tiddlywink jazz just kept right on trying to be cute and funny and happy and cool. Bailey squeezed my knee again. I sensed he wanted me to say something. That's when we heard footsteps outside on the porch, then the door opening.

28. More Girl Than Girl

Rita came in first, followed by Zaxy. His eyes were gleaming, and he kept shaking his head like he was trying to get rid of the big, slobbery smile on his face.

"Sorry I'm late," Rita said. "I couldn't decide what to wear."

She had on her skinny jeans, ivory-white sandals, and the green blouse she'd worn into town that first time we went. Her hair was tied back in a ponytail, and she had glittering green post jewels in her ear-lobes. She'd been careful with her makeup—low key. She was quite good at that, I decided. Regardless, she looked radiant and beautiful, lit up and sparkly. Her skin somehow had a perfect amber tint. I thought, here is my golden cousin. Could I ever look like that one day? I'm admitting that here. It felt weird to think like that. Was I being vulnerable or just giving in to something I'd fought my entire life?

Zaxy playfully pushed Rita forward through the great room to the table. There was an empty plate next to Mom, across from Uncle Edward. Rita sat down, with Zaxy plopping noisily back into his chair next to her.

"Boy, I'm hungry," Rita said. "Starving, actually!" She helped herself to some chicken. Del passed the hamburger and hot dog platter, then the salad bowl. Both times Zaxy held them for her while she served herself.

"Is there mustard and relish?" she asked. Del reached past Samantha for the condiments and passed them down, bottle by bottle by jar.

As Rita dribbled mustard on a hot dog, her mother, who was not looking at her, murmured, "Is that my top?"

"What? This thing? Why, yes it is, Mother. Of course, I don't fill it out the same way you do, but I could, you know, depending on the look I'm going for. Don't want to be greedy, though, or unnecessarily ostentatious. I'm happy with a loose fit. It feels wonderful, if you want to know. The material is so light and silky."

Rita took a bite of hot dog and chewed with a look of enchantment on her face. After swallowing, she went on.

"The color suits me somehow. Don't you think? It makes my skin glow, like perfect breakfast toast. It's something about this particular shade of green. What's it called again?"

Aunt Samantha had been looking down at her plate as Rita spoke. Now she raised her head. Her eyes swooped around the table from Daddy to me, then Bailey, Uncle Edward, then Mom, and finally to Rita, her daughter.

"Chartreuse," she finally answered. "You know that."

"Right. I know that. Because I helped you pick it out four years ago. At that shop on Rodeo Drive we liked so much. Our day in Beverly Hills. Just us. What was the name of that boutique?"

"Tory Burch."

"Right. Yup. It was going to be the year of green. Do you remember? We declared that. You and I." Rita smiled sweetly at her mother and waited a few moments. Then she went on quietly, carefully. "We also declared that it was a girls day out. Do you remember that as well, Mother? You said that. First thing, in the car. Girls day out in LA, you said. We talked the whole way up. I'd told you everything. We'd discussed it all. You said you already knew. You said you understood. You bought me this wig. I felt like we'd made it. I had no idea what came next, but I felt like we'd made it."

Maybe she was doing it wrong. It seemed like there was so much hurt and hostility on the edge of everything coming out of our cousin's mouth. This isn't you, I wanted to tell her. Not you at all, Rita!

There's no way to know if I was actually going to say that, but something was definitely about to come out of my mouth when Samantha burst into tears. So did Rita. My aunt covered her face and blubbered into her hands. Rita just shook at the shoulders a few times, then tears rolled down her cheeks. In the middle of all that, she tried to put relish and mustard on a burger. It seemed like Zaxy was going to start crying, too. When I looked over at Del, our eyes met.

I don't know how long we all just sat there. Bailey patted my knee twice and kind of leaned into me. The silence might have lasted just seconds. It could have been a few minutes. I had time to wonder who was going to break the dead air. The answer came soon enough.

"Why can't you just be yourself?" Samantha asked.

Rita sniffled a bit, stared down at the food left on her plate and sighed. "I am."

"I see. Are you sure about that?"

"What do you mean? Have you got any idea—?"

"Of course I do. I see this," Aunt Samantha waved the back of her hand in the air. ". . . this . . . other person you think you are. But what if you're mistaken? Who the hell knows who they are when they're just a teenager? It's like someone started a rumor and thousands of you believe it. *If you don't feel normal, then maybe you're the wrong gender.* What the hell? It's just a rumor!"

My aunt sat straight up in her chair. "You feel different, right? You don't like sports or competition or talking about girls like they're sex objects. Makes you uncomfortable. Right? You don't want, you *need* to wear girls' clothes. So you *must* be a girl. That's the only answer. Right?" She glared at Rita. "Please!"

"It's not like that."

Samantha wasn't done. "What do you know about feeling different? Makeup? Stockings? Short skirts? Skinny jeans? Jewelry? Painted nails? Perfume? Heels? Breasts? Look at me. That's *me*, Roberto! I do all of that so I don't feel different from other women. Is that what you're after here? To look like every other woman in America? Is that your solution? Do you think that wearing women's clothes and makeup lets you off the 'feeling different' hook?"

She swiped a tear off her cheek. "Of course you feel different. Every one of us in this family is different—except maybe these two old men here." With a sneer, she swept a hand at Daddy and Uncle Edward. Zaxy laughed at that. Delmore had this look in his eyes, like he was watching something very unexpected on TV.

"We're *all* different here," Aunt Samantha practically shouted. "Get it through your head. We're halfbreeds. We're terrible Quakers as well, I might add. We think too much, and we try so hard to care about everything. I spent my life being half a Latino girl for everybody in an Anglo school, smarter than everyone else and prettier, too. They were so scared of me. Scared! It sucked."

She wiped her cheek again with the back of her hand. We all waited for more.

Finally, Rita asked, quite calmly, "Why did you come here?"

"To bring you home. You're scaring me. Your father is scaring me, too. I've had enough."

"Mother, I'm happy . . . maybe for the first time in my life. Or I was, until *you* showed up. I'd been my *self*. My true self. It's pretty simple. Don't you understand?"

"That's what I'm talking about. That's why I'm scared." There was a hint of desperation in those words.

"Why? How can me being happy scare you?"

"You've brainwashed yourself. There's no happy in life. Not happy that stays. And there certainly isn't something called a true self. People watch too many movies and TV shows. The brain is much more complicated than that."

Her eyes swept around the table. Uncle Edward was leaning on his elbow with his hand over his mouth. The Modern Jazz Quartet continued to tinkle away in the background. I moved my hand and rested it on Bailey's knee.

"We thought you might come to your senses out here," Samantha said.

"I did. I have made my situation crystal clear," Rita said flatly.

"Do you have any idea how serious this is?" She looked again down the table at her husband.

Nonchalantly, Rita took a bite of salad, then said as she chewed, "You obviously don't get it."

"You keep saying that. Try me. Try all of us. Come, *Rita Gomez*. Tell us. Help us understand what you think we don't."

Rita took another bite of salad, then put the fork down on her plate. Slowly, she chewed then swallowed.

I noted the Adam's apple with that swallow. She blotted her lips with her napkin, then took a deep breath.

"I've been on the edge of something almost like magic my whole life," she said. "It's always been there, this sense that change is right in front of me and easy to grasp. It's like reincarnation could actually be a real thing here on earth, but you have to find the key. That's kind of what I'm doing here, right? It's actually quite amazing. But you don't *find* the key, you *create* it. That's taking so much energy, so much out of me.

"You may think I'm simple and naive, but I'm not. I understand. I understand too well. I know I can't exactly be a girl." Her eyes wandered from her mother to me.

"I try so hard, but it never quite fits. Once I looked like a boy, but I wanted to look like a girl. Now, I see how complicated the magic really is." She smiled at Bailey and me.

"And I'm not just trying to change me. I'm trying to change the whole world. That's what it feels like, anyway. I need to change everyone so that I can stop myself from feeling this sense of endless change.

"I wake up every morning and I'm a different person each time. Can you imagine what that feels like? Sometimes I just lie in bed wondering if I have some mental illness that makes me crave what I'm not. And it's never going away."

"You're a teenager," Samantha said.

Rita went on. "I have this problem with opposites. I don't see them very well. The opposite of a boy in my world isn't a girl, it's a dog or a pirate or a bottle fly or some new creature that's been trying to come into the world for centuries, a new form of human being that keeps getting shunned and left to die again and again—failed reincarnation."

"If you feel that way," Uncle Edward said, "why would you do this to yourself?"

"Because I know it's the right direction to follow. I just know it. There's someone out there in the future waiting for me at a mirror I haven't quite found yet, or on a phone screen—someone who got beyond all this doubt and uncomfortableness."

Aunt Samantha stirred in her chair. "But from what you say, this is causing you great pain and confusion." She looked almost tenderly at Rita, waiting for a response.

"Who knew, Mom, that so much pain and confusion could fill me with so much wonder and light?"

"No one can be as brave as you will need to be," Samantha answered.

"You don't have to be brave to be yourself. Just calm and foolish."

Out of nowhere, Daddy said, "And stubborn. Don't forget stubborn."

"Yes. Thank you, Uncle Scat. Calm, foolish, and stubborn. That's what everyone needs in order to be happy, Mother. Isn't it?"

"It's not enough to be happy. You need to be safe. Don't you see that?"

"Safe? I'm not a criminal or a drug addict or a prostitute. For that matter, I'm not a cop, either, or in the military or a fire fighter. What is safe?"

"People are cruel when you're different. There's too much violence out there. We all know that."

"But safe? You want me to be safe? Why? So you don't have to worry about me? So you can sleep at night?"

"I will always worry about you. I'm your mother. That's what mothers do. I just don't want to worry more than I should have to. It's complicated enough . . ."

Samantha's words trailed off, but all of us understood what she was saying. Is anyone ever immune from being selfish when it means protecting someone they love? Her selfishness was obvious, even normal.

The Modern Jazz Quartet was back at the beginning of their album. Was the CD player set to repeat? Certainly we'd already heard what was playing. I was about to say something when Zaxy piped up.

"Am I going to have complicated problems if I ever become a teenager?"

"Of all people," Del said. "*You* won't. You're going to be whoever you want to be and do whatever you want to do and no one is going to get in your way. Ever."

"Really?"

Del didn't say anything to that. He just raised his eyebrows and nodded.

Rita jumped on all of that, though. "That's me, too, now. I am who I am. I choose to be Rita Gomez and that's all there is to it. Ask me any question, I'll answer." She looked from one parent to the other. Daddy was grinning and nodding. At the other end of the table, I saw Mom reach out and pat Uncle Edward's arm.

"You know," Daddy said. "When you showed up and made this declaration about being transgender and told us your new name and made this big deal about being a girl, I thought it was really boring and kind of ridiculous."

He wiggled his fingers into his shirt pocket and fidgeted with his cigarette box. "You want to overcomplicate the jungle, kid. Most of the critters in here run in packs. And those packs are weird, often unbelievably heartless, ignorant, and cruel."

I leaned close to Bailey's ear. "Here we go," I whispered. "Prepare yourself."

"None of us understands what the deal is with the situation you're in," Daddy said. "Maybe some of us act like we do, but we really don't. How could we?

"Maybe there's some special code, some sort of trigger everyone's born with that's supposed to go off. I mean, we know that gender is the most fundamental aspect of being human. Girl or a boy? Pink or blue?

"So, did your trigger just get jammed the wrong way? Twisted? Inserted upside down? Or is the trigger fine and the code for the body what's incorrect? Or how about the code for the way society defines boys and girls? Surely that code is limited and inadequate. More importantly, are you actually *choosing* this? I mean, you just told us you've decided to be Rita."

He put up his hand to shush anyone who might want to comment. "I know. I know. It's not really a choice. At least, you say, Rita, that it doesn't feel like it is.

"But there will be so much effort and hard work required if you want to succeed at this. For the rest of your life. I mean, I thought it was difficult pretending I'm a writer. I know it's hard for my brother to pretend he's this important scientist. It's hard for everyone to pretend, because all that pretending entails a huge daily creative grind. But this? You? Boy to girl? Man to woman? Roberto to Rita?"

He crossed his arms and leaned back in his chair. "So, yes, I thought you were boring. Really boring. Trivial, even. Ridiculous. But I get it now. I understand. All of this is very interesting. *You're* very interesting.

"But your mom's right, Rita. Our family is stupid different. Each one of us walks around feeling all alone in the jungle unless we're with each other. And we're such a pain in the ass to everyone around us. That's the Scattergood way. It's sad, really, but that's who we are. Outsiders. Half-breeds. Misfits."

He glanced over at Bailey. "If you don't get what I'm saying now, you will soon enough, Mr. Cooper. That is, if you hang out with that girlfriend of yours much longer."

"I get it, Scat," Bailey said with a grin. "That's why I like her."

"Yes, well, I don't mean to say we have a monopoly on being weird. I saw some weird in you years ago, Cooper." Daddy looked kind of sad all of a sudden. "You have a secret, too. I'm still wondering what that is."

Before Bailey could respond, Daddy was talking to Rita again. "But you? What you're doing, Rita Gomez, is locking yourself in even tighter to feeling like an alien than any of us. It's like you want to prove to the world that you're a weirdo of the first degree.

"I get that. I really do. That's pretty much how I feel through my work as a writer. All writers who wish they were worth their beans feel that way. We are totally twisted. Every one of us—stuck-up, confused, self-important, assaholic. The whole idea of being a writer is to demonstrate how strange we know we are scrawling our graffiti in very ordered linear fashion. But I gotta tell you, proving to the world how weird you are requires proving to the world how weird *it* is. That can be a very heavy burden to carry, very messy, too, and chaotic. People generally don't like feeling life is complicated and strange.

"And now here we have you wanting to do the look-at-me-ain't-I-different dance with your whole body. That's crazy-hard to pull off. Harder than anything the rest of us will ever have to pull off in our puny little Scattergood lives—especially your dad over there."

He pointed at Uncle Edward. It was a pretty serious, mean, and accusatory way to point.

"The vessel of a boy coming to earth with a girl packed inside is certainly a perplexing dilemma, then. What are we to do with that? We've fought major wars over how bodies look, and thankfully, the good guys tend to win. Just because your skin is more pigmented doesn't mean people can make you a slave. Just because you don't have blond hair and blue eyes doesn't mean you should be rounded up and locked inside gas ovens.

"If you're really being honest with yourself then—and only you, Rita Gomez, my shiny new niece, know if you are—then first of all you have to understand what I'm saying here. They really did fight wars, horrible wars, because of people's fundamental right to exist in the bodies they were born with.

"And secondly, you need to understand that you're asking a lot of your parents. Probably more than you have a right to. There's no way around that. Still, if you're going through with this, I for one will forever stand amazed and incredulous at your fearlessness and your courage and strength."

He rubbed his forehead with his two middle fingers, then extended his hand, palm up, in my cousin's direction. The jazz seemed to be trying to tell us something we couldn't understand. We all just sat there.

"One last thing," he said when he looked up again. "Don't do this half-assed. Don't be a baby or a wuss about it—even a little bit. And don't be mean or angry either. I'm proud of you and I'm impressed because you seem committed . . . to *Rita*. Your parents will be proud and impressed, too, someday. They'll figure it out, eventually. As long as you're not going about it all half-assed.

"Your cousins already get you. I saw that in their faces when you walked in tonight. They were relieved to see you again. Good old Bailey Cooper here gets it, too. They all love you. They respect you. What more could anyone want in life?"

With that, our dad turned to head outside.

29. Eavesdropping

Before Daddy got to the door, Aunt Samantha stood up from the table and left the room, not saying a word. Mom said, "Zachary? Delmore? I need help clearing the table. And can someone put on different music? Ivy, how about you and Bailey do that? Okay?"

Delmore punched our little brother on the shoulder. "Bro, we're helping Mom. Come on." He too stood up, then partially lifted Zaxy from his seat.

"When you're done with the music," Mom said to me, "come in the kitchen to help dry and put away the pots and pans."

Rita and her father sat at the table watching everyone clear things. At the stereo, Bailey pushed the button to stop the CD player. The Modern Jazz Quartet went silent right in the middle of a song—finally.

"Did you like that music?" I asked.

"Sure. It's really distinct. You could hear every instrument clearly. It was both happy and kind of sad at the same time."

"It made me feel odd."

"Either that, or your odd family made the music sound odd."

"You think we're odd?"

He arched an eyebrow at me. "I love your family. Odd is good."

"I'm sorry."

"Don't be. Who gets to sit in on a conversation like that?"

"Thanks for keeping me under control there."

"I'm glad we were sitting next to each other."

Mom called us from the kitchen. Rita and Uncle Edward were still just sitting there staring at the walls.

"Let's put on your favorite music," I said. "What is it again?"

"Seriously, you don't have to do that. Play something *you* like."

"Bailey, it's just music."

"I know. I just . . . I don't know. Ever since you made fun of Katy Perry."

"Oh, my God. You said you don't even like her."

He shrugged. "I don't. Not really. I was trying to be cool. It backfired."

"Wait. It really is Katy Perry, isn't it? Your favorite music? Tell me." He was ticking through Daddy's CDs, not looking at me.

"No jazz," I said.

"Gotcha."

"Who's your favorite? Come on. Tell me. Jennifer Lopez? Elton John? Taylor Swift? I know. John Mayer. Girl's think he's cute. But he's also kinda macho. Very

Bailey-like. Still, I could see any of them being a bit embarrassing to admit to."

"It doesn't matter," he said, still looking through the CDs. "Here, how about Fleetwood Mac? My parents sing like guinea pigs whenever these guys come on the radio."

"Are *they* your favorite?"

He laughed. "No."

"Is your favorite in there?"

"Maybe."

"Then let's listen."

He slid the Fleetwood Mac CD into place. "One of these days we'll listen to my favorite group or singer or whatever. But not now. I know you like Fleetwood Mac because your brother and cousin told me a few weeks ago. That's going to have to suffice for now. Besides, I think this is the kind of music that maybe might calm everybody down and get their minds off all this heavy stuff." Guitars started to play. He took my hand, tugging me in the direction of the kitchen.

They were half done putting things away when we entered the room. You could barely hear the music, but Mom said, "Nice choice. This is the *Rumours* album. Very romantic for me and your dad. It had a lot of meaning to us way back when. It is actually the top breakup album of all time, but we heard it as music about liberating people to follow their own drummers. It may be old music, but it's always reaching out to new people. Makes me want to dance. We did that a lot back in the day. Spontaneously."

"Bailey picked it out."

"My parents like this, too," Bailey said. "Romantic for them as well."

"Yup. Old people's music," Mom said with a big sigh and a nod of the head. "Too bad there's nothing like this coming out anymore. Too bad your generation doesn't dance like we did. Now that was something special we had. No rules or anything. Just move the way you want. Do your own thing."

She had Bailey take over the dishes and said she wanted to make tea and put a couple plates of cookies together. I was sent to get a broom and dustpan to clean up the kitchen floor.

The pass-thru hallway heading back toward the dining area was fairly dark. We kept the cleaning equipment in the utility closet—the vacuum, brooms, tools, bottles of bleach and detergent, buckets, brushes, sponges. I opened the door carefully and stepped in to locate the broom and dustpan.

Rita and Uncle Edward had already been talking for a while. I could hear Fleetwood Mac singing . . . *you can go your own way,*" but on top of that I heard Uncle Edward say, ". . . hanging on to you as Robert . . . holding on to the past. Maybe . . . our marriage . . . She knows you're doing the right thing. Somewhere deep down . . . She has to."

"Why can't she just say it then?"

"Because she feels like this is all her fault—your happiness, our failed marriage, everything."

"Is it?"

317

"What?"

"Her fault."

I thought I heard Uncle Edward take a deep breath. It was hard to tell with the music in the background. "The complicated stuff in life is never one person's fault. I can't think about faults and reasons. Who ever really knows?"

They were quiet for maybe twenty seconds. I stood as still as I could, wishing that I could see their faces.

When Rita finally spoke, it sounded like she was crying a little, but I'll never know for sure.

"I still feel like it's my fault."

"I see that," Uncle Edward said. "I let myself feel like it's my fault, too, sometimes. But it isn't. Your mother and I grew apart somehow. I don't want it that way . . . but maybe that's what happens sometimes."

"I didn't help."

"Actually, you did. You caused us to come together and confront each other. We'd been running away from each other for years."

"But, if I hadn't—"

"Then we would have broken down some other way."

"Still . . ."

"Do you remember when you were young? We'd get you up at six every morning. There'd be the drive to McDonald's for breakfast. We'd wolf our food down on the way to Bounders Nursery School. We'd arrive right at seven when they had just opened, and then we'd pick you up twelve hours later at seven, just as they were closing. That was a pathetic, over-the-top life for all of us.

"We weren't bad parents we were just afraid. That never really changed. Somehow, we thought that if we dedicated ourselves to work, maybe we'd all survive. That's how we acted, anyway. Didn't make any sense, though."

"Maybe you didn't want children."

"Oh, we wanted children and we certainly wanted you, but we didn't know how to be around each other."

"But you seemed okay back then. In my memory, anyway."

"I don't know anymore. Like I say, it was all very complicated, and it still is. Three weeks ago, we were on our way to a meeting with our lawyers. We were going to make our separation legal. Sign the papers, you know? Out of the blue, your mother made me stop at a Starbucks. She wanted to go in and have coffee. You know how she can be. We sat down in this room full of people, laptops and cell phones open on the tables in front of them. Lots of folks reading the paper, chatting. It was mid-morning. A Wednesday. She said she couldn't go through with it. She still needed time. She said she was trying to figure something out."

"What?"

"I don't know. She didn't want to talk about it."

"You wanted to go through with it, though? Anyway?"

Uncle Eddie sighed. I heard that plain as day over the music.

319

"Right," said Rita. "Complicated. I forgot."

"She's not happy with me. Sometimes it's hard to figure out why. Don't get me wrong. I still love her. I just don't know if she loves me. I haven't known that for a long time."

They were quiet. I imagined Rita putting her hand to her forehead, leaning forward over the table.

"So, what happened next?"

"What do you mean?"

"After Starbucks."

"We drove back to campus and went back to work."

"So, you're actually still together?"

"I don't know."

"Complicated."

"We'd already split everything up. She'd moved out. A very nice condo about a mile away. I'm at—"

That's when Daddy came in from his smoke. "I've never seen anything like it. The sky is doing amazing things out there."

I took three steps out of the closet, then moved into the dining area. "The aurora?" I asked.

"You bet," Daddy said. "Come on, get everybody. Kill the lights. Right now! Tell Mom to bring some blankets. Turn the music up, Ivy. Who put this on? It's perfect. So perfect. Come on Eddie, Rita. You have to see this. It's amazing."

I started to head to the kitchen. I heard Uncle Edward ask about the color of the lights. Daddy's voice was already out the door, but I heard something like, "Come see."

30. The Sky Inside Everyone

It's hard to take your eyes off the aurora borealis. If you do, you feel like you're going to miss the best part. But it's *always* the best part. Over the years we'd seen it glowing off in the distance sometimes. But never anything like this. The sky was pulsing with light bursting all over. Occasionally, it seemed like you could hear over the music a faint crackling sound in the air.

Samantha was the last person to make it outside. We'd spread out two blankets. The kids were on one. Daddy, Mom and Uncle Edward were sprawled out on the other one. Samantha maybe thought about her alternatives, but eventually sat in the space open for her on the parents' blanket—right next to Uncle Edward (ha ha!).

There wasn't much time to think about where to sit, though. The sky fluttered with smears of moving color. It was like a big dream we were all having together. The same sky was inside each one of us. White and dark yellow kept shooting in rivers through big pieces of glowing pink and blobs of bright red. Swaths of lime green would show up for a few seconds, then disappear. Is it possible to be on a roller coaster of light? My whole body felt like it was moving with the sky.

Uncle Edward kept saying things like, "*Unbelievable*" and "*Not supposed to happen.*" We could hear Fleetwood Mac very clearly. I had turned it up pretty loud. It was a perfect soundtrack, somehow, for the strangeness above.

I can't really remember that first ten minutes very well, except that Fleetwood Mac went back to the beginning of their CD. Someone had definitely pushed the "repeat" button that night. The light pulsed more or less with the band's simple, constant beat. And most of the music, as I heard it that night, came from women's voices, although occasionally a man's voice would pop up, sounding as beautiful and ethereal as a woman's.

Every few minutes, someone stirred on their blanket, making slight murmurs of wonder and amazement. Each time that happened, it felt like that person was murmuring wonder and amazement at the sky and the night and the music for all of us.

The song "Go Your Own Way" came on. I let my eyes drift to the parents' blanket. Mom and Daddy were mouthing the words and waggling their feet to the rhythm. I felt a chill of happiness run down my spine. My arms tingled with goosebumps. Rita's face was turned skyward. Her long, dark, creamy neck was exposed. Right there, I saw the woman she was looking for in a mirror somewhere. It made my breath catch. I may have made a sound, I don't know, but she glanced away from the aurora. Our eyes met. Holding my gaze, she smiled shyly and nodded. In that unreal light, her beauty was almost impossible to look at. I closed my eyes and held them shut. I wanted proof of what I was seeing. When I finally opened them, her face had turned back to the sky, her lips were slightly parted, the aurora was flickering in her eyes. I tried to follow her gaze back out into the tumbling sky. She was still just as beautiful as ever.

A few minutes later, I realized that all the Fleetwood Mac songs were famous, and that I'd been hearing them my whole life. Watching the sky that night felt like something I'd been doing forever. What is that feeling?

Daddy finally asked, "Does anyone know what aurora means?" No one answered. And I'm pretty sure no one took their eyes away from what was going on overhead.

"Anyone?"

Mom said, "It was Sleeping Beauty's first name," and we all chuckled.

"True," Daddy said. "Princess Aurora. And for good reason. Aurora was the Roman Goddess of the dawn. She had two siblings. Luna, the moon, and Sol, the sun."

"What's broy illis mean?" Zaxy asked.

"Borealis," I corrected.

"Whatever."

"That's more complicated," Daddy said. "And boring."

"We don't want to hear it then," Zaxy said.

"Okay."

"Yes we do," I said.

Uncle Edward said, "It's a fancy way of talking about northern climates and the northern sky. There's also an *aurora australius*. Like Australia. That's for the southern hemisphere."

"The *southern* lights," Bailey said.

Delmore asked, "Why is this happening?" You could hear noise and chuckles coming from the parents' blanket.

"It's kind of like weather in outer space," Uncle Edward said. "Have you kids heard of solar winds?"

"Wind on the sun?"

"Sort of. Sometimes a bunch of magnetic particles, plasma, proton arcs, and cosmic rays shoot off the sun like a big storm. To be honest, scientists still don't fully understand the mechanisms or, really, even why these storms occur. But, basically, the sun throws off all sorts of chemical and magnetic energy at supersonic speed, and some of that eventually collides with stuff in our upper atmosphere, creating light storms like this."

No one knew what to say to all of that at first. There was no letting up in the sky. It definitely seemed like a light storm. Finally, Daddy said, "Nice to have a physicist in the family."

"Can sun winds hurt us?" Zaxy asked.

"No. Our upper atmosphere is protecting us. All that light is the stuff that shot from the sun, exploding before it gets to us."

"It sure is crazy," Del said in a dreamy kind of way. "How many ways can you light the sky, anyway?"

"There seem to be a lot of them," Bailey murmured.

"This kind of show doesn't usually happen so far from the North Pole," Uncle Edward said. "Sometimes you might get a big curtain of color off in the distance, but it's very rare for all these levels of light storm to happen at once this far south. Seriously. Very rare. Very lucky."

"I feel weird. Not lucky," Zaxy said. "I can't stop watching."

Daddy stood up. "I'm going to change the music."

"No," said Zaxy. "I like this."

"Then maybe you'll like what I put on next, too."

"What?"

"More Fleetwood Mac. Only better."

He trudged off into the colored darkness. I knew he was going to have a smoke. Still, five minutes or so later the music stopped. But a new song started up almost immediately. He was right. It was even better. Lots of bass and heavy drums rumbling out of the house.

"Wow," said Delmore. "This is what they call rock and roll."

All of a sudden our father came strutting across the lawn, turning slowly, twisting under the kaleidoscope above us. It was hard not to laugh at him. Did he know that? Did he care?

"I'd tell you all to get up and boogie," he said. "But when this song is over, it's slow dance time. That can be embarrassing."

Uncle Edward shook his head. Zaxy kept covering his eyes, then watching Daddy, then covering his eyes again.

Sure enough, the rock ended pretty quickly and a slow song started. Daddy high-stepped over to Mom and extended his hand. She put a palm to her chest and pretended to be shy, then took Daddy's hand as he pulled her up. I don't know if we'd ever seen them dance like that before. They were basically waltzing but there was so much more.

I snuggled in closer to Bailey, but I wanted to cry. My parents were holding each other close, swaying together slowly, gracefully, around a small piece of the mountainside that we lived on every summer, under a boiling sky of color. There was darkness, but somehow it wasn't dark. And we were all watching—knowing, strangely—those two dancing together had loved each other through so much and for so many years. How does that happen?

I looked over at my aunt and uncle. Did they see what I saw with my parents? Did they want to just let that same thing my parents had go for themselves? Throw it all away? They weren't that far apart, sitting on the blanket. Both of them held the same pose—legs out straight, crossed ankles, leaning back on both arms.

Aunt Samantha watched my parents. Uncle Edward kept letting his head move from the sky to the dancers and then to the back of his wife's head.

The music faded for just a second into silence. My parents came to a rest, still holding each other. Then heavy drums, bass, and guitar kicked in. Scat and Rikely split apart and began to dance like they had just flown in from the '70s, flexing their hips, flailing in rhythm together, circling each other, shimmying their chests and shoulders. They looked silly in a way. But they also looked free and happy and didn't seem to care what anyone thought.

Zaxy covered his eyes again. Delmore looked kind of baffled. Rita seemed amazed and transfixed by them. I turned to Bailey. "Do you ever dance like that?"

"Sort of."

"I don't."

"Why not?"

"I'm not sure? I don't know, actually. I never got asked to a school dance or anything."

We watched for a few seconds. It felt like I needed to just take the bull by the horns. "Want to join 'em?"

"Seriously?"

"Sure."

"Dance party?"

Just as I was about to answer him, the song ended. It had been so short. In the quick silence, though, Bailey began to get to his feet. And Mom said, "Come on everyone. Time to dance!"

The music kicked in. I knew the song well. It starts slow with guitar and bass. Then the singing comes in. Not exactly rock, or even normal dance music, but then I saw my mom. She was swirling and fluttering around my dad.

It was a song about a woman named Rhiannon. I felt what Mom felt. She moved so full of joy and love, so elegantly. There was the line about being captured in the sky. I felt it, but I didn't completely understand. Daddy moved, too, but mostly he watched Mom. I wanted to move like my mother, only feeling the music, something inside of me seemed strong and surprisingly beautiful, waking up.

When that song ended, I felt robbed—until the next song kicked in. All that unbelievable light. When I let my head come down, Bailey was right there, moving with me.

We danced. I realized I'd found something completely new about life.

And Rita was still plopped out on the blanket next to my brothers. I stepped over to her in time with the music and held out my hands.

"Come on," I said.

She shook her head.

"You have to," I yelled over the music. "It's the night of the amazing aurora borealis!"

"Can't."

The song was coming to an end. Another slow number started up. Bailey came over. I shook my head sadly at my cousin and moved off in Bailey's arms.

We watched my parents go over to Eddie and Samantha at the beginning of that song.

I wanted to ask who could possibly think up this music and what it was doing to us? We swayed together slowly. Daddy was dancing gently with Samantha. Mom was trying to be as encouraging as possible with Uncle Edward. Rita, Delmore and Zax seemed so lame, looking around, sitting there on their blanket, lost in their boring heads.

"I get it," Bailey said in my ear.

"What?"

"Fleetwood Mac. They're awesome."

Mom said, "Everyone up for this next one."

The three seated party-poopers looked uncomfortable. Mom went straight to my brothers, put her hands on her hips right as the next song started up, and kind of swayed as she waited.

Delmore was the first to rise. Mom waited for Zaxy as her shoulders and hips rolled with the beat. Slowly, but surely, the little guy got to his feet. Holding hands with each of my brothers, Mom started to move them out to Daddy.

Rita was on the blanket all by herself. I was about to go get her when I caught the blur of her mother floating past us in time to the music, holding her long skirt up a little, swaying and sashaying in her daughter's direction. Samantha didn't even offer her hand. She just reached down in the middle of dancing and seemed to levitate Rita onto her feet.

Bailey said in my ear, "Got a test coming."

Before I could ask what he meant, the song began to wind down. Samantha looked disappointed. So did Rita. Another slow song eased in. I was kind of unhappy myself. Rita needed to dance. I knew that now better than anything else I'd learned all summer.

The song is called "Landslide." It's definitely the most beautiful song on the album. There's a line in the song about being afraid of change. That's when Samantha took both of Rita's hands and pulled her out into the grass with the rest of us.

It happened naturally enough. You know how weird love can be, right? As Rita came close to the rest of us, we all joined hands and moved together with her in our center. We moved close in, then out. We revolved one way in a circle, then the other. And Rita, being Rita, surprised us all by flowing and twirling in the middle of that circle.

"Landslide" is too short, of course. As it ended you could already hear the drum beat for the next number—a chanting, funky, drum-focused song called "World Turning." When that song got rolling, we all split up and went crazy, dancing together, dancing alone, dancing as a family, like all the pieces of light above us. The sky roared, the music pulsed through us, and love, I guess, danced inside each one of us out there in a darkness that wasn't really darkness.

I didn't want any of it to end. That I knew. But there were only a few more songs left on the album. Daddy must have turned off the continuous play loop thing on the CD player. Our dancing eventually came to a halt in the quiet.

"More!" Zaxy clapped.

"Yeah," said Delmore. "Who knew?"

"More!"

But Mom said, "It's getting late. Why don't we go inside and have tea and cookies? I almost had everything ready before Scat called us out here. Plus, we weren't quite done with the dishes."

"No!" said Zaxy. "Boo!"

Daddy swooped him into his arm. "You need to be careful, Zaxamillion."

"Why?" said my little brother as he put his hand on top of Daddy's head.

"You don't want to wear out the batteries."

"What batteries?"

"Your dancing soul actually has tiny batteries. You need to take care of them."

I don't know if the kid got that, but I did. I turned to see if Rita had heard what Daddy had said. Everyone else was heading toward the house. She stood looking up again at the sky. The expression on her face was hard to understand. It was part fear maybe, and part hope. Definitely hope.

"Are you coming?" I called.

"Yup," she said without taking her eyes from the sky. "Just a minute or two. I'll be in."

31. Punching the Heart

Aunt Samantha and Bailey followed Mom into the kitchen to get tea and cookies ready. I think Bailey wanted to help out and finish the dishes, too. A minute later, though, he returned to the great room looking a bit confused. Rita was just coming in the front door.

"They basically asked me to leave the kitchen," Bailey said to no one in particular.

"What did you do?" I asked.

"Nothing. They wanted to talk privately, I guess."

"That happens with moms," Delmore said. He looked up as Rita moved across the room toward him.

"What music should we listen to now?" she asked. They were near the stereo and CDs and albums.

Over at the music center, Delmore had his back to us, whispering with Rita as he connected Rita's phone to the stereo. "You'll like this, Ivy," he said.

I had no idea what I was listening to at first. It started out with acoustic guitar, then big piano chords, bass and drums, followed by the same kind of bells you heard in the Modern Jazz Quartet music. A woman's voice that I recognized kicked in. She kept singing about diamonds. I didn't know who it was, but I also understood I should. Finally, a male voice took over and a light went on in my ears.

"Oh, my God. Is this Johnnyswim? These are my guys! How did you—?"

"We've been listening to this all summer," Del laughed.

"This is *my* song," Rita said. "Actually, it's everybody's song—everybody who feels rejected when in reality each of us is a diamond."

A streak of cold skittered up the back of my neck. "Wait, what is this? Where'd you get it?"

They laughed together. Rita said, "It's one of the bootlegs I got from my friend Stubbie. Every time Delmore the idiot here made fun of you for just listening to their one little itty bitty album I wanted to say something to you, but he wouldn't let me. This is their first full album. Supposed to be out next spring. Pretty cool, huh?"

"You've been listening to this all summer? Why haven't I heard it then?"

"Every time we see you coming, we switch the music."

"Why would you do that?" I didn't know if I should feel hurt or mad or what. The next song was starting up.

Rita said, "We were waiting for the right moment."

"I love these guys so much," I couldn't help gushing. "Amanda and Abner are the best. Such a team."

333

David Biddle

"And just like us."

"Yup, I guess so. Mixies. Golden-brown. Funny looking beautiful people. We're everywhere."

"Royals without a kingdom," Del said.

"There's an edge to them," Rita said. "But not mean or ugly. More like an in your face heart punch thing."

"They're calm, loving rebels," Del said. "But they're sad, too. That's the heart punch thing." It seemed like they'd been talking about them a lot.

"It's the way I feel all the time," Rita said.

"There's such a big feeling of love in their music," I added.

"Have you seen them on YouTube?" Rita asked. "Their videos and their Music Monday clips? They always make me happy."

"Of course I've seen that stuff," I said.

"Have you, Bailey?" Rita asked.

Bailey was sitting behind me. I turned to find him shaking his head. "I can't . . . I don't . . . You guys know so much more about music than I do. I'm an idiot."

I was ready to tease him again, when Aunt Samantha blasted through the back of the room heading for the bedroom side of the house. Her expression seemed so serious, even angry. It was hard to tell. All I know is that I once again felt angry with her.

The song changed. No one said a thing. We just listened. But I couldn't get my aunt's expression out of my mind. For a very brief moment she'd let her eyes shoot into the room, checking to see if we noticed her. It was like she was sneaking.

The music kept playing. I wanted to listen. Amanda and Abner, supporting each other, committed to creating beautiful, honest songs—together—for the rest of the world. I'd had enough. I needed to talk to my aunt immediately. It was time. Enough was enough.

I squeezed Bailey's arm. "I gotta do something. Be back."

He may have responded, but I was already on my way to a faceoff with Samantha Scattergood. Daddy always says, when the going gets ridiculous, have a little chat with the heart of the problem.

><

When we were little, we would play hide-and-seek or tag for hours in that part of the house. The hallway is double-width, lit by old hanging brass candelabra-like fixtures—hunter's chandeliers, I think they're called. Bedrooms are spread out on either side, along with several almost cavernous marble bathrooms. Near one of the cubbies I used to read in, I saw an extra glow coming from an open door.

Aunt Samantha was piling clothes willy-nilly into her open suitcase. I cleared my throat at the threshold. She kept piling. I couldn't tell if she was ignoring me or just seriously focused.

After another ten seconds, I asked, "So, you're leaving?"

There are times when really nasty words should be used. This was one of them—although, I didn't

quite feel capable of saying anything horribly miserable or whatever, so I just let my question hang in the
air.

Instead of responding, though, my aunt turned
and swept all the clothes she had on hangers into an
armful and lifted them off their rod. She spun to one
side and flopped the big bundle on top of the clothes
already in her suitcase.

"Packing and running?"

"Not now, Ivy."

Her expression was hard to understand. She
definitely seemed annoyed, and maybe even offended that I would confront her, but she was preoccupied, too. And yet, somehow, her eyes were shining at
everything in the room. She cocked her head to one
side. Her body seemed like it had just discovered it
was finally free of something. I felt like she was listening for something huge to happen so she could jump
in the air or even run away. Maybe it had dawned on
her that she was done with the Scattergood family
once and for all.

Still, she didn't say anything to me. She just tilted
her head again and stared at me like I was some odd
piece of art she was trying to understand.

"I don't get it," I finally said as calmly as I could.
"How can adults do this kind of thing and act like
it's okay? How can anyone? You're destroying so
much. You're just running away. You have a life with
a husband and a daughter, a whole future together. It
doesn't matter what Rita does in the end . . . or Rob-

ert. For the rest of her life, that kid is going to feel like it was her fault her mom ran away. And both of us know that's not true."

I tried to glare back at her ridiculous tilted head. It would have looked pretty funny if I had succeeded. Johnnyswim wafted down the hall behind me. At that moment, it seemed like music from a planet that was about to evaporate forever.

"Sometimes you seem like you're pretty cool, but other times you're so self-involved and full of beans. So, yeah, throw your clothes in a bag and run," I said. "Like you're nine years old, running away from home. Did you ever stop to think that maybe all of this is *your* doing, because you see things the wrong way? It took *me* a while this summer to figure that out, but I eventually did. How come you can't?"

She looked like she wanted to say something, but I cut her off by flicking my hand in the air. With a maddening smirk on her face, she closed her eyes and slowly shook her head

I went on in disgust. "It's like you're part of the group of people in the world who always have to have things their way. Your way or else. What is that? Did something traumatic happen to you when you were a little kid? I'm fifteen and I understand people can't be that way. You're just going to end up unhappy in life."

I pointed at the window. "Out there? Under that sky? Everything is good enough and beautiful enough, until people like you come along to ruin it."

Samantha took a deep breath. It seemed like she was either trying to remember something or counting to ten before she exploded at me. Her suitcase, big as it was, looked so ridiculous lying open, buried under stacks of bright clothes and lilac-cinnamon-scented unmentionables (sorry, I just had to use that word).

Instead of speaking or exploding, she reached under the lid of her suitcase and tipped it over the pile of clothes, then mashed and tucked everything together in a careless attempt to close it all up.

"I need help here," she said. "I'm glad you came along."

"What?"

She puckered her lips and blew air out of puffy cheeks.

"Maybe you're going to feel like you wasted a lot of energy just now, my dear niece." She paused, then tilted her chin up. "I'm moving across the hall over there to your uncle's room." She raised an eyebrow at me.

"You are correct, of course," she continued. "I don't know how people can do things like run away from their families. I don't know *why* they do, either. I don't know a lot of things. Anyone who tells you they have all the answers is a liar. And, yes, I like things to go my way. But I'm not so stupid, you know, as to miss the big picture. I like Fleetwood Mac, too. And dancing. And that sky. And I like my life. And I love my family."

"Wait. You're not leaving?"

She lifted her hands to cover her mouth and nose in that triangular praying way people have. That's when she broke down and collapsed on the bed, burying her face next to a corner of the suitcase, her shoulders quivering. Muffled sobs burrowed into the bedcovers, suitcase, and her hands.

I leaned back and stuck my head out the door to see if anyone was coming, but the hallway was empty except for the music. Moving into the room and sort of crouching next to my aunt on the bed, I didn't realize I was crying as well until a single, big teardrop splattered on the lid of the suitcase. I put my arm around her neck and tried to hug her. There's no telling how long we stayed like that on her bed.

When we were finally quiet after however much time it took, she gave the silence a few seconds then started laughing. First, she laughed with her face covered and buried, then she laughed sitting up and hugging me until I, too, was laughing, and then finally kneeling in front of me on the bed, my hands in hers, both of us maybe almost hysterical, even choking with relief that everything really was ridiculous and stupid in the world, she let out a long, slow sigh, then started laughing again.

She kept pointing at me and busting out in what I can only think of as Samantha guffaws. "You should have seen your face."

"Why did you let me go on and on like that?"

"What? Go on and on? My God. You're just like your father. No one can stop you when you get going.

Who would want to? You're like this magnificent little engine." She clapped her hands twice.

"So, it's settled. We are staying the week, plus those last few days. I have decided. Your mother and I talked. You and I talked. There is a need for time. There's always a need for time, isn't there?" She grabbed my hands again excitedly and took a huge deep breath. "I can be such a bitch sometimes."

Before I could respond she said, "Help me carry this case and all my stupid clothes across the hall. I don't want anyone to know. I want it all to be a surprise. To Eddie, especially, but also to my daughter."

We'd both stood up and had gripped her suitcase by two corners each. As we lifted, she said, "Only, she doesn't need to be surprised so much as to have it all just become evident and obvious. Sometimes when you're wrong, when you're really wrong, an apology or an admission of guilt is too little and too late. It's a native mountain thing from many places maybe, but I learned it from my mother and my grandmother. You don't regret the past, you just go into the future and wait."

She smiled at me as she wobbled backward out her door into the hallway. "Go into the future and begin to live in that better world. Wait for those you love to catch up. If you're lucky, all the effort it takes for them to figure out what's going on helps them forget their anger and pain. Sometimes they never even remember what happened. But usually in the end, with the strength of that new future, you eventually talk about what happened and understand how ridiculous you both were."

By this time, she was hanging clothes in Eddie's closet. We could hear some other music, new music, coming from the great room, and Scattergood voices laughing.

"Has this mountain people technique stuff got a name?" I asked.

With a stack of T-shirts between her palms, she stopped to think. "No. Actually, it doesn't. At least, I've never heard a name for it. It's one of those things that's so simple it doesn't need a name." She stuffed the shirts in an empty drawer, then went back to her suitcase.

"I'm not going to try any of that ancient wisdom on you, Ivy. I promise. Somehow I know all of this happened because Rita had you here with her. So, I will just say thank you—my stubborn, opinionated niece who doesn't know how amazing and beautiful she is. Thank you. And I'm sorry. And I was wrong. And I apologize to you from the bottom of my toes to the light that might have gone out in my eyes had you not been here. I thank you for my life and my love . . . and my daughter."

She tilted her head again and looked straight into my eyes. "I say all of that because you're here right now with me. We're in the future together. Do you understand that? We're waiting for people to figure that out and catch up to us."

32. What We Leave Behind

I spent the last days of that summer watching my Aunt Samantha holding the door of Rita's future open. I also got to watch Rita figure out the door was there and that she could just walk right through. Somehow Samantha held the door open for the rest of the family, too. I had a ringside seat. I tried to explain it to Bailey, but it was too hard. Some things really are so basic you can't talk intelligently about them.

One thing's for sure, it didn't take a lot for my aunt to get Uncle Edward on board with her new world. It was sort of embarrassing to be around them by the next morning. But that helped Rita figure things out pretty quickly. There were a couple moments during that last week where I caught Rita watching her mother, transfixed—stunned maybe, and surprised. You don't get to see that enough in this world—when people are startled by love. I could tell Rita was having trouble remembering what it was she was leaving behind. But we're always leaving things behind, aren't we? And forgetting? And finding that we're alive in the future.

We'd be out in the boat fishing or cooking with Mom or watching Bailey in one of his last games of the summer. Maybe Samantha would be telling a joke or explaining Honduran literature to Daddy. Rita's mouth would partly be open in some kind of wondering thought, maybe a bit of confusion, too. Confused by love. Confused by time.

And on the night Mom taught us all—us girls— her Norwegian sugar cookie recipe, I caught my aunt frozen in wonderment while watching her daughter. Rita was placing dough drops on a buttered cookie sheet. She had flour specks in her hair and a streak of batter smeared on her cheek like a single dash of white, sugary war paint. The guys were listening to Fleetwood Mac in the great room—really loud, playing team billiards. My aunt's eyes resembled those of a mother who knew she'd just won something really hard to win—something that maybe once seemed like you just needed the right combination of luck and skill to pull off, but in the end you discovered, no, luck and skill were nothing compared to the magic of dedication and commitment.

I don't mean to make it sound like everything was sweet and perfect and we were all just going to live happily ever after. Who the heck gets away with stuff like that? Nope. Delmore and Rita still managed to sneak off for smokes. Sometimes I smelled weed mixed into the scent of their tobacco when I got back to the little house. I really wanted to have a final talk with Rita about all of that, but I never did. That's a good thing, probably. What's the point of telling some-one twice in one summer that they disappoint you? She knew how I felt about her bad habits. My brother was a different story. I've left things that way for now.

And, yeah, I'd completely forgotten about the whole kissing thing by then with Bailey. Seriously. Forgotten. Phitt! Out of my little head. Squeezing his arm, his hand on my knee, his smell, his sweaty scent sometimes, that was enough. More than enough.

><

One of the last nights we spent at *Casa Cielo* I had a weird dream. Zaxy was the only child left in the fami-ly after Del and I had gone off on our own, and he sat in the back seat of the car by himself all the way from Philadelphia to Maine, staring forlornly out the window. He'd forgotten batteries along with the chargers for his screen gadgets. He kept trying to take selfies with some newfangled phone he'd invented. He wanted to send them to Del and me, but his phone had no power. He couldn't take a picture and he couldn't send one.

Once they got up here to the compound, he had a hard time opening the driveway gate. His sadness in the dream was like rain that wouldn't stop in the morning. Mom kept asking him if he was okay. Daddy kept correcting her, saying everything's a question of happiness.

"Are you happy, Zachary? Or not? Those are real questions."

It's funny. Zaxy was all by himself up there, somehow grown up, ready for college. But eventually, I wound up there, too. Somewhere. Hiding. Hiding and unable to reveal myself. Unable, that is, until Zaxy found a gun in the kitchen cabinet and put it to his head and pulled the trigger. Metal hit metal on the click. I appeared in the room. He was clearly disappointed that it didn't go off.

"What are you doing?" I demanded. "Why would you do that? After everything we've been through."

"I didn't know it didn't have any bullets in it," he said.

"It's a good thing it didn't."

"I wanted to know what it would be like to die," he said. "I need to know that."

I carefully took the gun out of his hand and put it back in the kitchen cabinet. When I turned around, he had shut the front door and was walking down the porch stairs.

"No," I said to the empty room. "You need to know what it feels like to *live*. To really live."

Through the window, I watched him running down the path into the trees, heading for the main house. That's when I woke up.

><

We said goodbye to Rita and her parents at the airport on a Thursday. I helped Mom pack most of Friday, and all morning on Saturday. In the afternoon, Bailey picked me up for our last walk together. We drove to the rail trail listening to a Fleetwood Mac tape he'd found at the bottom of a shelf in his parents' bedroom. I knew Bailey was tired that day. He had driven all the way to Blue Hill the night before for a fall racing group meeting, and then all the way home. Now that I look back on things, it's pretty obvious Bailey had a lot on his mind.

What a strange feeling the last day of summer romance gives you. Everything seems to happen so fast. It's so depressing. But you also have this growing, aching happy thing you don't really understand inside you as well. Maybe that's why I was excited. What I felt for Bailey was real, actually real—whatever that meant. We were the only car in the lot.

As we walked hand in hand, Bailey talked about growing up in Maine and being an only child. He talked about his dad flying airplanes for a living and Maine winters. We agreed that our parents were really important to us, but that they got on our nerves. He said he didn't want to be like some of his friends who said they couldn't talk to their parents, and then ended up lying to them, and sneaking around doing stuff they shouldn't.

On the way back, I started chattering away at him about baseball. I just wanted him to know how excited I was for him. I asked him one more time which schools he had on his list and how big a scholarship he thought he was able to get.

He let me go on for a while. I said I had always hated the sound of aluminum bats hitting baseballs. I added quickly that it didn't sound very real in softball, either. Aluminum bats were maybe ruining baseball and softball. I asked him if he knew anything about where to buy wooden softball bats. Then I brought up the Red Sox again and asked if he thought it was stupid for someone in high school to still have favorite players. I reminded him that I couldn't help it about Dustin Pedroia, but that Big Papi was like a baseball god. How could you not totally love that guy?

Then I told Bailey that it was okay he didn't like American League teams, but what National League team was his favorite, anyway? Cardinals? Cubs? Dodgers? It was forbidden to like the Mets or the Braves if you wanted to be friends with someone from Philadelphia. I glanced over at him to see if he was laughing. He wasn't. He looked like he was going to be sick.

We kept walking. I held my tongue, even though there was so much more I wanted to tell him. All you could hear was our feet crunching pebbles on the track and the birds and insects and wind in the trees.

Finally, he cleared his throat. "I need to tell you something, Ivy."

He looked down at me, then straight ahead as we kept moving.

"I hope you still like me after this," he said.

"Uh oh. That doesn't sound good. What?"

He hesitated for a few steps, then said, "I don't like baseball." He took a deep breath. "I kind of hate it, actually."

I noticed that our hands, pressed together, were all of a sudden really sweaty. I felt a drop of sweat run down my cheek, too. I tried to rub it away with my free forearm. He let go of my hand.

"I didn't want to have this discussion today," he said. "I promised myself I wouldn't."

"You hate baseball?"

"Yup. Pure and simple. I hate all kinds of games. Isn't that funny? I've been the star of everything— baseball, hockey, football, soccer, tennis, sailing, you name it, and I hate all of them."

"But why?"

He didn't respond. We kept walking. He seemed to be working hard to compose himself. I wiped my hand on my shirt. Did I feel weird? Did I feel like I was just learning that maybe I didn't know this guy that I thought I knew because he was so cool? What do you think? Honestly, though, I just wanted to keep holding hands. Instead, he was mad at me.

"I want to be a doctor," he blurted into the afternoon air.

"And that makes you hate baseball?"

"Yeah. Yeah, I guess it does."

"How? I mean, it's just a game."

He let out a barking laugh. "That's kind of the point, Ivy. First of all, sports—all sports for me anyway—aren't *just games*. You have to work really hard to be good at them. They were all just games up until I was thirteen or fourteen, but now they're hard work and commitment and all that crap." He looked down at me. "But that's not all of it. There's all these expec- tations— especially with baseball, which is my best sport." He snickered and stopped walking.

Staring off over the trees towards the lake, he explained, "That's exactly how things went with you? You just *assumed* I was this baseball whiz. Everyone's like that with me.

"To hell with all of that!" he yelled. "Screw it all to hell! I don't want to go some place like Harvard because they want me to play sports for them. What kind of baloney is that? It's sick. I don't want to go to Harvard no matter what, but if I did, it would be be- cause they want my pinky, low-class Maine-woods ass as *a student*. Not an athlete."

"I know all this may surprise you, but there's a lot more important stuff in the world than baseball."

He was breathing a bit hard. And, yes, I felt a little scared of him. If you'd seen us from a distance, right then it would have looked like he was really mad at me. His fists were clenched and he was towering over me.

I started thinking about how small I felt there, and our age difference. In my head a voice kept say- ing, "So vast. So, so, so vast. You are so young. And he is so much more mature than you are."

A bird flew close to us. I don't know what kind it was, but it was quick and dark, like a huge shadow zipping by our heads. I hadn't wanted to think at all about how things would be for us once I got home to Philly. No matter what you say to each other when you're young, no matter what promises you make or plans you intend to carry out, you always know things will change. And there we were, already changing. Bailey showing me his dark side, and me realizing I wasn't good enough for him.

I wanted to tell him something, but just as sound began to come out of my mouth, my legs began to shake. I tried as hard as I could to hold it all in. But then I was dropping to the ground and crying all at once, covering my face with my hands, sobbing like I was six years old.

Those tears were brimming with everything—so much more than the effect of Bailey's anger—like what Daddy was doing to himself with his smoking and drinking. And how that made my mom tense and worried for him. And I knew my older brother was maybe doing something similar to himself, and Daddy seemed to know that too. Delmore was scared of school. But he was so good at figuring people out. And Zaxy was always lonely. He didn't have any real friends.

Then there was the partially self-destructive cousin of mine who couldn't figure out who she was but was also strong and lovely. What was in store for her? What was going to happen with her parents? It felt like the decisions she had to make weren't just going to determine her life, they were going to determine mine, too. All she had was her brains and her stubbornness. That's all I had too—not as much brain power as her, maybe, but just as much stubbornness.

I sat at Bailey's feet in the dirt, unable to control my sobbing, afraid to look at him, a little first grader, proving I was too young for him, realizing that the whole summer had been a horrible mistake and a waste of his time.

After a minute or so, though, I felt him sit down next to me. I felt his arms wrap around me, pulling me, somehow, back. He put his face on the top of my head and held me. We rocked there together in the middle of the trail all alone under the warm afternoon sky. I was determined not to cry anymore, but I kept it up anyway. I knew this would be our last real time alone together.

Sob, sob, sob goes little Ivy Scattergood. Boo hoo hoo!

I don't know how long that went on. I'd kind of curled into him and felt like he was protecting me from myself, like he was a warm, thick, comforting bear person who had just showed up in the middle of nowhere.

"I'm sorry, Ivy," I heard. "I'm so sorry. I didn't want to upset you. Sometimes I can't help myself when I think about all that stuff. It gets so frustrating. I never talk about any of this to anyone."

His face was in my hair. I loved feeling his breath against my scalp. That stopped my tears.

"Really, Ivy. I didn't mean to hurt you. You of all people."

I let my body adjust against him a bit. He wrapped himself around me tighter. My arm was caught in an uncomfortable position under my body, mashed into his belly. I pulled it out and rested my freed hand on his forearm.

"Maybe I'm wrong," he said. He seemed to be waiting for my response.

"Wrong about what?" I finally asked.

"Baseball. Maybe it actually is more important than I think. Clearly you think it is. And if we're going to spend more time together, I'm going to have to re-think my priorities."

I might have started crying again, but he kissed my head and then he kissed my ear and then managed to try to kiss my cheek, but I was moving into him by then and all of a sudden we were really kissing.

I'm sure he tasted my tears, but I was tasting his sweat and his mouth and I loved it. I wanted more. It really is a hunger thing, somehow, maybe.

There was a lot of kissing there in the middle of the track, and facial parts blurred together if I opened my eyes a little, and warmth everywhere, good warmth, cool warmth, soothing. It felt weird and thrilling, and something else quite happy that's hard to explain, having his tongue in my mouth and mine in his, all mixed up and both of us at once together. I hadn't ever imagined anything like that could be what it is.

He said my name three different times. I wanted to respond the last time, but just as I opened my mouth I heard a scraping, rustling sound come at us fast and hard.

Someone said, "Ridiculous!" And bolted by in running shorts and fluorescent blue shoes. Over his shoulder, the runner said, "Get a room!"

We laughed together at that. Those words made me feel proud and grown up somehow. But it was also enough to snap us back into reality. Bailey said, "We probably look a bit scary, especially from a distance."

Sitting there, tangled together, I looked one way and he looked the other. A few stray cry spasms hit me. So did a question.

"Are we really going to spend more time together like you said?" We were unwrapping ourselves and beginning to get up. "I'm going home tomorrow."

"It's up to you," he said. "You just found out what an ass-butt I actually am."

"You weren't an ass-butt," I said. "I was just surprised, and then I started thinking about everything. I'm not myself today. I was the ass-butt, just blathering on at you like that. An ass-butt baby."

"That's why you started crying? Nope. *I* was at least an ass. I'm sorry. I get carried away sometimes. My mom says I make her want to run out of the room when I get like that. I make her cry, too, sometimes."

"Did I cry? I don't think so," I said. "Ivy Scattergood does not cry. You have me confused with someone else."

We walked back to the car slowly. Every so often one of us would stop and we'd have a long, slow gluttonous lover's kiss. Then we'd walk some more and talk about the year to come.

We planned phone calls and weekly Skyping. He said he wanted to come down to visit schools in the Philly area—Penn, Swarthmore, Princeton, and Haverford College. He wasn't sure he'd get accepted to any of them.

He said that Penn and Princeton both had decent baseball programs and that recruiters from both schools had talked to him. I reminded him he didn't want to play baseball in college. We kissed a lot in the middle of all that. It was hard to catch my breath. I wanted more. It was a bit worrisome. Bailey kept himself under control, though.

When we got back to the parking lot it was still empty. "Got a surprise for you," he said. He pulled a cassette tape out of his back pocket. "I made this for you." He smiled down at me.

I couldn't help laughing and clapping my hands. He handed me the tape. "There's no writing on this," I said. "What is it? Who is it?"

"Hmm," he took the tape back. "Let's see." He opened up the passenger door, then went around to the driver's side, leaned into the car, and put the key in the ignition. "We need the doors wide open for this," he said as he slid the tape into the cassette player.

Tape hiss started up. He scooted back out of the car and looked at me. "The other night? Last week? Dancing under the sky? I wished it had just been you and me. I've been . . ." He stopped as the singer began to sing, then held out his hand. "Will you please dance with me, Ivy Scattergood?"

I'd heard most of those songs my entire life. My right hand was tucked into his left hand. His arm on my back held me close. I had my left arm around him, too. At first, I felt small. His ribs and back muscles were so huge moving to the music. My hand grabbed at his shirt in back. Something in me was convinced I might lose him forever if I didn't hold on right then and there.

You need to hear Van Morrison to know how it felt out there in the parking lot that last late afternoon in the middle of August 2013. I know you've heard the songs. The first one was "Brown Eyed Girl."

Neither of us really knew how to dance. Certainly not close and together as we were. But it didn't matter. The music was all happy and jaunty, but we moved to our own rhythm, at our own beginners' speed. I rested my head against the soft part of his chest where the shoulder connects. He put his chin against my temple. I could hear him breathing. We swayed in small circles, tiny lovers' steps. Can I say that? Were we lovers? I was fifteen. He was two years older.

"I wanted to listen to this music with you at the right moment," he said. "I've always loved Van Morrison. Van the Man. I grew up with him, I guess you could say."

"I get it," I said. "This is your secret."

"I like other stuff, too, but Morrison's music is important to me. I worry that people will think I'm stupid for it."

I didn't know what to say to that.

"'Brown Eyed Girl' got to me first. I was thirteen, maybe, which would have made you eleven. I didn't understand what I was feeling. Not really." He looked down at me. "Is that perverted? Having a crush on a fifth grader . . . with big brown eyes?"

We danced as the song "Moondance" began to play. Bailey held me closer.

"This is the song," he said in my ear.

"I love this song."

"I've actually dreamt a lot of dancing with you while this plays."

"Moondance" is a jazzy, happy song with flute and piano. We tried to pick up our pace.

"Is this stupid?" he asked in my ear.

"Shhh."

When the song ended, we came to a stop. I looked up at him and waited. He looked down at me, blinking. I thought, *it's nice to know I'm not the only big dummy in the world*. As the next song began, I reached up and tugged on his head a little to draw him down to my hungry mouth. As we kissed, I felt him tremble. His eyes might have been brimming with tears. It was hard to tell.

"I've never felt like this before," he said finally.

I leaned into him and the song "Tupelo Honey" started up.

He said, "I always think of you when I hear this."

We danced there in the late afternoon warmth of that parking lot. I tried so hard to feel *everything* about us in those last short moments alone together. I loved the scent of his hair, the feel of his heart beating on my cheek, the way his chest had trembled when he cried, his gentleness, his angry frustration, how big he was, and, actually, how sweet he was and able to still be a boy, unsure of himself and vulnerable even.

How big is love, really? Why is it scary and sad and happy and hungry all at the same time?

The song ended. There were others. Some fast and happy. We danced touching the whole time. Some were slow and heartbreaking. Some were in between. Van Morrison wrote a lot of beautiful love songs. It felt like he knew he would be there in that very moment with us—our moment. But I suppose that's the way it is for everyone. You have to forgive me. It was the first time I understood that kind of thing with music.

And then we were driving back to *Casa Cielo*.

33. Closing the Gate

We left the next morning. Bailey was there to help pack the car. I'm not going to bore you with what it's like to say goodbye to someone who makes you feel all the things you ever heard about summer romance. That last kiss is something, though, isn't it?

I listen to Van Morrison all the time these days. My favorite song right now is "Into the Mystic." It gives me chills. I think it's partly just the fact that the song is about a "we." And Bailey listens to Johnnyswim all the time. His favorite song is "We Can Take the World." He says it's a song that makes you feel lonely when you're happy and happy when you're lonely.

We probably talk on our phones too much—at least twice a day—mornings before school, in bed before sleeping.

We have lots of Rita discussions. I keep searching Facebook for her Rita Gomez page. Nothing pops up. I text her, but she has only responded back to me one time. Delmore and Bailey have gotten nothing from her at all.

We do know she's still Rita Gomez. Aunt Samantha is at least in touch with Mom. Rita put her wig in a closet and had her hair styled before school started. Samantha took her back up to Beverly Hills to buy clothes and shoes. I will never understand why girls need fashion. Bailey says he likes that about me.

And I got my hair cut short—very short. It's more kinky and curlier than ever. That's my African blood. I would hope so.

⋋

When we left *Casa Cielo* that last morning, it seemed like our whole family had grown up a lot. We let Bailey drive out first, waving until we couldn't see him anymore. Then we started off ourselves, rolling slowly down the driveway, our houses getting smaller, disappearing behind us.

The sky promised rain before lunchtime. Clouds hung low and dark. The trees pulsed with that blue-green haze they get in cool, muted daylight. We couldn't see the sun at all. I realized I like that for the last day of summer in the mountains and lakes of Maine.

Our van slid through the gate and came to rest just past the property sign that read "*Casa Cielo*" with *Scattergood* printed underneath. Before Daddy could tell Delmore to get out and close the gate, Zaxy said, "Ivy should get to do it."

My older brother happily slumped back in his seat. Mom turned to me from the front and raised her eyebrows. I got out of the car and felt the thick air on my face and hands and legs. It had a ticklish kind of watery feel. As I moved through damp grass to lift the gate and iron rod out of the ground, something seemed to sigh for just a moment. I don't know if it was just a sigh inside me or the wind in the trees. A light rain began to fall. When Daddy drove through, I walked the gate back to its closed position, dropped the rod in its slot and flicked the latch down to hold everything in place until we returned.

Once I got back in and closed my door, we seemed to float the rest of the way down the gravel drive until we came to the paved road leading to the boat club. But we turned the other way and headed up to the main road. I always feel like we have to re-solve some simple puzzle in order to get back to the highway that will lead us home to Cliveden and Philadelphia.

I missed Bailey at first on our drive. But by the time we were on I-95 heading south with a bunch of other cars, I was thinking about school. Sophomore year is when you have to start getting serious about college. That's pretty much a tradition at Cliveden Friends.

After an hour or so on the highway staring out the window, I turned to check on my brothers in the back. I expected them to be staring at their screens. They didn't disappoint. Zax had earbuds plugged into the sides of his head, slowly turning his iPad from one side to the other. He glanced up with a self-important grin. "I'm driving us home," he said loudly.

I nodded as his little face returned to its connection with the screen. Delmore, of course, was gazing lovingly at his phone. He kept tapping the screen and swiping his finger from one side to the other, then he'd tap again.

They were staring into little pools of light. I could see tiny sparkling beads dancing around in their irises. One brother's eyes were bright blue, sometimes white-blue. The other brother's eyes were brown. Mine are brown, too, touched with flecks of orange. My dad's are blue and gray. Mom's are the deepest brown in the family, like melted chocolate glazed over into a glassy, agate or obsidian. Rita's eyes are golden brown, like her skin almost, only shiny with liquid and light.

I slept a lot on the drive. I dreamed about Bailey and Rita and my brothers. At one point, we were trying to dance up the side of a mountain, knowing the whole time it was pointless. A whole mountain? You cannot climb a mountain by dancing. But we didn't care.

><

When I finally got that one text from Rita, school was well underway. The Red Sox were in the playoffs by then (they would go on a few weeks later to impress me so much by winning another World Series). It was mid-October. She sent a photo of her sitting at a cafeteria table with two other girls along with a brief comment. One of the girls was kind of Gothy looking, wearing dark lip-gloss, with a pierced cheek, weirdly pale skin, and straight black hair buzzed short on one side only. The other had dreadlocks, a nose ring, and tattoos on both arms. Rita, with her short, styled hair, stared straight into the camera. Those golden-brown eyes were enormous, like she was watching for something about to pop out behind the camera. She'd definitely done something to her eyes with makeup. Her cheeks were slightly rouged, and she had on soft red lip-gloss. The photo was definitely taken at her school, but she had an unlit cigarette between the fingers of her right hand, dangling a bit behind her slightly tilted face.

If I tried hard, I could still see Robert in her, but it was mostly that long, rail-thin body. The face was almost all Rita Gomez. She wasn't smiling. But she didn't look sad, either.

It took a few more seconds for me to notice two things: First, her left arm was bent on the table in front of her. She held her thumb up at the end of that left hand.

I had to make the photo magnify in order to see the second thing clearly—a dark marking on the side of her left bicep. Spreading my fingers on the screen, I pulled the mark closer. It was one simple, clean, tattooed word in stylized cursive: "Ivy."

Her texted comment read: "The only one I'll ever need."

I texted back: "You are crazy." She didn't respond.

Later that day I texted again: "Next summer?" No text back.

And why should she respond? She's busy being a totally new person. Maybe she has a girlfriend. Maybe it's that Peggy girl. Maybe not.

One thing I know more than anything: no one's messing with her, or teasing her, or making her feel bad about herself. She's having the time of her life just being Rita Gomez, looking for that girl in the mirror somewhere, or on the screen of someone's phone. Who knows—maybe she's already found her.

Acknowledgments

I want to thank early readers of *Old Music for New People* for their advice and encouragement: Gary Miranda, Nancy Bevilaqua, Will Terry, and George Record. I am grateful as well for the long-term friendship with my pen pal and colleague Paula Silici who has been there as a noble critic and willing editor of almost every early draft I've concocted for the last twenty years. Huge thanks as well to Allison Maretti of The Story Plant for her editorial acumen, and Stacy Mathewson for his copyediting skills. Lou Aronica's willingness to take me on as a new writer in The Story Plant fold can't be emphasized enough. Lou's editorial advice has helped make this book much better than it ever could have been without him. Also, I am astonished at how lucky I have been over the past thirty years receiving the support and love of my three sons. Sam, Jesse, and Conor; each in his own way, has been an inspiration and a mentor to me. They know how to take on big stuff in life.

Ivy Scattergood showed up narrating this book one morning as I was walking up the stairs to my office. Her voice stayed with me for two years as I did my best to transcribe her story. I'm lucky to know so many astounding and unconventional young women unafraid to follow the beat of their own drummer. I couldn't have written this book without the respect I have for every one of them. Some I coached in baseball; some are part of my extended family; some I worked with in the environmental and energy worlds; some I went to school with in Missouri and Oregon; some I dated over the years. And one is my wife Marion, the love of my life, whose enthusiasm and humor are always surprisingly fresh and authentic, whose intelligence constantly astounds me, and whose common sense about what really matters is often poetic and profound.

About the Author

David Biddle has lived in Philadelphia for almost forty years but grew up in a Midwestern academic household during the 1960s and 1970s. His family traveled around the world in 1965 and again in 1969 with long-term stays in Australia both times while his parents did research. David studied anthropology at Reed College in Portland, Oregon and received a master's degree in Energy Management and Policy from the University of Pennsylvania in 1984. He had a thirty-year career in sustainable development and served as a contributing writer to both *In Business* and *Talking Writing* magazines during much of that time. His fiction, essays, and articles may be found in a number of online and print publications. *Old Music for New People* is his first novel. You can find him on the internet at davidbiddle.net.